Bringer
OF THE
Scourge

M. DANIEL McDOWELL

First KDP Print Edition: March 2024

Typeset: Alegreya HT; chapter headers: Aboreto
book logotype & map elements:
The Mariam Story by RQF Type Foundry
other typographical map elements: Unlucky by RetroSupply

Typesetting, map artwork, logotype, & additional
interior decorative typographical elements by
Jay Wolf at Flamespeakers Union
https://jayxwolf.carrd.co

To all my friends, here and in the Realm of Dream:
Thank you for sacking this particular castle with me.

—M.

the unconquered plains

Tajorr
seat of ruin

bereft of the living
Stonebrake

Imperial Derebor &
the Known Jands

Zalandan
the Astral Circle

the prince's folly
Cascada

Stardowne
that ghastly tower

Estuary City
the Independent's Guild

Broadcoast
Bay

inland pass
Devere

Riverbend
Drought's End

annotations in TEVINT

TABLE OF CONTENTS

CHAPTER 1
THE END

VIERRELYNE AWOKE TO THE SMELL OF FIRE IN THE CRISP NIGHT
air. Not the soft kind of fire that lit the hearth; this was
something bigger, wilder, a fire wicked and unnatural, with
a tarry note of grease that ran behind it, and a sharp
undertone of burnt hair.

On peering through the single southward-facing
window in her parapet cell, it was clear: a building blazed in
the village beyond the gates of Castle Talorr. No—it was
two, three, a dozen... Fabric, thatch, and beams all alight in
the darkness, crackling with deliberate violence.

The sudden explosions that accompanied this great and
growing conflagration served to add more terror into the
air. The screams of townsfolk in panic could be heard even
at this distance, and Vi cursed as she watched the heart of
this fire advancing rapidly toward the siege gates of the
castle itself. Would anyone come to her aid, up here in her
lonely tower, if the fire spread up from Tenvale?

She shook off the mantle of fitful sleep as best she was able, laying aside her terrible recurring dream about a disfigured boy with the eye of a demon, its piercing green gaze fixed on her, across an endless river of darkness that churned swiftly between them.

As she set herself into motion, she put on her only shoes, a threadbare pair of thin-soled black slippers; one of the bitter hallmarks of her interminable interment. . From where she stood, she was still unable to do anything but prepare, and *hope*. The words of the prophecy that had dragged behind her like an anchor all her life now rang with force within her.

That jeweled tower of her broken heart can only stand forth as righteous so long as the Flower of Hope remains, Rose in the Tower Eternal, else that flower of hope become crown of all ruination.

What dire nonsense.

If Talorr could fall... it would, and she'd known this since her youth, even as her paranoid father claimed he would prevent it by stuffing her into this fretful tower, hoping to forestall the inevitable. The walls of this castle were built on the shifting sands of fate, and Brabinghar, warlord and holder of Derebor, would be its last king. Not because of this fool prophecy, but because he was at once cruel and dull, shaped by a long time caring for nothing but his own wants—and his many and varied wants had brought ever greater suffering, as her tutor often told her, in whispers between her other lessons.

Vierrelyne knew enough of that cruelty herself, though she had seldom seen her father in the fifteen years of her imprisonment. She'd spent more years in that tower than she had in the light of the sun, at twenty-seven.

Decades of his unchecked tyranny had wrought much suffering in all his vassal states, and now it was visited upon

Castle Talorr in kind. She had heard as much, in whispers, in idle chatter no one thought her attentive enough to hear, that now the collective power of the Merchant Principalities was taking its vengeance.

In the Eye of Chaos, in the fall of the great empire, will be reborn the Crown of the World Unbound, the voice of Unspoken Ages anew, awaiting the return of the Sundered Throne.

It was his own fool deeds that had brought them to this place, but as it had always been, the last princess would bear the blame for her father's descent into ruin, all because some drunken sod with his own sectarian religion believed in the sacred truth of his dark imaginings. The baseless belief that every castle in Derebor, every kingdom in the Known Lands would one day fall to bloodshed, and all because of one lousy girl. It was worse than ludicrous in retrospect.

She wondered if it was worse to know the folly of the prophecies. It had been the king's own decision to bring her a teacher, someone who knew a world far outside these towers, and whose instruction had only honed her long resentment at her seeming fate. She had learned only that this castle held nothing for her, despite her aching wish.

In the firelight, down the hill, the vague shapes of riders on horseback bore torches and siege equipment, bound for the walls of the castle below. No time. If there was to be any change, any alteration of the star-sworn testimony, it would be by her hand. If she found her mother's crown and ran for Stonebrake *now*, there was still a chance she could set things right and escape this miserable tower once and for all. Better worlds she could live with, if only her luck held long enough. If only she was fortunate enough to flee at all, for that matter. The moment she'd anticipated for fifteen terrible years had descended upon them all at last.

Only by the oblation of the Shepherd in Shadow... She tried to remember the rest of the words. She didn't believe in any of it, but it'd haunted her for so long. *The Bringer of the Scourge, the Crown of the World Unbound...* All of it strange, unhelpful in the face of the oncoming blaze.

Only by the oblation of the Shepherd in Shadow will the Bringer of the Scourge free the Crown of the World Unbound.

It didn't matter anymore, did it?

As she shed the rest of her night clothes and cursed the ever-encroaching darkness, Vierrelyne du Talorr readied herself for the battle that had finally reached her door. She donned her training clothes—a gambeson and some other padded armor—then reached for the training sword Kharise had brought her...

Kharise! Where was she? The clamor of dire panic and the clashing of blades in the yards below filled Vi with an acute terror as waves of riders breached the siege gates. She steadied her mind, as she had been taught by her curious mentor, silently mouthing the words that accompanied the meditation of the blade. *I control only my response, I control only my breath, I control only my destiny.*

She suspected the destiny bit was her tutor and sword-mistress's way of critiquing the same prophecy that had brought her into the princess's circle, teaching and training her in secret, between lessons in music and histories known only to the folk of the Unconquerable Plains.

It was reassuring that the bardic woman from the distant steppes innately understood the preposterous nature of Vierrelyne's circumstances and regarded it with the same skepticism.

Vi slipped the pocket bag from her day-dress into the only gown that fit over her thin selection of armaments, the night-dark blue velvet masking her sturdy curves. Her tatting shuttle and a spool of black silken thread; a handful of rare gems loosed from their settings by diligent, hidden picking; a signet ring with a crest she dared not allow anyone to see upon her finger, for it was a token of a shattered time; all of these disappeared into those confines.

The shrill whinnies of spooked horses and the harried cries of night guardsmen in the courtyards below sharpened her resolve.

"Maybe they've forgotten me." It was not a wish, but it sounded like one, spoken aloud.

The burning odor accompanied the ozone of illicit mage-thunder from the ramparts; no way to tell which side had fired off such wicked spells. She threw herself at the locked door, anxious to be found before the unholy fire crept up the ivy trellises, equally anxious not to be apprehended by her father's guards if she sought escape. She drove her weight against it, shouting for Kharise, for anyone who'd hear, but it held fast despite her every effort.

Wild violet-blue flames erupted in the sky above her window, and a foul, alchemical scent flooded the room. She screamed for help, for mercy, her shoulder against the door frame as she bellowed herself hoarse and pounded the latches with her fists, trying to be heard over the din of the suffering below.

Damn them all, the superstitious and the gullible and the complicit, every single one of them, the ones who believed her only place in this world was this singular cell. Overcome with a terrible shuddering sensation as the air grew thin, she collapsed, heaving dry, gasping for breath.

An overpowering drowsiness came over her, as she thought she heard the faintest sound of her dearest mentor and friend, just outside the door, but she could not make out the words.

As the first wave of enemies crashed against the gates, The first thought on Kharise gen Valuure's mind was of the princess Vierrelyne; the Rose in the Tower, the young woman whose whole world was tied into that damnable old man's worthless prophecy. With the castle under siege, the tower prison was an undeniable target, taller than the rest of the castle, than even King Brabinghar's spires.

The dense wooden beams that held the interior scaffolds ribboned with the first vestiges of fire as the siege on the castle gates gathered momentum. A spray of rocks arced above, catapulted over the outer walls. Kharise took cover under an immobile wagon until the cascade slowed. The shouts of soldiers in motion mingled with the din of horse hooves on cobble, the clatter of metal and stone.

More than once, in the shouts and cries she heard a sentiment that filled her with dread—*find the princess, capture her, take her to Cascada!*

She gritted her teeth and redoubled her efforts to get to the tower before the hordes at the gates made it through.

This was not the first siege the plainswoman had ever borne witness to, but it was the first for which she held such specific responsibilities. Her calling was to aid the princess, in whatever capacity was required, but it seemed to her wary mind that tonight's unspoken mission was to extract the young woman from her confines before anyone else noticed. Perhaps the poor creature could be freed of this misbegotten belief system at last.

She cut through a side courtyard near the tower and stopped short. An arc of glimmering alchemical fire ripped from the ground level toward the princess's window, then a second, and a third—three arrows of magenta flame tinged with blue, aimed at the highest spire. None made their mark, she noticed; all clattered in sparks like the glint of a bright-carved amethyst before bursting outward into billowing clouds of vile smoke.

In an instant, her attention was on the figure standing beneath it, shrouded in a grey cloak with a deep hood. The figure bolted around the tower toward the doorway, into the spiraling stairwell, Kharise hot on their heels.

"Hey! What are you doing here? I saw you fire those strange arrows!" She bellowed.

The cloaked figure vaulted the tower steps ahead of her, two at a time, and she struggled to keep pace, on shorter legs than her adversary, but not shorter by much.

"Get back here!"

The figure turned, a rag hiding his face.

Kharise took the note, pulling her shawl over her nose, and it seemed to help. The air stank of acid from that rotten spell. She drew her dirk from her hip sheath and pursued him up the spiral staircase.

She rattled him with her persistence as the two climbed the formidable tower. He was not immune to the miasma, either; as they ascended, his eager gait drew shorter until she caught him by the shoulder and pulled him down. He tried to wrench free, and the pair went tumbling over and down several stone steps.

The intruder groaned and clutched his arms to his chest. She panted, drawing to her feet, and took control of the situation.

"Who are you?"

She yanked the fabric from his face. He gasped, flinching away from her, his head tilted down to the right. She held out her dirk, angled at his chin.

He trembled in terror and held out his palms.

"I-I'm a friend," he stammered, "I know the t-truth, ab-b-bout the princess. I was sent here to help her by Tobin—"

"The Heresiarch?" Kharise scowled. "Tobinarde l'Ete? He's dead. Try again."

He was younger than she expected for someone capable of such threatening spellwork; yet foolish enough to try something so brash as this. In his late twenties, she thought, by the first hard lines of age engraved at the creases between his cheek and nose. Another thicker line only became visible when his upper lip twitched, a deep tissue scar like a winding river, up under the long mop of shaggy black curls which settled over the right side of his face, his left eye a bold brown ringed in gold.

"N-n-no." The man clenched his jaw and slumped forward, flinched away from her again. "He went into hiding, after the t-tower collapsed, at Stardowne. He still leads the Circle, he t-told me where to go. He m-made the plan—"

"The Circle?"

"I c-came here f-from the Astral Circle. At Zalandan."

"You fired this alchemical spell up here, didn't you? What does it do?" She held the cloth taut to her face with her free hand, her blade still menacing the cloaked stranger trembling on the stairs below.

"Ssssleep," he said, unable to stifle a yawn as he sagged with alchemically induced exhaustion, closing his eyes, mumbling. "Not long—j-just a few minutes—I just n-needed to sneak up, help her, find the prism, r-rescue..."

He nodded off, leaning against the stone wall as if it were a pillow of goose down. Kharise broke away from him with a shake of her head, cursing every last alchemist as she wound her wrap over her face a second time and then a third. Madmen one and all, those foolish wizards from that damned cult, not a care in the world for a bystander.

She had to credit him once, though; he'd made quick work of the guards' tenement, the floor below Vierrelyne. Kharise strolled in, past two slumbering kings-men, and walked out with the key she was ever less frequently permitted to use, as the prophesied darkness drew nearer and the princess' superstitious father, the bastard-king himself, welcomed fewer of the bardic plainswoman's intercessions on Vi's behalf.

"Princess! Vierrelyne, I'm here!" she called out, and nearly tripped over the poor creature as she stepped inside.

Kharise tutted over the young woman she had come to quite admire, in her decade-long stay as the young lady's mentor in language, in music, and in swords. The red curly hair of legend was tucked into chained and beaded cauls of silver silks, links of maille, and bright glass beads, as her battle-maven mother had done when she was at war those many years before. Her dress was worn over what little armor she was permitted to keep in her tiny but well-appointed tower. Kharise suppressed her pity; for even at less urgent times, pity wasn't useful.

She grabbed her charge by the shoulder and shook her, without much hope, but Vierrelyne stirred back to life. If the spell was this temporary, they did not have long at all until the guards—and that wretch in the hallway—woke up.

"What's happening?" Vi groaned, hoarse, groggy, as she turned over on the stone floor. "Is it all as we feared? I thought it might—"

"Worse than that, I'm afraid, and your fool father has spread his own soldiers too thin. The siege walls of Talorr are falling. We haven't much time and we are surrounded by enemies. We must evacuate the castle, head for higher ground, maybe in the outer cities where the merchant infantry have yet to intercede—"

"We can't allow their foot soldiers to take the northern wall… Not until…" Vi faltered, and Kharise dug through the princess' wardrobe for something that might suffice to keep her clear of the lingering poison smoke.

The spell dissipated, but now the tower window was taking on soot from billowing black clouds, and those would be far deadlier if they did not flee now.

"Here," she said, holding out a long scarf.

Vi sat herself upright with a dreadful groan.

"We shall have to hurry, if we want to search the catacombs, but…" Kharise paused, searching for the right way to say, *you can leave all this star-sent foolishness behind and just run*, but she found none.

"He locked me in this tower for fifteen *years* to prevent this," Vi sighed, her deeper anger muffled as Kharise delicately tied the scarf over her face. "And no amount of prevention could forestall what was to come. I'm sorry, I shouldn't talk like this."

"But it's true. Vierrelyne, we must go. They are here for *you*." Kharise patted her shoulder. "Is there anything else you require from your long isolation? I daresay this is that last day foretold, so we won't find ourselves here again."

"I have Alaina's signet ring, and some things to barter." Vi contemplated. "I should have my papers."

The princess's diary, wedged under the sideboards of her bed, was so small it fit inside her pocket beside her lace tools. How strange, to have so few things of meaning and purpose to her name that it would all fit in a pocket-bag, but the princess had, after all, been prevented from having either meaning or purpose outside this tower for so long.

"Now," Vi said, so quietly Kharise strained to be sure she understood the princess's intentions. "To the northern wall and come what may. I have to find my mother's circlet, the one my father refused me after she died, the one she said was to be mine."

Kharise hesitated. "Are you *sure* you don't—"

"It was her wish that I take it, and I will."

"You m-might want some help," the wizard in the cloak called out as he stumbled through the open door, arms laden with pillaged armor. It spilled from his hands to the floor in a crash. Kharise drew back, blade in hand again, but the young man stepped away from the pile, palms raised.

"You came here from the Astral Circle, you said?" She strode toward him, and he flinched backward as Vi perused the pile of metal pieces. "Why are you helping us? Don't they believe in that old foolish prophecy from that heretical bastard? Why did he send you now, after all this time?"

"No, no! Tobinarde says the princess is the key to fix it all, he insisted it was the only way."

He leaned on the door frame, still woozy from his own foolhardy spell, tilting his face at an odd angle to the right.

"Milady, Princess, so long as I'm here, I intend to set things right, b-by the astral clock and the words of our leader so long ago, a history distorted by old beliefs. I will aid h-however I may, to get you to the P-Peridot Starprism, and to safety."

"We've little need for another dose of that noxious spell of yours," Kharise spat. "And even less use for that damned stone. Come on, Vierrelyne."

"Are you the Shepherd, then?" Vi whispered.

"It's not for me to say such things." He demurred, solemn as a priest, head bowed nearly to his chest, "Just the one who was called to the task by the—"

Angry shouting echoed through the stairwell.

"I blocked them in with a b-broom handle, but I couldn't bolt the door from outside. They're detained, but not by much." The wizard bent down to shoulder a vest of maille, and refastened his dark, shadowy cloak around it.

"We've got to go." Kharise swiveled toward her charge.

Vi had donned a helmet and a chest plate and braced a shield in one hand. Her practice sword in the other, she sheared her velvet skirts to shin length. She hadn't lost her wits from this smoke bomb, then; she knew she had to run.

Kharise winced to herself at the idea of fleeing in such dainty slippers as the princess was forced to wear, but it couldn't be helped here and now. She quietly seethed anew at the king and his advisors but perhaps, she hoped, this miscalculation would be their last.

"Onward," she called out, and slid the other helm over her cocks-crest of short-shorn greying curls. The wizard led the way, Kharise followed Vierrelyne, and together the three charged toward whatever destiny intended for this dark night.

The princess had pictured this cataclysm in her mind many times over many years. She'd sworn her closest confidante Kharise to secrecy over her plans to escape, but she had never thought it might be under such dire circumstances. It was another thing, entirely separate, to finally enact such a plan. Vierrelyne hadn't expected any of the legends to be true, but the dull false truisms of the prophecy that defined so much of her life had hung over her in such strange ways. Three armies had come for the end of the empire, and her only chance at safety now was to be party to this wretched end. It was a hideous numb feeling, one that ran from her temples down, a cold shock that she harnessed as best she could to get herself out of this damnable tower and into the catacombs to find her mother's gift.

Her legacy, her ancestral crown awaited there, in her mother's tomb. She just had to get there—and get out, perhaps to take the diadem back to Stonebrake, her mother's ancestral home. The power of the stone would do the rest, so long as she remembered the words... and so long as she could get her hands on it.

Upon the queen's brow lies the untold strength of armies from beyond the sun's reach.

It was fitting, if overwhelming, that Vierrelyne's first descent of the spiraling tower steps was into the fray of what would surely be the downfall of Castle Talorr.

It seemed that anything that could burn was in flames.

There were loud shouts and skirmishes farther down the courtyard, and everywhere seemed to be clouded with hideous shadows. She did not like to look at them closely, for it seemed to her as if the night itself were alive above her, a tremendous writhing beast of night with black wings unfolded over them.

It was oppressive, the overwhelming sense in the back of her mind that something, some dark entity, thirsted for this bloodshed and was nourished by the conflict at hand.

The blood rushed to her ears the first time Vi raised her sword and shield; a tidal sound, like waves on the shore when a man in a dark blue tabard rushed at her, his own sword raised. She knew the dance and had done it so thoroughly in practiced routines over her long confinement that battle contact with an unknown, maneuvering enemy challenged her at first.

Centering her mind, centering her vision, her dull trial sword was still a sword, and its blade was no less dangerous for its relative dullness—as a device of bludgeoning, more than adequate, until at last she got under her first adversary's chin and thrust forward with the point. She cast him to the ground, and stared at the reality of what she had done until Kharise shook her shoulder and broke her of the dark spell that crossed her face as the man's life rushed out of the gash under his neck.

"Quickly now," she intoned. "He earned it, and so did you. Never forget what that means."

Vierrelyne nodded, silently, thinking of countless nights practicing what to do, but not always remembering what it meant. A cold comfort in practice—but she knew it now in such a way she thought she'd never forget.

The silver-gilded armor of the soldiers at Talorr gave the three of them plausible cover to a point. The figures charging at the gates wore the colors and banners of three different, collaborating armies, former vasssal states of Derebor; the burgundy brocades of Cascada, accented with gold; the dark blue of Devere, that far inland kingdom oft forgotten by Brabinghar and his counsel; and the drab palette that adorned the many different merchant soldiers of Estuary City, men dressed as grey as the rivers that surrounded their principality, across the Broadcoast Bay. They had all traveled long to be here, and it was this notion that troubled Vierrelyne the most—that there were so many who'd travel so far to ensure the destruction at hand now.

She and her flanking pair darted out of the tower's open passage and around the courtyard behind the alehouse, along the outer castle wall. Around them surged such miserable apocalypse that they drew little more attention than the intruding horsemen under all of those Merchant Principalities banners.

Vierrelyne screamed the next time she truly had to raise her dull and blunted sword against another soldier, a hapless grunt in her father's armor. She hadn't anticipated how familiar it would quickly become, either, the strange and wet metal smell she associated with her own femininity, in a dark way—the unmistakable odor of blood—as she drew back her weapon and brought it crashing down upon that young man dressed in the silver heraldry of Castle Talorr, and he did not spring back into action but instead collapsed and fell still, the life of him pouring out a deep and dark gash she'd left behind despite the pathetic dullness of her blade. A cut was a cut, Kharise had told her countless times, but it had never sunken in with such detail as it had now. *He earned it, and so did you.*

She would need a sharper blade than hers. She traded with the dead man in her father's armor. It was the least they could do for each other: the dying empire, and the living symbol. It was still a wretched sword; the reach heavy and uneven, but how often had she said it to herself, under her breath? A blade was a blade. It would do as it was meant to do, for now.

Kharise scooped up a poleaxe from a fallen Cascadian, a man nearly twice her size, and while the weapon was unwieldy, in her capable hands she readily drove back a wall of others from Cascada charging toward them. The Astral Circle wizard held only an arrow-sling, but on more than one occasion interceded with a well-timed spell—dreadful little bits of magic laced into the feathers of short arrows. His aim was strange; seldom dead-on, and his eye for distance was questionable at best, but when he landed a good shot with his arrow-sling, it cleared two or three charging figures at once to the ground in paroxysms, even breaking whole rows of well-organized mercenaries.

Vierrelyne charged at the guards before the chamber at the northern wall, on the walkway that led to the catacombs at the heart of the castle.

A long-imprisoned fury burned in her heart, one as violent as her incarceration was futile. The fall of her father's throne need not be her own, but on the mark of her freedom, she had four enemy states, not three. Talorr itself felt no love for her, yet it was slow to recognize her as an enemy, thanks to the swift thinking of that strange wizard; their armor provided cover more by its familiarity than its true purpose. Under her own silver banners would she wrest her freedom from the Dereborean empire.

If she could make it to the catacombs in the stairwell below that highest tower, she might be able to turn the tides such that the invading forces would be swept away, even if the stronghold in this castle did not hold.

She hadn't ever realized the full shape of such a day in her mind's eye. No. There was nothing to *save* in this wretched place, she knew that. The first and only objective now was to reach the crypt where countless other ancestors had been laid to rest and take her mother's mantle: the Peridot Starprism.

That ancient weapon had wrought the great glories of the empire through the ages, not to correct this great wrong but to forge forward.

It was that crown which those superstitious old men truly feared, an ageless weapon of incalculable power, a symbol of something once held in highest reverence, the anticipated feats of a destiny unbound. It was that fear she wished to possess now, in this darkest moment.

M. Daniel McDowell

CHAPTER 2
THE BEGINNING

"THERE ISN'T MUCH TIME," THE OLD MAN SAID, AND MEHREN
nodded, silent. "After this, we won't have another
opportunity to change the world that is to come. It must be
tonight, when the Three Armies converge upon Talorr once
and for all. It is as I foretold. *Three armies fall upon the dying
empire and call forth that dread soul lost to ignorance.'* We must
ensure it happens as I know it to be."

Mehren cast his gaze away, into the middle distance, as
Tobinarde l'Ete continued his nigh-endless list of prophetic
instructions. It wasn't enough for him to be so certain of
himself and his beliefs about the universe, he also seemed
convinced that he alone could change the tides of the
burgeoning mercenary war with the coastal empire, with
the help of one warded mage who owed him a debt. Only an
elderly wizard alone in the mountains, addled with
overconfidence in his own strange predictions, could be so
demanding and so interminable all at once.

"You understand how to render the portal? You will have to do it twice in short order, you won't have time to calculate the foci—"

"Yes, sir," Mehren said, and did his best to suppress his frustration-borne sarcasm.

He had made it this far under Tobinarde's tutelage, but the longer he stayed, the more acutely he was aware of the sage's grandiloquent leanings and self-centering within his own band of prophetic teachings. Mehren went over the steps in his mind, trying to cement his own resolve. *Make the portal, find the princess, get the gem, return to the circle, and all creation will be spared the perverse devastation of the wizard-prophet Tobinarde's wildest projections.*

End the war before it starts.

The march on Castle Talorr had departed on all fronts over the past two weeks, by land and sea. It'd be mysterious to no one observing the political tenor radiating from Cascada of late: the wavering empire was at a threatening precipice. Moreover, it was tantamount to a death-wish to jump into the center of it at such a tempestuous juncture.

But Mehren was the only one in Tobinarde's collection of talents that the old man was willing to send for this mission, and if he played his hand correctly, after turning over the girl, and the stone, Tobinarde would have no choice but to let him go. His mind was so full of potential energy, it was hard to focus as the old man paced the room in front of him. Freedom beckoned with glittering claws in the dark.

"I need you to promise me this time, Tevaht. None of your damned excuses. I need the princess and the gemstone back before the night is over, just as the castle falls. We must find it before Prince Erenth's fools. We have only this chance to change the world to come."

M. Daniel McDowell

"I understand, sir." At this, Mehren drew his fingers over his face roughly, his thumb tracing the deep, nerveless fold that ran down his cheek to his lip. "If you wanted a mage with perfect poise, you wouldn't have asked me. You know as well as I do, I'm no hero of your made-up legend. You thought you could mold me as you liked. I'm not half as gifted as—"

"I know you are a man of discipline and tenacity," Tobinarde countered. "Few can survive the crucible you did, and with such strength of will. I expect more of you, but it's not without cause or reason. Rejecting any guidance is forever your greatest weakness, not the limitations of your sight. I trust no one else with the work to be done this night."

Mehren scowled. "So, the princess of Derebor is really the secret to your legend? What if I get there and she's nothing like you said?"

"Oh, I expect she will be nothing like either of us can anticipate," the old man replied. "She's a survivor, not unlike yourself, though her crucible is a different sort from yours. You might have more in common with her plight than you know."

He gazed out the far window, at the horizon Mehren could scarcely make out with his left eye. There was an odd glow in the far distance, across the ridgeline of mountains that stood between the tower of the Astral Circle and the castle at Talorr.

"Time is dwindling. Stonebrake has fallen, and Talorr is next. If we intend to be on the leading edge of the world yet to come, we must be swift. I need the crystal in hand before the next day dawns. I chose you over everyone else in this fated circle for a reason. I'll not be the only one who takes any failure quite harshly."

Tobinarde l'Ete bustled him out of his quarters and down the narrow steps, into the evening dark of the courtyard.

"Onward, to glory. Do not disappoint me again."

It was neither a hard spell, nor particularly intricate, but with only one eye that saw the World That Is, Mehren Tevaht forever worked twice as hard as anyone else in the Astral Circle to prove himself.

It was Tobinarde's constant changing of stakes, his insistence upon tampering with his own prophecies, that made Mehren the most resentful, more so than the mention of his lost right eye. That loss, that trauma of his youth, had been but one of the dire costs of his survival. Each of these new desperate errands for the *prophecy* had come with a promise of eventual freedom that, to Mehren's reckoning, stretched ever further into the future, as they had done since the old wizard first took him in.

He traced the sigil for the portal he would require: an intricate double ring of bright powdered chalk on the dark flagstone walkway. The incantation was all nonsense, near as Mehren could tell, just words Tobinarde had taught him only the sound of and not the meaning, only meant to attune the traveler to the deep-song of the folds, the places where the walls were thinnest between the realms: *the realm of bodies, the realm of beasts, the realm of spirits, the realm of dreams.* All the places that comprised the Scourgelands, the realms governed by the eldritch whim of demons, places no ordinary person could see; but Mehren, with his everlasting curse, could see them all, as they overlaid his own vision.

As he lowered his head and pressed his hands to the edges of the circle, the bottom dropped out, and though he screamed as he fell through the vast blackness, for once not a single soul heard him. Usually when Mehren crossed through any of the Scourgelands, by whatever means, he did not find himself alone. All eyes, demon and otherwise, must be on the various battlefronts to the west, across Broadcoast Bay; things were worse than he imagined, then.

It was a hard drop into and out of nothingness.

He landed roughly, as he usually did; this time, it was in a damp and driven grainfield on the outskirts of his marked intentions as the sun was setting. Thankful at least that he hadn't fallen far from the village he'd indicated in the spellwork, just south of Castle Talorr, he brushed away mud and blades of grass and set off in the general direction of firelight on the deeply wheel-rutted dirt road.

At least this time Carina couldn't gut him with the usual fish-knife; he'd arrived exactly where and when he intended to be. The always-impeccable Carina Betrel liked to taunt him, especially when he fouled up tasks she considered to be beneath her own station.

She'd stared daggers at him every morning at prayer for days over this assignment; it was *her* turn to prove herself, she'd said, but Tobinarde had insisted on sending Mehren, because of something to do with the particulars of his prophecy; that Mehren might be the latest Shepherd in Shadow, that it was Mehren's destiny foretold. For his part, Mehren did not especially believe he was the figure in Tobinarde's own prophecies—why could he not simply make up a *new* Shepherd? Perhaps one with Carina's tumbledown blonde curls and aggressive smirk—but he did believe in the power of *barter*, and once he had fulfilled Tobinarde's mission, once there was no further need for his prophetic Shepherd, Mehren could leave the fold of the Astral Circle free and clear, in charge of his own destiny once more.

As he drew closer to the village, his throat went dry. Men on horseback bearing torches; voices screaming from all directions; the thunder of catapults... He put his chin to his chest and gritted his teeth. This was different, not like *before*, not like it had been back *home*... but he could not cast aside the wave of nausea and fear as it struck him.

Run, now—you can't fix this—you can't stop *them—*

He could not stop the voice in his head; the last words beloved Istven ever said to him, before his voice was broken, before the *rest* of him was broken—

He could no sooner stop the fire that surrounded him than he could stop the memory; nor could he let that horrible memory stop him now, not after everything. He'd thought about the night that changed his life every day since, but none of it prepared him for how it would feel to be on the precipice of Tobinarde's prophesied future.

His heart hammered for a moment at his thoughts of the end. What he'd been promised. What he was *owed*. What the old man didn't know, couldn't know; what no number of prophetic visions and hypnotic smoke could possibly reveal—what Mehren intended to do, once his word was truly kept.

Mehren steeled himself, tied his scarf over his face to mitigate the fire as it swiftly overtook the thatched roofing throughout the village. Girded with the armor of his own fear, he made for Castle Talorr, on the well-beaten path of the ambushing crowd in the hope he might go unnoticed in the fray, shaded in his cloak. He weaved through the bodies at war with keenness. He was seldom glad to be so slight and wiry, but here, under his own cloak and the cover of encroaching darkness, he was able to cross the courtyard in pursuit of his precise target with little attention from the armed figures clashing around him.

There it was, the high tower, *the Tower of the Rose*, prison of the missing princess from the old man's mutterings. He notched an arrow in his sling, enspelled with a sleeping-draught that carried through the air with the slightest spark of surface impact. It missed the narrow window, and his next effort was no closer; it clattered off the high stone walls. A third such arrow was risky, as by the time he'd fired it he was drowsy from handling the wicked little device, but the resulting plumes of purple and blue magic encircled the tower. He ran for the stairwell, doing his best to shake the temptation to curl up in his cloak and sleep off the spell.

As he pivoted on his heel, though, he turned sharply and realized he hadn't been so hidden as to go unnoticed. A short grey-haired woman with a plainswoman's shawl gave chase, yelling madly at him until she had caught him and pulled him down hard on the stone steps.

His heart pounded in his ears, and he tried to pull away from her, tried to make her understand, he was only here to protect the princess, he was here to *save* her, just like Tobinarde said—

"He's dead. Try again."

But he *wasn't dead*, he'd survived the fall, it was all a horrible misunderstanding—

The short-tempered plainswoman's questions were too much, he just wanted to lay down, please. He yawned, and tried to tell her what was happening, but he wasn't sure she understood him as he nodded off in the stairwell, his weary head against the cold stone wall.

He came to, alone, the starkness of the chill flagstone beneath him a sharp reminder. The stairs... the tower.

The princess.

He heard the plainswoman's voice, trying to wake her.

There was still time. He wasn't too late.

Further up the stairwell, the guardhouse door stood open. Curious; an opportunity. On peering inside, he found the guards had taken the brunt of his sleeping draught; he had some resistance now but was still cloudy from the residual effects. He tied his scarf taut to his face so he wouldn't be drawn into another involuntary rest on the tower steps.

Mehren set himself to the task of stealing anything that wasn't nailed down, anything that might help them escape. Bits of armament, sacks of coin, the guards' helms, a scrap of hide parchment with a wide map of all Derebor and the Known Lands. This last, he figured, might well come in useful once he was done with Tobinarde and his schemes.

He wedged the door closed, the guards still dozing inside. Arms laden, he trudged up the narrow stairwell that led to the princess's chamber. Was it mad of him to try this? If he could keep her safe long enough to find the stone and escape?

He had to try.

Tobinarde had been clear with him—he had no choice but to recover them both. He knew the stone must be hidden, that something about its power must have been inaccessible to the reigning throne in Derebor. No. Something about its power had become relevant in this moment, through the old man's scheming, and Mehren was uneasy at this.

Vierrelyne thrashed her way through allied and enemy soldiers alike, with her mentor and their newfound ally at either side. The man had spells little more than parlor tricks, to her eyes, but he was able to distract and confound better than any courtly conjuror she'd known, back in the years she was permitted to attend. Kharise had marshaled a strong rejoinder to the proceedings. The wizard did his level best to follow them through the fray, nimble enough in his evasion of weapons that she suspected there was an illusion over his cloak.

As she threw down another soldier in her father's armor, she reflected on how she hadn't known what it would be to subdue a foe from her damned tower; how could she, from the comparative comforts of her castle cell? She suppressed the faint sickness in her gut, the cumulative tremors, the innate responses she'd done her best to ignore, over those first crumpled figures at her feet, some of them her own people.

She roared with half a lifetime's anguish in one single, unearthly howl. The very sound set a dozen lesser soldiers, under any marching banner, scuttling for cover.

Three stood before her now: the guardians of Abenelle and her crypt. Sturdier men than the rest of Talorr's standing forces, but with Kharise at her back, together they cornered one guardian swiftly, breaking the formation before he could even alert the other two. Kharise diverted the attention of one, her eyes pleading with Vi, to no avail. The princess would have what she was owed, at whatever it cost her now.

Standing in the archway, clouded by the haze of smoke and ash that blew around them, her father's most loyal and trustworthy lieutenant stood between goal and glory. Rolande du Tremaine drew his sword and raised it.

"Back away! None shall pass!"

"I shall *never*," Vierrelyne snarled. "You know why I'm here. What was taken from me."

"Vierrelyne!" He called out in alarm.

"It is. Stand aside, Rolande, and let me inside."

"This is a wretched mistake," he insisted. "Take cover with the rest of the court! You'd have no complaint from them—"

"The ones who boxed me away?"

A holy fire surged within her, one she could neither shake nor tame, one she could only ride to its apex, her stolen sword and shield in hand, bellowing in fury at what fate had wrought. She threw her full weight into a hard, jarring blow.

"Stand aside or die, Rolande. You let her die and pled your case to guard her damned bones and I will accept nothing but your submission in penance."

His eyes went wide as he parried her every strike, measured in his response, but he was older than Kharise, and his reflexes would surely betray him, if she pressed his weak points.

"You might accuse me in her death, but you know not the truth!"

"What truth is there? The king of Derebor envied the victories of his wife and sought to emulate them in the only way he could!"

"You can't know that." He deflected her with a sweep that kept her at a distance. He was prepared for her strength, but not for her speed. Perhaps, like the others, he still thought her the useless girl in the parapet; perhaps he was simply too proud to admit that his place as the late Queen's guardsman had softened him.

"I know my father well enough to know the blood on his hands. He used the prophet, and the prophet used him, and for what? Jealousy? Revenge?" She spat. "What does it matter now? Why would he swear *you* to defend it if it were not rightfully mine?"

"It's not too late to halt this madness!" he shouted at her. "I forever told his lordship it was a great injustice to pen you in his bloody tower."

"The key was never hidden from you!" Vierrelyne snapped back, catching his blade on the guard of her miserable stolen sword. "Nor from anyone in your command, Rolande. It was convenient for an entire kingdom to believe it my role to play, the cowering creature brought out once a year for their pathetic rituals, or on occasion to celebrate their empty victories, to sing the ancient songs of the lands of Derebor against the scourge of the demon provinces! It was for *nothing!*"

Sensing his hesitation, she wrenched her own worthless weapon slightly outward and slammed him with her shield, rewarded with the clatter of his blade on the stone stairwell. She backed him against the wall at the point of her unbalanced sword before he could drive her off.

"Abenelle, forgive me," he called out in futile prayer. "Forgive us all!"

Vi snatched his discarded blade from the floor, trading up her sword for a second time that day alone.

"She can't hear you. None of them can. None of the ones you were willing to destroy, only to forestall the inevitable! You'd rather let my father live his miserable lie than stand down, Rolande, and for that I offer you nothing but the edge of your own sword."

"You know I cannot allow you any further—" His voice faltered, and Vierrelyne lunged, his clean-polished blade swifter than her dull tester had been at its zenith. There was no mercy for him, nor any of her father's army, left in her by the time his blood sprayed from the wound in his neck. He collapsed, and she stepped over his body.

Nothing more than a lapdog to the declining throne. He had no further use for it.

She dashed down the stairwell, into the shrine her father had preserved most holy at the behest of that damned madman, a shrine to his nihilistic word, in the deepest reaches of the Talorr crypt.

Kharise tried to keep one eye on the princess and the other on the stranger who had incorporated himself into her rescue. Vi had taken to combat with a furor that threatened to open her to vulnerabilities; she was strong, for someone kept as she had been kept, and she was surprisingly swift for her size and frame. She watched as the strange man flung another arrow into the oncoming crowds, another that landed short of the estimated distance—clearly, he could see, but he had no sense of

M. Daniel McDowell

depth, no eye for long distances. She snapped to attention when she realized she'd lost her view of Vierrelyne.

"Princess?" She swept her surroundings, but the fighting seemed to be coalescing at the front gates. Not good. It'd be nearly impossible to get her out that way now.

"Here," Vierrelyne called out, as she charged through doors whose sanctity had been preserved by spells that would do nothing against her. "On to the catacombs."

Kharise trailed her into the foyer, the wizard following at her elbow, but hesitated there.

Why was he so determined to hang close? There was something uncanny about him, and she did not like it at all. She grabbed him by his sleeve.

"I'd go no farther, whatever your beliefs," she warned him. "If you're trying to hurt her, in any way—"

"I'm trying to *save* her," he snapped back. "As soon as she finds the Starprism, we have to get out of here, before everything falls apart—"

"What is it that you aren't telling me?"

The young man stared at her, and she realized his hair was not simply obscuring his view. The right eye, under the long black forelock, remained closed. His expression sullen, he turned away from her. "Did you not hear them? I was *not* the only one who came to this castle in pursuit of Vierrelyne du Talorr, and I *am* the only one who wants to see her out safely."

Kharise stared back at him, not wanting to admit he was right, but she had heard the Cascadian soldiers, and she rather wondered what their motives were.

"We must leave. The sooner the better. Please, I'll take you both, I'll make the portal. We can escape before the whole castle collapses, but it must be now, before Talorr falls to ruin."

"I don't even know your name, you odd little weasel. I'll *not* let you set the terms."

He did not offer his name, not even when presented to him as a means to negotiate. Kharise narrowed her eyes as he stooped forward, rummaging in his cloak.

"I'll explain it all once we get to Zalandan. P-promise. Tobinarde is there; he knows w-what to do, how w-we can stop it." He began tracing figures upon the stone floor with a round brush he dipped into a sack of pale powder. "He can f-fix it all."

The young man's hands shook as he sketched out concentric circles in chalk over the time-polished stone atrium.

Kharise stonewalled him. "Zalandan? Absolutely not. We're going to ride out to the castle in the south. Stonebrake. Her mother's people. We'll get her an audience there, and—"

"Stonebrake?" He looked up at her, his left eye wide with alarm. "The castle at Stonebrake has already fallen. We can't go there. There's n-n-no one left to make an audience. We have to go east. Zalandan is safe for her—"

"We would have heard something by now," she countered. "Stonebrake is at the edge of Talorr, the seat of the southern reach, the other hand of the empire. Surely some messenger would have escaped the fray?"

He shifted his gaze away from her and returned his attention to the glyph he'd drafted upon the dark stone. He wasn't happy with it, she thought; he'd be contented with one line and need to redraw the next, in a manner she thought hopelessly fiddlesome. When he looked up at her again, his expression was curious.

"You are a daughter of the endless grass. How did you come to care about an *empire*?"

At this, Kharise pursed her lips and squinted at him. "I care about Vierrelyne du Talorr, whose education during her ghastly captivity has been my responsibility. You are a stranger who has inserted himself into the makings of multiple fronts of war. How did you come to care about empire, impudent little death cultist?"

A strangled, furious cry from the chamber below pulled both to attention.

"She needs help." He pushed up from the floor.

"*My* help," Kharise cut him off, and then realized she did not want to leave the strange man alone drawing arcane ciphers in the vestibule. She couldn't trust him, but he'd proven useful once so far. She grabbed his wrist, and he yelped in protest.

"Hey! My chalk!" He hurried to bind the bag closed and secured it in a deep pocket of his cloak. "Be careful with that. Without it you'll never be rid of me."

She sighed.

"Grab a torch, wizard. We're going in."

M. Daniel McDowell

CHAPTER 3
CATACOMBS

BOTH OF MEHREN'S EYES STRUGGLED TO ADJUST IN THE DEPTHS OF the crypt, with only the torchlight to aid him. This place was thin, its connection between the many realms of the Scourgelands overlapping in this great and grim expanse of underground darkness.

The crypt at Castle Talorr held generations of the princess's ancestors. Sheltered here were her empire's holiest adherents as well as her lauded emperors and noblest soldiers; it was a place carven from the dark stone depths below the castle itself. The centuries of accumulated skeletal remains were ornamental in some chambers and more subdued in others. Derebor had long been a land of suffering and death revered, and this was most apparent in her catacombs, adorned with the bones of the fallen in ceremony and in decoration, in memento mori that none the less defied actual remembrance; legion upon legion of the nameless and forgotten dead.

Mehren expected the sound of their boots to echo through the tiled stone tunnels, but there was an eerie dampening to it, a softening he attributed to the ink-dark banks of crepuscular moss that coated some of the oldest surfaces and structures. A faint odor of wet earth carried throughout the silent halls. The sounds of the strife above did not carry down below, but none of the Scourgelands were far from view, if one had that particular and unfortunate second sight, as he did.

Mehren and Kharise walked briskly, trying to find where the princess had gone. In the judder of torchlight, the shadows stretched into sinister, yet eerily familiar otherworldly forms.

Mehren parted his forelock with his free hand, holding it away as he opened his right eye, the one forever sighted only in the vast liminal places—the folds between the portals, the grey space tangled up somewhere inside of himself wherein he could push against the bounds of reality. He gasped.

Everywhere he looked, shimmering beasts from beyond the Cairn of Shadows—the gravelands beyond even the Sundered Lands, beyond even the human Realm of Dream—lurked in the gloom, but none approached, nor even took much notice of them, as if they were waiting for some inscrutable signal.

They sat in vigil, in reverence, uncaring at his intrusion into their proceedings, even as he waved the torch before him.

The plainswoman turned her attention toward him. He settled his hair back into place as he closed his right eye once more.

"Why are you truly here, wizard?"

"You said it yourself. Your loyalty to the princess transcends your other responsibilities. As does mine."

She tilted her head at him. "My loyalty to her is not in question. What is yours?"

"It's not that simple." He sighed and stared up at an archway crafted from a lattice of femurs as he struggled to find the words. "I am here to *protect* her, sent by the only person who knows how dangerous and precarious this situation is. I'll do whatever I must to keep her safe."

Hell, for all Mehren knew, Tobinarde's old passages about the Shepherd in Shadow, the sacrificial figure in his grand tapestry... Perhaps Mehren had been short-sighted in his acceptance of this task, but he suspected even the old man was not so cynical as this.

Kharise snorted.

"If you lift one finger against her, you'll lose them all."

She brushed against a shadowy figure, unmoving in its reverence, and jumped back.

"What was that?" She wiped her arm as if she'd met with a grisly spiderweb.

"We need to be careful," Mehren said, weighing each of his words. "There are things you were never meant to see lurking between every sepulcher down here in the tombs."

"What do you mean by that?" she asked, holding out her poleaxe with apprehension. "I see nothing strange here. Not stranger than the burial rites of the Dereborean elite, anyhow."

"Most of them can't see you any more clearly than you can see them," he said, trying to keep his voice low.

Some of them, after all, could *absolutely* see him.

She surveyed the room with her woefully ordinary human eyes under the brightness of the torch, but her face read with the same skepticism he'd come to associate with her.

"A lot of the ones who can see you haven't got any interest in you," he continued. "There might be some demons who want to frighten you, and they should; you don't want to get near them."

He paused, scanning his surroundings as they crept ever deeper inward. Every eye from another realm was fixed upon a single doorway at the end of the passage before them: reverent, obedient, waiting. He could not distract them if he tried.

"The ones you really need to watch out for are the ones who want your attention."

"Demons?" She shrugged, with a laugh. "I don't believe in any of that."

"Well." Mehren laughed with a grim humor. "Some of them don't believe in us."

He wondered, though, why it was that a congregation of such eldritch creatures had convened upon this unutterably *human* place, when they heard another loud shriek, in one of the catacombs ahead of them. This time, the princess sounded disappointed or deeply frustrated more than dismayed. More yelling. Furious.

"My lady!" The plainswoman called after her, as she bolted forward into the gloom. Mehren struggled to keep up; it was not easy to hold the torch aloft and run at the same time, especially in his heavy cloak.

Something slithering and dark followed after him, and he tried not to pay it any mind.

If he did not look, he would not have to see.

Vierrelyne had never before been to this particular antechamber of her estimable family crypt, the place where her mother and her armor had come to rest. The creation of this remarkable enclosure was the work of a decade, begun not long after Vi's destiny was decided, completed at some time during her interminable captivity. The assembly of the bones stretched across every rank of the many loyal soldiers under the watchful command of the Great Lady of Battle, the most fearsome Abenelle.

Vierrelyne's skin crawled with revulsion and distaste for the mockery of opulence in this quiet place, this theater of grief.

To Vi's way of thinking, it was designed to mask a sinister truth: a queen overwhelmed by the loss of her daughters—two to a terrible accident, one to a terrible destiny. The legend wrote itself, did it not? A queen whose life ended in emotional agony and heartbreak, but VI knew too well that was nothing more than a story, not well told.

Vierrelyne never questioned it *aloud*, for fear His Majesty might choose to add her to the crypt as well, but the thought never left her. In visiting this space by torchlight at last, the grandiosity of this sepulcher spoke to her father's dramatic performance of over-elaborate grief.

For such a holy place, no warmth emanated from the echoes of the past that surrounded her now, the plinths of plaster and hand-polished bone, hewn from what remained of enemies and allegiants alike. The figural forms of the ancient and sacred ghosts fused together with the great legends of her family's vast empire, a mosaic of the consecrated soldiers who served under Her Most Holy command.

Left in her father's hand, what remained was an empire of bones.

Twin figures in alabaster stood at the sides of the carven stone sarcophagus, one dressed in the fine and fair fabrics Abenelle preferred at court—silks and beads and corsetry, little of which had survived the years unblemished. Evidence that the profundity of Brabinghar's grief did not persist endlessly through time; the queen's finery had gone to tatters in this unvisited tomb.

Only the high, elaborate lace ruff at her symbolic mother's statuesque neck remained intact. Vierrelyne took it, a fine emblem of her late Majesty with which she did not wish to part. A pile of amber beads rested on the floor at the statue's feet, the string rotted. Vierrelyne pocketed the centerpiece: a single heavy perfect golden teardrop, the color of her mother's eyes; the color of her own.

The other standing stone figure held Abenelle's armor upon her sculpted statuesque form, the figure carved in effigy to the battle-maven, rendered with a reverent eye to the exquisite details of the enchanted metal. The steel spider-lace that draped over her sharp-curved pauldrons, the gentler lines of the cuirass beneath, the fauld of three lames that rested above the heavy belt slung low at the hips, the tasset belt, and the greaves and sabatons, all impeccably polished for having been kept in a cold, dark place. The pieces were exquisite, feminine, but eminently threatening, touched with an eldritch power that radiated from them even after nearly two decades of disuse.

Atop the gleaming, polished stone brow, Vierrelyne expected to see the thorned crown which paired with this armor, the diadem said to be the eye of a demon prince who lurked there still. The optimistic, youthful visage, pallid and pure, was unadorned above the chin, her battle raiment incomplete. Would that coward have hidden such an important piece of Talorr— for he could not keep it himself—or would he have laid it to rest with the late Abenelle?

She searched the room by torchlight. It burned within her that this was a single refrain in the litany of wrongs against her by her father and his sycophants.

He'd listened to the hysterics as they warned him of the stone's darker properties. The violence of their paranoia was fresh in this moment, though their deeds were the work of a decade past. That superstitious old bastard. Let the armies of his enemies have him, for she had nothing left. Even if she found the weapon of her salvation in time, it would not be for him.

The Peridot Starprism holds the undoing, the endless rain of torment.

Least subtle of the prophecies; the wellspring from which was drawn the worst of her father's fears, the catalyst for Vierrelyne's imprisonment. Likely the catalyst of her mother's untimely death, though she dared not follow that thought, not now, not when all apocalypse was nigh at hand.

In the depths of the catacombs, Vierrelyne could not help but shiver, knowing this was not merely the resting place of her mother and countless untold souls of the crusades that defined her. This space was an end, a haunting certainty, and it shrouded her with unaccountable doubts. It wasn't simply her own grief that rang through her bones now. The immense losses her mother had suffered before this last great indignity: Vierrelyne's elder sisters. She was older now, at twenty-seven, than either Revica or Nianne had ever been. She had been twelve years old when her father locked her away; she'd spent fifteen more years in that dismal tower, the youngest of three rendered into an only child. Her sisters had been older than her at the time, only in their late teens, when their carriage overturned in the dark during a cataclysmic storm, the kind of tragedy that makes even a sensible man believe in the sinister words of a ghoulish prophet:

The last becomes the only, the herald of blood.

Even as she counted herself a heretic, it was the final great insult her father could lay upon her, to exclude her from her mother's tomb.

Brabinghar was nothing but a coward. It was this cowardice that had led him to this grand precipice, where he would part the princess from the queen, forever, all in the hopes of suppressing the herald of blood; the endless rain of torment; the Bringer of the Scourge.

He'd paused none of his agitations against the merchant cities within his dominion, and not even the word of their unions, their rising tide of forces, could sway him from his usury, but he felt safe in his choices, for Vierrelyne was contained and thus, the prophecy could not be brought to bear. The destruction of an empire, for which she would be the herald.

No. All that mattered to her now was the power to leave him, and this, behind forever. If she only had the damned crown of her mother's personal thorns, she could leave all of this. Break the old and crystalline world of the prophecy, lead any who would follow into the new.

For if she held the mantle of the Sundered Throne, they could doubt her no longer.

That it had been hidden from her, she knew as plain as day. She could not stop herself from howling in rage as she scoured the catacomb shrine, the room whose heraldry in bone spoke to Abenelle's dark legacy, the shroud-bearer of the last age, whose many warriors had given everything to the land of Derebor, whose blood enriched her soils, whose bones were inlaid throughout this vast cathedral.

There were no obvious hiding places here, but she surveyed every last panel in the hopes that some secret might wait beneath. Soon there was only the stone sepulcher at the center of the room, surrounded by the late queen's alabaster figure. Even if Vierrelyne were to don the ancient armor, with its untold powers, she suspected she could not lift the lid of that stone table without the assistance of several hands. Kharise was small, but strong. If only she had anyone else. Perhaps that odd wizard. He seemed bent upon reconciling the prophecy; she pondered if that extended to robbing the queen's grave for her benefit.

She screamed once more, still not finding words for the commingling of terror, grief, and hope that rang within her. She would not let this last slight against her be her defeat.

In this grand hall, so far below the chaos, she heard nothing but her own agonies, the beating of her heart in her ears as she stripped away pieces of the captive girl she had been, shedding the mismatched protective layers stolen from her sleeping guards in favor of the suit she would require, escaping this dreadful place at last. From the rituals her mother taught her, the strength imbued in such a glorious set of armor—fused with the deep-magic of a time long before, its scrollwork enspelled by wizards whose very souls were laced through its crenellations now—maybe be enough to wrest free the stone slab that held her apart from the only place her mother's thorned diadem could possibly rest.

The layer of clothing she retained fitted her closely under the pieces she now donned; the gambeson and shirt of maille, sabatons and greaves, tasset belt, cuirass, pauldron, bracers, gloves. A holy might surged through her; different now from the one that had kept her alive through the smoke and fire of the siege. This was something righteous, something alluring, something truly powerful in a way Vierrelyne had been expressly forbidden since that fateful day. Once she was no longer third of three, once she was the cursed only child of the king and queen of Derebor...

She shoved at the stone slab, and it did not budge. A lip extended below it, catching against the edges. Vierrelyne cursed, and dug her gloved fingers underneath it, snarling as she lifted it over its edges, pulling it, inch by inch, scraping stone against stone in an agonizing noise to create a gap where she might push in the opposite direction. She thought she might shed blood from her pores at this rate, for the impossible weight of this stone was meant to secure this kingdom against her, to prevent whatever destiny would come. She strained, and cursed, and bellowed, as if the stone itself would bend to her will with the right persuasion. The gloves shielded her delicate fingers as she concentrated on levering the lid from the stone sarcophagus. She roared, enraged, as the great heft threatened to crush her fingertips. What a fool her father was if he believed this enough to stop her.

"Princess!" Kharise called out behind her, and at last, beyond the conch echo of blood in her ears as she strained to lift the stone, she heard two pairs of boots scuffling on the cobblestones.

"In here!" Vi called back.

"At your word!"

Her mentor and the wizard both appeared at the door. It was curious to see how they responded to her mother's tomb—Kharise with the mix of reverence and revulsion writ across her face as she often had for the cult and custom of the kings of Derebor, the wizard with an expression that seemed to be vast with wonderment, underneath the cascade of dark hair that shrouded half of his face. She wondered again what it was that had brought him through this gauntlet of horrors to be here, why he was as determined as Kharise to make her plans come alive. He was so strange, but she could not reject any ally at this point, no matter how odd his manner. Together, the three strained to lift the lid, Vierrelyne and her force of will doing the bulk of the work.

With a second pair of hands, the stone was no lighter, but it skimmed over the lip of the carven box more readily, scraping and gouging against the rim as they shifted it. With their combined effort, the heavy lid gave way, and the lingering odor of something foul, something unspeakable, laced the underground room. The liquid of the corpse within, sealed by the heavy stone, was imbued with something else; some foulness of magic, she suspected, some dull sorcerous thing done to prevent precisely what the princess herself set out to accomplish, another barrier to the theft of the demon-bound trinket she sought.

"Is that..." Kharise started but would not continue. She wrapped her shawl tight over her face once more, the beads in its fringe clanking against the cuirass she had strapped over herself to brave the pillage outside. "Vierrelyne, we can leave without *any* of this—"

"—I can't, and I won't," Vi shot back, between deep breaths and heaving efforts to shift the stone lid, inching it across the lip of the sepulcher. "If I am to be punished with this nonsense for the rest of my days, I will strike back with the future that was denied to me by those meddlesome priests. I will have my mother's crown."

"It—it was foretold," the wizard offered, before he bound his own face against the strange air. He at least did not fear the grave before him and lent what strength he could offer to the task. There was a gap, now, one wide enough to allow Vierrelyne's gloved hands entry. She dared not look at the putrefaction, the leather, the bones beneath, but her fingers met something wicked and sharp, and she gently lifted, upwards and out. The only resistance she met in removing the diadem were the strands of the late queen's silvered hair through which they had entwined, through her interment, her settling.

Vierrelyne spoke the words of a prayer in solemnity. Kharise breathed not a word, and the strange wizard only stared, his left eye wide and dark in the ever-dimming torch light.

It wasn't much, and she could not be sure she remembered every word, but she did know that she must speak with this demon if she ever expected him to open his eye and smile in favor over an anointed brow, however haphazard her approach to such power was. She recited the words of her mother's prayer-hymnal, a rite half-remembered from years spent at the warrior queen's knee, a rite which had long existed only in Vierrelyne's dreams.

Nothing. The stone blinked and gleamed in the firelight, but there came no rush of magic, no sudden alertness, no obvious cataclysm within its shimmering confines.

"Don the crown, my queen," the wizard said. Was he as impatient as she was for the dawn of a new future? It was most unsettling. "We must leave this place, and fast, before it becomes the tomb of our own. Please. There is no time."

She raised the odd, pointed thing over her head, the dream of fifteen years gone at last renewed by peculiar circumstance. In the fray above them, she knew that if the besieging forces had done what they do best—and the tremors in the ground itself spoke to that certainty— Brabinghar du Talorr would be dragged from his fine chambers, then marched down the roads of every merchant city, to be gawked and spat at by their denizens, a spectacle of rightful ignominy in death.

It wasn't hard to picture what else they might choose to do, and while it was a grisly thought, she could not contain the thrill of victory at the thought of her father's head upon a pike at the shores of Cascada, or upon the walls of one of the neighboring villages or paraded through the dark alleyways of Estuary City or the brilliant promenades of Devere. The thought filled her with nothing but fresh contempt for his grand ignorance, and something like revenge colored her every thought of him. The shuddering of the whole structure set upon them; bits of stone plinked against their helmets and the tile within the chamber.

"Princess, we have to go," Kharise insisted, her wrist over her mouth and nose, even as the shawl covered her face. "This place was never meant for such..."

"Come with me," the wizard insisted, "I'm here to get you to safety, Princess, and your companion, but we must hurry!"

Kharise shook her head as she exited the chamber, coughing. "We don't have time for this strange ritual of yours! Vierrelyne, let's regroup, somewhere far away from the walls of Talorr, on foot."

Vierrelyne felt a strange surge throughout her, nothing like magic at all, simply the blood of the fight renewed. She did not wish to concede her unbearable disappointment that the demon within the stone, the one who was purported to awaken at the first opportunity to lend his grand and unspeakable force to his bearer, lay silent.

Kharise insisted that they run; it was not safe to linger underground, not when they still had to make a mad dash for the safety of the southern keep at Stonebrake in the cover of darkness. As it was, there was precious little she could do to keep Vierrelyne safe, as the princess was insistent upon running headlong into the shadows of her own mother's path.

The wizard followed after them with the torch, as if he were watching for an ambush behind them. Quite nervous, for someone so bold as to call himself the assistant to a heretical prophet arisen from the dead.

"My name," he called after them, his words in fits and spurts as they ran through the hideous maze of crypt chambers. "I'm Mehren. Mehren Tevaht."

Kharise looked over her shoulder at him.

"That's a warded name."

"Aye, it is, for I walk the Scourgelands." He huffed, and she got the sense he was trying to keep pace, but also to prevent them from leaving him behind. "Th-that's the only way out of here alive tonight. I-I can shield you through the folds and get you to the temple at Zalandan. I can help, Princess. I p-promise. *Please.* I've started the spell; I only need to—"

He was so desperate, but he left so much unsaid. Why? Kharise did not trust a word of it. This wasn't the first piece of Tobinarde's miserable legacy she'd ever encountered, but it was the first since the fall of the towers at Stardowne, where it was widely rumored that the heresiarch himself, the founder of these wretched prophecies, had been slain.

She'd rather preferred the idea that the old man suffered and died for the hideous fate he'd set for Vierrelyne—for her whole empire, collapsed as it was now.

The idiot-king Brabinghar had misread the glorious past as a glorious future. He had mistaken the tragedy of his eldest daughters for the tragedy of his entire people, and now, he had no people and no empire.

There was nothing to be done about this bizarre set of circumstances but to stand aside and let them wash over the world before them. Now this strange little cultist wanted to drag the princess back through such a profound and excessive waste.

"Ignore his utter foolhardiness," Kharise insisted, but it was as if her insistence only reassured Vierrelyne that it might be the safest way forward.

"Can you get us to Stonebrake?" she asked him, her face flushed, her words breathless, as the three staggered toward the vestibule where the wizard— Mehren—had first offered his odd little wards. "Please. To my mother's people."

"Zalandan," he insisted. "It's safer there. Stonebrake has already collapsed, Your Highness. If anyone remains there, it is forces of the Merchant Principalities who are at this moment marching through on the route to the high castle at Talorr to destroy us all."

"We cannot truly take our chances now," Vi said hoarsely, and Kharise was startled at her swift agreement. "But I want to see it for myself. Please, to Stonebrake—"

"There is nothing to see there," the wizard said, with solemnity to his words as he pulled out his small satchel of chalk and continued to draft the periphery of what Kharise knew to be a portal, a passage through the demon realm. Her skin prickled with radiant distaste.

"Princess, he is mad," Kharise pleaded. "We cannot do this—"

"We cannot stay here." His insistence was unnerving. "None shall survive the ambush at Talorr. You know as well as I. The gate is blocked, the fire encroaches. I want to *live*, don't you?"

He painted the floor with the strange chalk: more concentric rings and runes, using a soft brush that left a delicate counterstroke. These faint marks were magic enough to transport three people across the continent, far beyond the frayed borders of Derebor and into the Sunward Free Cities? She'd only made that journey once, in the days after her beloved had departed this world, and she did not relish the thought of returning to a place her heart held in such shadow.

It was one thing to believe in the impossible; it was another thing to doubt the truth before her eyes. Mehren Tevaht alleged he had come here by the same such circle by which he proposed they should leave. Could they trust him with such absurd claims?

"Hold my hands," Mehren said, tucking the chalk bag into his voluminous dark grey cloak and extending his palms. "We only have one chance to make this work."

The plainswoman regarded him coolly but extended her palm. The princess held out her heavy, armored glove, and he bent his head, speaking the words to pull open the seams of reality for but a moment. The lightless gap in time and space swallowed them whole.

When the world dropped out beneath them, Vierrelyne gasped in alarm; Kharise drew in a sharp breath but said nothing. As they fell through the portal, with Mehren's arms outstretched to hold their hands, he kept both eyes closed and concentrated on their destination. Soon, they would be in Zalandan, where the chill of autumn had already begun to twist into place, the air cold and crisp instead of the last harvest days of summer here in the west. The leaves on the mountain trees would be sparse but colorful, the morning still bright...

He'd deliver on his promise to the old man, and he would be free, his obligation to his so-called rescuer finally met by this one last errand.

The notion of freedom might've been a burden, under different circumstances, but—

They landed hard on stony ground, long before they were supposed to, and tumbled several yards down a steep hill. The violence of the fall shook loose a cascade of graveled coarse dirt, and a plume of smoke-like pale grit went up behind them as they tumbled to the foot of the hillside. The three collided on the ground, sharply, violently, at the bottom of the slope, coming to rest not far from the embankments that surrounded the tall and forbidding fortress beyond.

The other two seemed not to be in such rough shape as he, but then, they hadn't already done this ritual tonight.

His face hurt, and as he put his hand to his nose, he observed in abject terror that he'd sprung an excessive nosebleed. From the violent entry or simply from the temptation of fate by having done two trips through the folds of unreality in such short succession, he could not say, but as he looked at his hands, palms and fingertips coated in his own blood, he went lightheaded.

Oh, damn it all, not again—

CHAPTER 4
STONEBRAKE

KHARISE STRUGGLED TO HER FEET ON THE COBBLESTONE ROAD AT the base of the hillside. Southward facing, she deduced, from the wind and the light. Something wasn't right about this. It should be deeply autumnal, nearly ready to snow this time of year in Zalandan, but here the leaves had scarcely begun to turn.

The wizard collapsed, his hand and face covered in blood. Was he... dead? Could she be so fortunate as that, she wondered with a dark humor as she knelt to inspect him. His chest rose and fell, so she knew it could not be so simple. He still had a steady pulse, however erratic. It did not seem to be seismic nor a stroke.

Had he simply *fainted*? How quaint.

Vierrelyne was slow to rise, and held her head, as if she were burdened with a foul headache as well as the shock of a hard landing, somewhere far from the terrible tower the princess called home for such a wretched long time.

"Have we made it, then, Princess? Zalandan awaits?" Kharise muttered, shaking each of her limbs to do away with the curious, rubbery sensation that came with the sharp impact. "Whatever remains of it, anyway."

Vierrelyne's eyes, though, welled with tears as she surveyed the landscape around them, with only the wind in the trees making a sound.

"This isn't Zalandan," she whispered. "It's Stonebrake."

"Isn't this where you wanted to be?" Kharise replied, trying to comfort Vi, trying to understand her own unease.

"It is," the princess cried. "But he told the truth. Look! It's all gone. Not a soul remains."

She felt keenly the sense of loss from Vierrelyne, but she could not help but wonder what it was they'd stumbled into, and how. Surely there was something more here, something sinister, and she would not be satisfied without at least another look to see what yet remained. It gave her no comfort, at the moment, to know that the wizard Mehren was right.

Vierrelyne tried her hardest not to crumble under the weight of her own expectations, but the tears came unbidden. How could she not be devastated at this, her hope of a safe haven, her beloved Alaina's childhood home, before she came to the court at Talorr, her mother's homeland in the times before? No, this was worse news than she had dared to dream.

He'd tried to tell her, to take her elsewhere, but her hopes, her wishes—were they too powerful even for a wizard to overrule? Perhaps. Did he do this on purpose, just to prove her wrong? Something so cold and hateful as to deposit her on the rocks above the abandoned castle.

Even as she thought it, though, even as the spiteful feelings welled in her gut, she knew she could not truly blame him for this. It had been *her* wish, not Kharise's and certainly not his.

Why in all the stars had this been the only one of her wishes she'd ever been granted? It filled her heart with sadness and dread.

The castle at Stonebrake still stood, her crenellations and buttresses sounder than even the walls of the great castle at Talorr, but the silence that engulfed her was absolute and harrowing. There should be noise and firelight at this stark hour, some sign of human activity, but the fortress at her gates was shrouded in shadow, and so were the rest of her vast grounds. Not even the sounds of animals reached her; no stray pigs or goats, nor a single horse to whicker in the soft darkness. Absolute destruction.

That strange wizard had told the truth, then. Stonebrake lay in ruin, and she had refused to believe it, perhaps out of spite or pride. She would not bend, no matter how anguished her heart at the sight of this lifeless place; pillaged, emptied, voided. Let it forge that heart into hardened steel, to know the enemies of Derebor would stoop to such excesses as this.

"Where do we go from here?" Kharise's voice was solemn, her expression contemplative. "If this is what's come of Stonebrake in such short a time, I think it is fair to say that we face far graver odds than any of us anticipated."

"True," Vi replied, and she gnawed her lower lip. A fever of anger dwelled within her mind, but she could not figure out what she was to do about it.

With Stonebrake abandoned, with Talorr naught but a flaming husk, nothing remained to tether her to the worlds of her forebears at all.

"We need a shelter for the night and a plan for the morning," Kharise prodded her.

"Yes," Vierrelyne agreed, wiping her face. She had survived one apocalypse already; she might as well throw her weight into survival of the next. What legacy had once hung over her was vanquished as surely as the various capitals of Derebor. If both of the highest castles had fallen, it stood to reason that the other city-states standing between Talorr and the Merchant Principalities had been taken as well. How swift this change of fate, she reflected, that none of the fallen did so much as cry out in the dark. Someone must be assisting the Three Armies, some greater force at play whose aim was the end of Derebor.

She shuddered at the notion, but she held the picture in her mind for a long time. Pawns in some larger war? Hills of ants stomped upon by some infantile godling. The ants might swarm out, but that made them no less insignificant in the eyes of the uncaring above and below. Perhaps this was the justice of the Scourgelands, for the capture of their grand demonic prince, his imprisonment in the very diadem she now wore.

Unseemly, but not without potential.

How, though, had all of these armies made such a swift entrance from the Merchant Principalities? For all three nation-states to rise up at once in such fury, something must have gone awry for much longer—possibly longer than Vierrelyne had been alive. She wondered, as she stared across the vast and empty structure, what else had gone before. She tried not to despair, but it was no easy task, not when she had been so humiliated. It wasn't her fault, exactly, but she knew it must have been something she'd done to unbalance the wizard's portal.

Mehren stirred at last, with a heaving sigh. The wizard gingerly wiped his bloody fingers and palms on the edge of his dark cloak, flinching away as he did, as if the sight of his own blood troubled him. Slowly he pushed himself to his feet.

"I tried to tell you." He grumbled, groping around his person for something, increasingly agitated as it became clear that whatever it was had gone missing. "How did we get here, anyway? I clearly marked our passage and set my mind to it..."

Vierrelyne sighed, miserable. "I set my whole heart on Stonebrake."

"The wishes of a lone princess are not enough to re-route a portal through the Scourgelands—" Mehren froze, and began to scale the steep, rocky hill they'd fallen from, inspecting every stone and surface.

A fine white powder settled over the hill. He swore under his breath, and stooped down to pick up his chalk brush, snapped in half at the middle length, the handle embedded between some coarse stones in the hard ground. The chalk pouch, which was meant to hold it, instead sagged open, its entire contents little more than a faint smoke over the whole of the hillside.

He picked up the empty container and snarled. "Not even enough chalk left to draw a single glyph, let alone an entire portal."

"Can I help?" Vi asked. She understood that other people experienced miserable crises, but having her own rather protracted miseries, she had little skill in navigating them for anyone else.

Mehren seethed, a murmuration of words in a language she didn't know; when he turned to face her again, his long, heavy forelock of dark hair had blown to the side, and she caught a glimpse of his deeply scarred face, the eye he kept so well-hidden under that thicket of hair.

It was the same violent green as the gem that graced her diadem; an acidic, poisonous color she had always thought of, however errant, as *demon* green. It reflected the light strangely, with a faint shimmer. It did not glow, but it had a lightness about it that chilled her.

She realized, with startling clarity, the other times she'd seen this particular eye, this intense expression of anguish and regret. The hideous dream, with the demon-eyed boy across a dark river; she'd seen *him*, the wizard who called himself Mehren.

She couldn't say it, not here, not now, to him, that he had appeared to her before. Her heart sank anew at the idea that there was some substance to the long-reaching tendrils of the prophecy.

As if he felt the weight of her stare, he swiftly closed his aberrant eye, but his anger did not recede.

"Princess, I don't know how you led us so far astray, but I can alter none of it. My chalk is gone. I can't get us back to Zalandan now."

"Then I suppose we aren't meant to be at Zalandan now, if this is all going as your precious prophecy foretold." She said it coldly and brushed off what remained of the dirt from their calamitous fall. "I suppose I must have made this dreadful wish, and now we shall have to find out what comes with it."

A castle carved from the Stormwrack Mountains, Stonebrake had long been the home of a people Vierrelyne always thought of as her own. If her future hadn't been such a wretched calamity, perhaps she might have returned, one day, to the castle her mother had once inhabited, for it was the place her beloved Alaina had once called home as well. A bitter thought, in the moment, as all thoughts of Alaina had become since her wedding to that boor in Cascada, the odious Erenth Remaryn, whose armies were the very same that had marched upon Talorr.

The emptiness of this place was hideous, forbidding; her skin crawled at the absence. Not even a stray pack of bandits roamed her halls. She had been hollowed out and left to a terrible nothingness—by Erenth's men and their allies? Or had something even fouler still happened to the people of Stonebrake?

It was cold comfort to feel somewhat safe within her walls because of this great void; because there was nothing left, not even an enemy force. It was not a defensible position—not now, at any rate, not while there stood three armies at Talorr. Why had Stonebrake been so swiftly and thoroughly abandoned, so hollowed out that even her top-level cellars were barren?

A mixture of exhaustion, dread, and raw hunger led the three to explore her stockrooms with torches in hand. Mehren led the way, insisting he should take point on any task that involved a delve into the subterranean darkness. Vierrelyne followed him, with Kharise at the tail. It seemed quite absurd to think that someone might follow them here, but Mehren was convinced they were not as alone as they seemed, and Kharise was forever attuned to threats imperceptible to the sheltered princess, so Vi simply agreed, and let him walk on ahead.

More than once, she thought she saw him brushing his hair back, and she wondered at what that might mean. She could not shake loose the notion that she'd seen something she wasn't meant to, something *illicit* about the strange little wizard who had inserted himself into her escape route, who was still quite put out that they had landed so far from the place where he felt certain they'd have found some safety, and in so doing they had lost his precious spell chalk.

As time went forward, though, Vierrelyne was more and more curious about that. What did this odd stranger really want from her, that he would invoke the name of someone like the formidable legend himself? Tobinarde l'Ete had fallen from the tower at Stardowne; that was the whole genesis of this curse she'd found herself living through. This man Mehren believed him alive but didn't question if that *meant* anything else.

To her way of thinking, if the old man lived, all his foreboding words were null and void.

The words that had ruined her life, yes, but also the ones that secured her some strange future now. It was an unsettling feeling, to be so unsure of what yet remained before her when so much of her life had been governed by this curious portent.

The possibility that this wild and eccentric sorcerer might truly be the mage whose very existence was meant to entwine with hers, to follow that same path she must also

M. Daniel McDowell

walk, now, *that* was interesting, even as she felt a revulsion at the idea that this man had supposedly been sent to help her by the Heresiarch himself. All the same, he was so nervous and strange, so much *more* frightened than she was, regardless of how sheltered she had once been, that she realized she no longer saw him as a threat.

He was willing to walk with his back to them both; it certainly spoke to what did, and did not, frighten Mehren Tevaht. He ducked into one of the narrow stockrooms and disappeared from view for a moment.

"I've found something!" He called out. "Looks like someone didn't clear all of the stock from the smokehouse."

He emerged from the shadowy room with a log of aged hard sausage under his arm, its teal-green protective rind of mold leaving pale smudges on his grey cloak. At his knee he carried a wheel of hard-shelled cheese larger than his head, which he struggled to balance.

"Well, we won't starve tonight, at any rate," Kharise replied with a soft chuckle.

"We must leave this place, though, and swiftly," Mehren said, foisting the cheese wheel upon the plainswoman. "We're drawing attention we do not want, and I cannot understand why. I've warded us with a gesture spell against the deep shadows, but..."

Vierrelyne internalized the soft blame for having led them astray, but she did not know how she had accomplished such a thing. All the hells, her diadem didn't even *work*, not really. She had felt so sure, when she was searching for it, that this was the key to her mother's manifold powers of armament, the command of force. She'd been so sure of her mother's promises that she never once questioned them, even when it became clear they were only tales.

Having the diadem in hand, she realized she'd simply acted on a wishful dream of her own: her desire for control of a dark magic that might set her free of a generation's worth of nonsense.

The three trudged back to the surface level in relative silence, this time with Mehren focused on the tail and Kharise taking point. He asserted that something wretched lurked behind them, but it wasn't until they'd left the hold that this threat became clear to Vierrelyne.

A susurrus of whispers emerged from the shadows, a locust-like cloak of sound, a tremendous wave with its own physical form. Mehren fixed his gaze on something in the middle distance, and Vierrelyne observed once more that he had opened his right eye.

He held out his arms, using his torch for some short-range offense, and some unseen thing from the formless dark swatted at him, for he dodged with a deftness: he saw something she and Kharise did not, at least not clearly in the dim torchlight.

"This place is infested. We can't stay here—" he started. Vi realized with slow-dawning horror that she could, in fact, see what beckoned beyond Mehren. A tremendous, coiled thing had followed them from deep within the cavernous holds. In the flickering torchlight, she made out the shimmer of bright-blackened scales and claws, an interminably long body, a squirming spiny creature unlike anything that roamed freely outside the protection of darkness. Its many eyes glittered in the dim light, but it did not lunge after Mehren again, instead ululating at a low, near soundless pitch, a hideous foreboding reverberation.

He recognizes you, said a voice behind her, mellifluous, rich, from somewhere she could not be certain. *He wishes you great tidings, Your Majesty. He apologizes for his grave error.*

Vierrelyne shrieked and spun around, searching for any sign of the speaker—or of other terrible things awaiting in the gloom. Mehren had not lowered his torch, but the creature scuttled backward on uncountable thin legs, its head bowed, its warbling pitch rising, and she could not help but feel powerless against some deeper force.

Oh, said the voice. *It's been too long between us, Abenelle. My humblest apologies.*

She shrieked again, and scoured the room, desperate to understand where the sound originated. Mehren stared over his shoulder at her, and she could see, even through his hair, that both eyes were transfixed, but he said nothing that might give her any peace.

Vierrelyne watched as Mehren returned his attention forward, and backed away from the looming creature, as the creature in turn backed away from him. The odd détente captivated her, and all the while she could not help but stare in her idle horror as the thing *groveled.* She was certain of it— prostrate posture, long body heaved downwards, head bowed, before it inched backwards and away from them, into the darkling gloom.

"You saw it, didn't you?" she said sternly to him. "What was that?"

He bent his head, chewed his lower lip in contemplation, and his hair fell forward over his face once more.

"Well, depending on who you ask, that was one of the minor dignitaries of the shadow realms, far beyond even the Scourgelands. Don't ask me to pronounce his name. At first, he thought we might offer some sustenance after his long journey, but..." He paused; his expression was unreadable, between the tangle of his hair and the cadence of his words. "His lordship wishes we forget his *grave* error, for he realizes his mistake, Princess."

"His long journey?" Kharise cut in, bracing the wheel of cheese on her hip. "Vierrelyne, what in all reason is he talking about?"

"I..." Vi swallowed hard, trying to find the right words for something so strange. "I heard a voice that isn't mine. Just now."

Mehren stared through her, and while she could not see it, she knew both of his eyes were open again. She could not read the expression on his face; anger or sadness, something deeper she wasn't able to untangle for herself.

"We need to talk, once we're out of this place," he said.

He envies you, my dearest, said the voice, and she flinched, but did not cry out this time. *Why have you forsaken me for so long? Was it that terrible warlord of yours? Be honest, beloved. He was never good enough for you. For **us.***

The voice had not simply invoked her mother as so many of her servants had; the voice had mistaken her for the bon vivant battle queen of Derebor, uniter of the Westward Reaches. The voice believed she *was* Abenelle. And that she was... She refused to admit the thought.

She concentrated. *Abenelle is gone.*

The voice tutted at her, as if she'd made some error.

You wear her raiment well. Where has she gone? I need to hear her voice. Tell me where she roams.

Vierrelyne did not know what to say, so she focused her attention on Kharise and Mehren. "Let's get to level ground and see what's left. Maybe we should camp here until daybreak. I'm not sure what other horrors await us below and I'm not keen to find any."

Mehren gave a slight nod as he scanned the room.

Kharise led the way; the others followed closely behind. Once they were upstairs, they sought out a room where they might make camp within the castle walls, along with enough scraps of wood and fabric to rough out a fire and a modicum of comfort by which they might rest as the night stretched over them.

M. Daniel McDowell

CHAPTER 5
HESITATION

MEHREN TOOK THE FIRST WATCH ALONE, LETTING THE WOMEN sleep as he sat silently next to the hearth, warming himself on the broad flat stone and feeding whatever stray shards of castle detritus would yet burn across the blaze. He'd wake Kharise in a few hours, but until then, he had the time to brood, and the inclination. His bottled anger overflowed.

If only I hadn't made such a stupid mistake, if I'd just...

It was useless to scold himself now; the errors had played through, but that didn't stop him from the litany of recriminations.

They'd all been in such a hurry to escape the siege that he'd been careless, trying to flatter her into action. He should have made her surrender the crown to him, but it had been too much, too fast; it was all he could do to coax her into the circle in time to escape, at the last possible moment. He could've told her to let *him* hold it, just in case, for the spell—no, he'd probably helped her rouse the demon, if the evening's proceedings were any indication.

Mehren had ruined everything, again, and now he did not know what to do.

He was sure Carina would have secured the Peridot Starprism immediately; she'd never let him live down such an ignominious failure, and the high wizard Tobinarde would also be full of soft accusations as to why Mehren could not. A failure in his constitution, in his convictions... And yet, how could he have anticipated that the demon in the stone would be so interested in the princess that he'd willingly give her his power? It wasn't part of the plan at all. He had heard the grim whisperings, down in the cellars, and it made his skin crawl to think of it again.

Tobinarde wanted the stone, and possibly the girl, if only because it worked in his curious puzzle box, but for the princess to have made her own designs upon it was grave. Neither he nor the old man had expected the princess to know anything about the stone, much less to have an emotional attachment to it. He'd have needed to steal it from her, and that felt worse to think about, in light of the depths she'd driven herself just to find it—to pluck it from her mother's sepulcher, to violate the regal grave.

One thing was certain, in the aftermath. Princess Vierrelyne had clearly awakened the demon prince within the diadem. *One* of the demon princes, he corrected himself. There had once been three, and which was the lone survivor was a subject of scholastic debate among the few who cared for such things—unsettling folk like Tobinarde, in the main. Was it the vain Margandrys, the conniving Egrendelys, or the brutal Avadamrys? Did it matter *whose* eye peered out of that sickly green stone, in the end?

The imprisoned demon had heard her pleas, had taken advantage of Mehren's portal, and now the last of his spell-chalk was gone, smeared halfway down the Stormwrack mountain range, near as Mehren could tell. What else could he use in its place? Every warder in Tobinarde's coterie could use his infernal chalk, and in theory anyone with that special skill could deploy it with one's own blood, but...

Mehren swallowed his dread at the idea of that. He was such a coward he could not bear even the *sight* of his own blood, not since the witchfinders had beaten and burned him as they tried to wrest the nature of his magic from him.

Nothing he could do now, so long as the demon was comfortably nestled between Vierrelyne's ears. His skin prickled with the foolhardiness of letting her *wear* such a powerful thing. Tobinarde would rightly tear him down over this, and yet, in his own pity-wallowing, he realized he didn't know where else he could turn for help now that the end of the Dereborean Empire had come.

Not without the stone in hand, at any rate.

The demon's presence had drawn an unexpected audience. There had been a vast congregation of Sundered folk here in Stonebrake, demons from the Scourgelands, lingering in this cavernous place not long before their arrival. The obsequious Grand Lord whose name Mehren dared not speak had been only one among dozens of mid-level minions who had swarmed out of the Scourgelands, and now Mehren understood why: they'd sensed the grand unbalancing for themselves. No wonder he'd passed through their shadowed world so unattended during his journey to the castle Talorr. On the auspices of a prophesied apocalypse, even the humans were of added interest to those who walked the thin places between the planes. There was plenty for the demon realm to gawk at, in the dawn of their awakened prince, the first revival of the Sundered Throne in fifteen years. Their vigil would soon be ended.

The soldiers marching on that tower had been looking for Vierrelyne, too. It was not as if he hadn't been thinking about protecting her, in light of that. He had stolen one victory from the Prince of Cascada, and that was likely Tobinarde's true intention, anyway. Protect the princess of his grand prophecies, and maybe that would be enough.

Tobinarde would surely wonder where he'd gone; the Principalities would doubtless make their victories well-known in the coming days, and Mehren...

Well, Mehren was detained, and now every last shard of his plan was shattered. He'd make the case for hiking to Broadcoast Bay in the morning. It'd be a burdensome journey, but if they hewed close to the river north of the mountains, they'd bypass some of the militias returning along those same roads.

How *had* Vierrelyne awakened the old demon prince, anyway? It made little sense that the petty grievances of the mortal world made even a dent in theirs. Perhaps he could ask her, before he fetched Kharise for the next watch. What she did, how she roused the stone, what she intended. Get the truth before his defeated march back to Tobinarde.

The diadem rested on the floor next to her pile of discarded fabric and her metal shell. If he were less of a coward, there would be *nothing* stopping him. He'd take it. Make his way to the tower at Zalandan. Prove himself to the mad old wizard whose prophetic visions had sent him down this deranged path to start with, end this whole quest.

In the hearth light, the Starprism gleamed, eerie, eyelike, and Mehren was certain beyond all doubt that as he stared at it, it blinked. He shivered and turned away. He'd have to think of some other way to fix this.

Vierrelyne woke to the thin breaking dawn with a stabbing pain in her brow, the likes of such a headache as she'd only had once, in the weeks before her imprisonment, when she drank too much mead at the last midwinter festival at court that she was allowed to attend.

She had been visited by that terrible dream again, the one with the strange boy she now knew had to be the wizard who had come to her aid. A broad dark river flowed between herself and Mehren, but once that river was crossed... He had screamed, and sobbed like a child, but she could not get close enough to help. She didn't want to upset him with what she had seen—for it *was* only a dream, of course—but it troubled her twice over.

Her companions had let her sleep in, but the two of them shuffled about with such irritating fervor that once she was aware of the breaking light, she could rest no longer. She sat forward, dimly aware they had made a nest of remnant draperies in which to rest that evening, rueful of how little support and warmth they had been. Her every bone rang with the first cold autumn air.

What to do now? Surely there would be sorties searching for her; all of the merchant cities were full of superstitious little tyrants who would love to bring an end to the coming age by the meager deed of murdering one lousy woman, however highborn she might be. It was too much to contemplate on such a miserable morning, though, especially one with such a raucous din in her ears and a headache drummed upon her forehead as if by some lousy beer.

Kharise dragged an unburnt, unbroken bench from an adjoining room to the lone table next to the fire, where Mehren had taken on the work of preparing something proper to eat.

"Now that we know Stonebrake has fallen," Vierrelyne murmured, "I'm not sure where there is for me to go. Where do we have left?"

"We shall have to think harder about your alliances," Kharise mused. "It's been long since I have returned to the plains, but I suspect my kinfolk want even less to do with this than I do. Even so, I dare say the plains would be safer than anywhere in Derebor, considering what's happened at Talorr. I can't imagine anything but the bitterest end for his majesty."

It was nice to be freed of the obligation to follow such a statement with *'may His reign be unblemished with suffering,'* or any other such preposterous and obligatory niceties.

"Maybe we could set sail for the Crystalline Cities," Mehren said, as if casting about for a suggestion. "Maybe we cast off to the north, and you can plead your case in Beryl or Garnet—"

"Or maybe we stick to the mainlands," Kharise retorted, "while the merchant arsenal expends themselves of a fantastic array of weaponry. Not much of a seaward strategist, eh. Besides, the Crystalline Cities are still beset with their fixation on witches."

"The Merchant Principalities are spread thin right now, too," he replied, setting a cast iron pan on the grate above what remained of their fire. "They aren't going to trifle with one vessel full of religious adherents on pilgrimage, are they?"

Kharise gave him a strange, startled look. "The only religious adherents going to Beryl would be coming from further east through the Rimelands. The Frigid Sea's waterways are the other direction."

"I suppose you're right. Just wishful thinking, I guess." He shrugged and turned his full attention to his pan. "I just think that going across the bay would draw less attention than marching there on foot, which we might well do, if we don't find another way."

Kharise gave him a hard look. "Are you trying to take us back to Zalandan, still?"

"I don't know where else to go. Suggest away." He sighed. "In the meantime, let's eat."

Mehren had sourced an unattended hen's nest that morning, and over their woebegone fire, he did the work of cooking the handful of eggs he'd found, mixed with carvings from the dry sausage and some chiseled bits of the hard wheel of cheese ground fine with a carving knife. Scraped together on three wooden plates, it was nothing much to look at, but for Vierrelyne, who hadn't eaten a meal made especially for her in fifteen miserable years, it was unaccountably grand for the circumstances. She inhaled the delicate aromas of crisp- fried salted meat and the sharp tang of hard-rind cheese, marveling as if they might be only her imagination's hard work, instead of the wizard's. She'd gone without comfort for a long time, but she'd never been so hungry as this morning found her, so empty as this.

"Not so much as a crumb of bread nor even a grain of flour left in the pantry here," he groused as he set out their servings.

"I wonder what must have happened here," Vierrelyne mused, momentarily forlorn at the vivid image and scent of fresh bread in her mind's eye.

"Three armies marching as one," Mehren answered. "Reckon they licked the floors clean and kept moving. Lucky someone missed a single shelf in the deep pantry, or we'd be out hunting pigeons on the moors."

"This whole movement strikes me as one born of madness, frankly," Vierrelyne said with a sigh. "Something we aren't seeing, something moving the pieces along the board."

"You wouldn't be alone in that finding," Kharise agreed quietly. "It seems to me that something's happened to push along the dread vessels of prophecy, such as they are, of late."

"I could have told you that much," Mehren said sharply, and turned his full attention to his food. Kharise ate hers swiftly and set to work on the scrap fabric she'd mustered their bedding from, fashioning herself a traveling pack not unlike the custom on the Unconquered Plains, and once she'd finished her first attempt, crafted two more.

Vi savored every bite of their haphazard morning meal. Who knew when another such plate might come.

Mehren stored the remainder of their spoils in the pack Kharise made for him; he wrapped his heavy cloak and placed it inside as well. The first leaves were yellowing in the foothills, but the sky was bright, and his cloak would only make the sun hotter on his back as they hiked away from the ruins of Stonebrake.

Hefting the pack onto his back, stretching his legs, he thought of another such sojourn of his, at the far eastern reaches of the continent, where even Derebor held little sway. There, the weather was cold and strange, but seldom freezing. The sharp cliffs down to the ocean held the clouds in a grey pattern, one which made him forever nostalgic for a sudden squall, however inconvenient the rain might be.

It was one such storm that had led him to hide in the cliffs with his dearest friend Istven, after all; an afternoon of hiking and foraging interrupted by a downpour,which brought on a heartfelt conversation by the side of a poorly-made campfire with damp branches that scarcely offered any light or warmth, forging a connection between them ever after, beyond even the solemn stone cairns Mehren had seen only once, in passing, before his departure from the eastern vale forever.

To say he had regrets would be inadequate, but those regrets existed because they came attached to his brightest memories, and he was not willing to give those bright memories to anyone.

This new journey might prove fruitful, anyway. Once the princess was safe in Zalandan, his obligations to Tobinarde met, he could take his leave of the Astral Circle for good.

The weight of this abstract transaction was not light on his shoulders and had not been since they'd begun. It was not easy to admit to himself, but he had found himself fonder of the princess and the plainswoman in her company once they'd got past the immediate distresses of their unplanned landing in Stonebrake.

This detour was only a setback. Under other sets of circumstances, Mehren might have been angered by this, but in the depths where he presently found himself, it only gave him a distinct unsettling sensation. Too many possibilities, nowhere near enough certainties, and several prior certainties had been obliterated. His spell-chalk on the wind, he had no way back into the tower, save on foot. No way to salvage the disaster he had made of Tobinarde's grand plan.

At least he'd gotten the princess to see sense about traveling eastward. If they made it to the southernmost of the harbor towns, perhaps they could ferry out of what remained of Derebor and into the harbor cities, unnoticed by the power structures in Estuary City. It was still a voyage from there to Zalandan, but if they hewed toward the tower, due east from the Principalities, they were less likely to encounter the types of creatures that loved the thin places in the far southern mountain ranges, the valleys above which Stonebrake had once stood valiant.

Well, once he was free of Tobinarde's follies, he'd go explore those thin places for himself. He might have scoured the whole of the Scourgelands if only it might give him the chance to see Istven once more— even if only to wave farewell, at a distance, maybe in the Realm of Dream, if both men were so lucky one day.

There were gaps between the known and the unknown, and Mehren was going to try them all, once the last of his outstanding balance sheet was clear. There was a new age dawning, but he didn't care to see it one way or the other, not if he might find a way back out, into what he yearned for most. He need play no more of Tobinarde's games.

He shouldered the pack, and went out to the courtyard, where Kharise stood examining the winds and the horizon.

"If we cross into the valley," she said, "we might make one of the outer settlements by nightfall. Possibly earlier if we hit upon the Bent River on the way. I found the drinking well this morning, and a few unbroken jars, so we ought to survive even if we don't find the river."

Mehren nodded, absently contemplating. He had the map he'd taken from the tower, but it would be of little use once they were on foot. His sense of direction was honed by the intangibles of his arcane craft, and by his notion of place. It meant that he often had to accept fluctuations and unexpected detours— seldom one so complicated as his present embarrassment. It was neither precise science nor established practice; Tobinarde's teachings were a singular dark art.

"Once we've found our bearings, we could always travel west," Kharise said, gazing at the ridgeline, beyond which lay the expanse of what Mehren knew to be her homelands. That passage would be no easier, even if they went northward to skirt the mountains. Their ridge was arrayed with the ancient ruins of a people whose towers rivaled the height of the peaks in some places: the Bleak Pillars. Beyond there lay the Conquered Plains, the domestic grasslands; beyond those, the vastness of wild forest and meadows meshed with deep grasses—the Unconquered Plains.

Vierrelyne approached them, much of her armor in the pack over her shoulder, but the unsettling diadem rested once more on her brow. Mehren was dismayed to see how lively the stone seemed in the bright morning light. The reflections in the acid green stone made it shimmer and dance with what Mehren read as gleeful abandon.

If he stayed with them, at least to the river, he ought to find swift passage to the east, and with luck, by then, his charges might be truly sick of this adventure and prefer to see things his way without much in the way of grief.

"I haven't any supporters in the west, save you," Vi told Kharise, her voice confident but quiet; she was practiced in such a specific form of grace.

"You haven't any here, either, my lady," Kharise replied dryly, her tanned face creased with a knowing grin. "I know the free cities won't stand behind the empire, but it may offer you a place to start... if you know what you want."

Mehren thought it interesting that the princess did not have a ready reply to Kharise's comment. Maybe he'd done more to sway her opinion than he initially thought.

As she stared out over the mountains, though, her silent contemplation took on a quality he found reflective, melancholy. That was fair enough, he supposed, for a woman whose world had been the span of a single room until mere hours ago.

"Towards the bay," she agreed, finally. "We should find civilization and shelter, and perhaps an ally, if any of my father's holdings still remain."

The three embarked, once the path was set, the sun still rising overhead, and as they hiked down the slopes and cliffs into the valley, Mehren was reminded of how swiftly such sunny days could turn for the worse; but in the company of his quiet companions, he settled into a rhythm he'd once thought lost to him. It was not long before he was lost in his thoughts of hiking hills far from these, with companions lost to this world, at a time in his life forever distant now.

CHAPTER 6
DROUGHT'S END

KHARISE GEN VALUURE WAS BUILT FOR WALKING. EVEN HAVING traded her supple boots to Vierrelyne in exchange for a truly woeful pair of slippers, her feet were well-used to the dirt beneath them, and the thin soles gave her enough cover against the sharp stones.

Vierrelyne du Talorr, on the other hand, throneless heir to destiny thwarted, captive of her own castle, was unprepared for the distance they would need to cover even if she'd been dressed in the most comfortable and form-fitting footwear. As the three trudged onward together, Kharise tried not to let her deep frustration at the princess' slow pace and delicate footing set her off guard. Truly, it wasn't Vi's fault that she was soft in this specific way. She had taken off her crown, for it was too heavy as the day progressed, and placed it in her pack once they had descended into the foothills.

Even with the weight elsewhere, Kharise could not help but notice her pace had only slowed.

Off the beaten path through the mountains, they had descended—slowly, painfully, carefully, with Vi's lack of conditioning—into the broad pan of the river valley, leaves making their slow seasonal progress through the arc of possible colors, the air still warm but no longer sweltering.

The Bent River itself was still heavy with the summer rains and smelled faintly musty in the high floes where the water churned the mud against the rocks. They found a footbridge across the river that led toward what Kharise expected would be a small farming village, one of the many settlements whose farms fed into the imperial granaries. What was at first a single footpath spread into a proper roadway; small farms, mainly, though Kharise noticed that an assortment of the houses appeared to be abandoned. It was not immediately clear why.

In the town center, at the crossroads, was a tavern inn. It was a well-kept place from the outside, brightly painted woodwork in the regional style, with signage in several local dialects she recognized as soft resistance to Dereborean rule.

The tavern was well-attended that evening, just as the sun set on the second day of their travels. The stables busy with horses, the taproom bustling with customers. Kharise wondered first if there would be any rooms left, and second how dearly such rooms might cost.

They drew closer, and she realized a third, distinct problem: on a pole leaning against the long wall of the tavern, a marching banner from Cascada stirred in the faint breeze; on the signposts, more flags of the Principalities hung proudly. A convocation of marching enemy soldiers from distant lands was openly welcomed here. Any place sympathetic to the Three Armies was in no measure safe for Vierrelyne, not even if the princess ostensibly agreed with their hatred for His late Royal Highness. She had heard voices directing their soldiers to search for her.

Vi, by her nature more curious than fearful, did not see the risk inherent in this stark place. Mehren, whose nervous constitution was already tightly coiled, shook his head in dismay at the sight of Cascadian banners.

"We need to find another haven without such clear hostilities, Princess. There's bound to be some place less violently opposed."

He had seemingly ceased his baying about Zalandan now, Kharise observed. Something else had shifted weight. There had been no miracle of the Peridot Starprism when the princess had donned the band of stone and claws; nothing reminiscent of the legends had happened at all, as far as she saw. Whatever bits of prophecy to which he'd clung so fiercely that he was possessed of this strange quest had crumbled as swiftly as the last vestiges of the empire of Derebor.

Vierrelyne stood with her back straight, her shoulders aligned, a stance of surprising confidence. It was a subtle note, Kharise thought, but she had earned at least some conviction in herself even as they had fled the grand tragedy of Castle Talorr. She'd grown, in such a short time. Perhaps it was the great hope of finding her destiny, the damsel in the tower freed.

It was a slow process, for such stories always were, but Kharise was impressed by the swiftness with which the sheltered young woman had adapted already. It was hard to picture that past history so far from the spot where the three of them stood, when not even shelter for a single night was at hand, but Kharise felt the threads of past songs tugging at her, expressions of times long lost nonetheless salient in the moment if only she might evoke them, but none of the ones she knew seemed to fit.

"There is no place but this one, and we have come from so far away," Vierrelyne said with a loud sigh. "I dare go no farther than here, come what may. I intend to sleep until dawn anyway."

Kharise did not care for the idea of staying in this particular tavern whatsoever, but it was hard to argue with the notion of a warm bed and something to eat prepared by someone other than herself or the strange wizard.

The signpost outside the tavern was written in three different languages Mehren recognized and at least one he did not. The name was a pun about drinking away sorrows in Dereborean that did not carry over into any of the others—*Drought's End*; that was bleak enough. The banners of the rivaling mercenaries did little to assuage Mehren's concerns.

There were still rooms to be had, and at a generous rate, even with dinner service. He parted with two silver crowns from the guard house to gain them room and board, with the evening's stew and a pint of ale each. He declined the coppers the tavern-keeper passed back; it was simpler to spend someone else's coins when one did not have to track them.

Upstairs, he deposited his travel pack and did his level best to look like he fit in with the haggard fellowship of mercenary soldiers mingling downstairs— though it gave him a weak stomach to think of the rime of his own blood in the crease of his wrist, it added the suggestion of recent, yet distant, combat, so he left it be.

Vierrelyne and Kharise both insisted on rest and took their trenchers of stew upstairs. Mehren was too nervous and alert, so he went down to see what he could do about dinner and ale on his own. Once he was inside the busy taproom, he was thoroughly occupied with the project of eavesdropping on every conversation of which he could avail himself. The steadfastness of the soldiers from a given contingent might be significantly more fragile than the united front of banners leaning on the walls outside made it seem.

The groupings were uneven; a loud, long table of rowdy folk who could only be from Cascada, judging by their accented words, jingling coins, and cardinal-red garb, and they occasionally spilled over to a smaller section full of quieter folk in the dark blue dress of the soldiers' front from Devere. In the knothole nearest the bar, a smaller cluster of patrons kept close, and it was that contingent in what he assumed where the Estuary City dress grey cloaks that Mehren suspected would offer the densest conversation but was also the hardest group to surreptitiously observe.

Each of those men wore a jeweled badge—the grim visage of a skull whose eyes were inlaid with glittering gems in all colors, with chevroned ribbons that hung below the skeletal jaws. They had a weariness about them lacking in the others. Their capes were a similar color to Mehren's cloak, but he did not feel any safety nor comfort in the possibility he might be mistaken for one of their ranks.

For the moment, at least, Mehren felt safest sitting at an adjacent table, listening for the signs of a conversation with sharp edges, something that might tell him what some of these men had seen in their journey from the Merchant Principalities. He ate his stew slowly, sipped his ale to make it last, leaning against the wall so his right-hand side was in shadow.

"I'm telling you, Darrek—they went to find the girl and the tower was empty. I know what I saw when I was in that castle chilled my blood, but I don't trust these ghouls from Cascada. They were looking for more than blood. They want that girl for *somethin'*."

"Who?" the man called Darrek sitting next to him jostled him with an elbow.

"That muckety-muck prince from Cascada with all the wives. Is that what he wants her for, you think, another wife? Or does he just want that magic stone—"

"Just eat your roast and sit quiet, for the *last* time, Teven," called out one of the voices further down the table, paired with a meaty fist that jolted every plate and pint on her sturdy joinery. "No one cares what you think. You can barely lift a poleaxe you're so hammered."

"You think it's *not* strange, Graves?" Teven replied. "You think what rotten old Brabinghar was doing in that moldy old cathedral of his was normal? You think what they did with 'im when they was finished is normal? You think lettin' them creeps from Zalandan tell you what to do is normal? These 'estlanders are weird and I say to rot with them."

"I didn't *say* any of that. I said eat your roast and sit quiet, you pissant."

"And you en't my *boss*," he said, turning away from the louder man in the middle. "Not even if Reyser Gorum said so. An' he *didn't*."

Mehren tried to point his attention elsewhere. A pack of louts, likely no more invested in this than in any other

M. Daniel McDowell

endeavors which might carry a sack of crowns. Bored, indifferent mercenaries. All the same, they had mentioned enough he could hardly *ignore* them, either.

A sloshy fellow from the overflowing red-cloaked clutch of Cascadian soldiers settled at the table directly across from Mehren and tipped his head in a gesture of false-fronted politeness.

"Oi, didn't I see you in the fires?" he asked, his voice wet with foam from the latest pint to cross his lips. He was curious-looking; high-cheekbones, finely-carved features, fair-haired and red-faced with ale. A distinctive visage, but not one he recalled in the slightest.

"You must be mistaken." Mehren tilted his head to keep his right side in shadow.

"Oh no, I never forget a face," he said, jovially. "Just appeared out of nowhere when we was lightin' the hill village up. I wondered what a wizard was doing there on account of we didn't bring one. You with the other greycloaks? Didn't think they had any wizards anymore."

"N-no," he said, too fast, too nervous, but he couldn't stop himself from stuttering. "J-just had an independent interest in the balance, that's all."

"Independent, eh," the Cascadian said loudly, swaying slightly in his seat. "You're a *tradesman*, are ye? Just here to make what's owed you and tuck your tail after like this lot?"

"Not in whatever manner you intend," Mehren replied, feeling his heartbeat in his throat as another soldier from Cascada approached the table, not nearly as drunk as the first one.

"Then I reckon you ought to explain yourself," the first Cascadian said, loud enough to siphon attention from the other conversations around them.

Mehren demurred, which only made things worse, as he now had the full attention of both tables.

"Y'with them cultists from the east?" said the awkward fellow called Teven.

"What'd *they* want with the war in Derebor?" the drunk Cascadian laughed and shook his head.

"The prophecy," said one of the other greycloaks, at the far end of the table. He had a neatly cropped beard and gently receding hair line, finely silvered, with warm dark eyes that spoke to a lot of study. "In the days before the fall of the Astral Circle at Stardowne fifteen years ago, where the scholar Tobinarde l'Ete disappeared from the record evermore, he said his emissaries would ensure that his personal truths would come to pass."

"You an' I both know there en't no such thing, sir," Teven said with a snort.

"Oh, there is. Where you and I differ is in whether we believe the prophecy is *true*. A minor distinction, but an important one." The greycloak stood, his arms folded. "So. Why don't you tell us what you were doing there?"

"Me?" Mehren deflected. "W-whatever you were hoping for—n-n-none of it happened, save the fall of Brabinghar, and even that... no prophecy was ever needed to say such a man could rightly fall."

"You don't deny it, though."

"There is n-nothing to deny. Three armies fell upon Derebor, as it was foretold, and now?" He silently cursed his stammering, stuttering jaw, desperate to lose *any* of the attention his presence had drawn around him.

The tall greycloak smirked at him before he cast his gaze upon the Cascadians. "Now those three armies have to do their best not to fall upon *each other*, I suppose."

The drunk Cascadian in turn glanced between them and pushed himself to his feet with a grunt.

"This is boring. Maybe I'll understand what you're on about if I have another pint."

He sauntered off with the other Cascadian, and Mehren breathed a single sigh of relief. The grey-cloaks lost interest in him shortly thereafter, though he could not shake the notion that their leader—the well-read fellow who quite understood, at least, that some supernatural factors had arisen with the armies from the other side of Broadcoast Bay—was aware of far more than he let on.

All the same, Mehren nursed his pint of ale for the rest of the evening, and only felt free to take his leave once the Estuary City fellowship had cleared away from the table in slow attrition. Only the cadre of Deverish soldiers in blue remained in force; the Cascadians had gone to bed once their leader's drunken antics had tapered into exhaustion.

All the same, he felt the silence in the room as he stood, a blanket over the whole taproom as he made his way up the narrow stairwell.

In the relative quiet of her room upstairs, Vierrelyne heard a strange groan, a miserable grumbling. At first, she thought it might be coming from the taproom below, or the adjacent spaces, but it was too loud—and too unusual. She emptied her pack, each piece of unworn armor in its own place, in the corner of their room, until she came at last to her mother's diadem. It shrieked when she picked it up, and she wobbled to catch it in her fingertips, scarcely missing the floor.

She studied the Peridot Starprism, the bright green gem winking in the lamplight, when it flickered like the eye of a lizard. She heard a muttering that sounded somewhat like the voice from the depths at Stonebrake, so distant she could not make it out.

It blinked again, and the sound became more insistent but no clearer than before. Testing her own maddening uncertainty, she put the crown on and waited for something, anything to happen.

I was starting to think you'd forgotten about me.

Vierrelyne caught her reflection in the pane glass of the small vanity mirror above the dresser and shivered when she saw a shadowy, statuesque figure standing just behind her, to her left. She jolted and turned around. No one.

No, it's true, I'm not there, darling. It would be nice if I stood at your side once more.

"You keep saying that. I told you, I'm not Abenelle, she's gone."

I have not been asleep for so long that she'd have left me across the seas of time. Why would she not seek me out before departure? Where could she have gone?

"I can prove nothing of it, but it's my belief she was murdered." Vierrelyne's skin prickled, a chill on the back of her neck.

It hurt more than she expected, to say it aloud instead of letting her belief boil within her. It was nothing she could ever prove, not least of which because she had been kept, by that time, so far away from Abenelle.

Murdered? That damned fool Brabinghar. I told her never to trust him... I'm only sorry I was right.

The prickle at the back of her neck intensified. She had yearned to speak with this demon since her mother's untimely demise, but now that she could hear him, she understood better what Abenelle's divided heart had endured over such a long time. The voice was soothing, assuaging, tempting. She had longed for someone to *understand* her, especially since she'd lost all contact with dearest Alaina, and it was impossible to deny, however strange it was, she felt in this moment most deeply understood by someone as wounded by Abenelle's death as she. It was a most curious and uncomfortable sensation.

Does she not walk the Realm of Dream evermore? Is that not the path for your kind?

"I don't know." She drew a deep breath and tried to compose her thoughts.

There is a sumptuous banquet at Talorr this very day, I hear.

The voice sounded as if he was trying to boast, but she was not certain what it was about.

The concordance of the grand Sundering has begun to arrive, from the outer realms, though it is early yet, and we still have far to travel.

Vierrelyne did not know what to make of this. "Talorr has fallen, yes. I wish I were not so glad of it, but I must admit I am not sorry to leave it behind forever."

*We are of a kind, then, daughter of Abenelle. I see a great wound in you, a long and slow festering, a time of waiting and longing, a time that has ended. I, too, have waited an unthinkable time for some measure of justice, as I wait in this prison even now, but I would serve that time but gladly to offer you the fullest of my powers, from the vantage of this gemstone prism. My **every** ability is yours for the taking.*

"It is true, then? You are the prince of demons who served at her whim?"

Some would know me as Margandrys. It would please me if you did.

"Margandrys, then." She said it hoping to close the conversation without offering him the same fuel.

You should look closer. See what I can offer you.

In the dim, silver-foiled reflection, Vierrelyne made out the silhouette of an unaccountably beautiful man, taller than her sturdy frame, with a flowing mane of hair. Upon his brow, he wore a crown of antlers and thorns, his gleaming eyes the same peridot green as the prison within which he rested. She could not make out the finer features, in the light which remained. It was clear from the sheen of his highlighted profile that he was a well-sculpted creature of devastatingly handsome proportions, and she knew without question that every one of these details was a trick of the light, but that did not protect her heart from the obvious temptations.

She yearned to be *beautiful* in a way that radiated, in the way that he was beautiful.

*You **doubt** me, dearest. I would hope for something more.*

"You don't know me at all." She did not like that he would call her *dearest* so easily.

I'm learning. You are the very likeness of your mother, you know.

Vierrelyne fumed. "Is it true, what they say, that you gave my mother her gifts? Is that what this exchange is supposed to be?"

*On the contrary. She asked it of me as her dearest love, and I could never refuse her. I love Abenelle, and always shall. Even now, she lives on through you... **Vierrelyne.***

Her blood ran cold.

"I didn't give you my name. Do not use it."

Margandrys's reflection bent his head in unsettling obeisance.

Of course, my lady.

She stared into the mirror, at herself, in a mixture of pride and fear. She did look beautiful, in a way she had seldom seen herself in fifteen long years, her heart-shaped face flushed with angst. The rising peaks of the crown seemed taller at this angle, more elegant than they had mere minutes before in her hands. That was troubling. She still could not refine her image of Margandrys whatsoever. He was a fine and alluring shadow of a form at the edge of her vision, whose lovely voice echoed in her ear as if he stood right behind her—and if the mirror told her any truth, it was that she should not trust those rich and mellifluous words.

But she could not deny that, at her core, she wanted to, more than *anything*.

M. Daniel McDowell

CHAPTER 7
ON FOOT

Kharise went to bed early upon their arrival and found a hideous, grey autumn morning when she awakened with ravenous hunger well before dawn.

She'd missed the bell at the door the night before, and cold stew and room-temperature ale were all that she was likely to find at such a time of day, so she tucked into that bland fare that had been left in her room with resignation once she'd pulled on her clothing and boots. Better than an empty belly, but it made her wistful for a hot flatbread with the last of the summer's ripe berries and chai.

When the morning drew on into early daylight, Kharise swept herself together, her strange few items bundled into her pack. It was nothing new for her to travel with so little provision; she regarded the circumstances with some amusement.

She had been born under a wandering star, said the soothsayer attendant at her birth, in the druids' huts, somewhere farther west than she'd traveled in nearly fifty years. In those long-lost misty ages, she remembered how many people had said to her, in some wonderment, some variation on:

When the wind finally catches you, it will never let go.

None of them were wrong, much to her chagrin at the time; she'd met a nomad she liked, and he'd met a road he wished to wander, and over that long time, they had. Noruk had left her too soon, from a bloating, starving sickness. Not even a long convalescence on the warm southern coasts could give him back his vitality once it took root in his belly. In her aimless grief, she'd been hungry for purpose when that Dereborean noblewoman from that strange mountain stronghold reached out to her, with a most unusual inquiry: to stay on at Talorr, to teach the lonely teenaged princess of the wider world beyond the imperial threshold.

Truly, the strangest thing she'd *ever* done was to stay put in that wretched castle, but Vierrelyne's plight had caught her off-guard. Such a bright girl, done such a profound wrong by backwards tyrants.

Downstairs, as the bakers bustled for the morning's bread, Kharise sat in a corner of the taproom waiting on the kettle.

Mehren staggered down to the tables and harrumphed. His face was writ with acute misery, his forever-messy mop of black hair shadowing both his eyes. He set his rough rucksack in the corner.

"What happened to you?"

"Didn't sleep much." He seemed loath to discuss it further, pushing his hair out of his face and squinting around the common rooms before he was satisfied with some minor detail. She caught a glimpse of something brilliant green beneath the curtain of his hair, but thought it best not to mention, despite her burning curiosity. At last, he sat down across from her. "I don't know how you did."

M. Daniel McDowell

"You get old like me, and sleep comes right to you after a long day on foot," Kharise replied with a dry grin as she fetched up the kettle and poured herself a cup in a rough-hewn clay mug. "Like a cat to the wharf when all the fishing boats come in for the evening."

"There was a nonstop processional upstairs last night. I reckon I was the only one watching if it did not disturb you."

"More of your ghosts and ghouls?"

He sighed. "Spirits. Demons. Visiting deferential Lords of the Scourgelands, dignitaries of dismal places beyond any mortal ken, yes."

"And what, pray tell, was that about?"

Mehren contemplated. "Well, the reawakening of the Lost Prince of Demons has turned the tides, in a war that ranges far outside the ragged borders of someplace so quaint as Derebor. His allegiants are lining up now, after untold years of watching and waiting to see if he would ever emerge from the crypts at Talorr."

Kharise squinted at him, neither willing to give him the match point nor able to summon up an alternate theory.

"And they just... walked in?"

He nodded. "Once dusk draws in, the waking world is thin and the demons slip through every shadowy crevice as they please, until the first edges of dawn, when they retreat from the light. Most of them are gone now; they won't return until the twilight begins."

"This isn't like any culture I've studied before."

At this, he laid his head down on the table; if there was anyone about, it would have been unaccountably rude, but so far, they were alone. Perhaps they'd be on the road not long after daylight— that gave them better odds of reaching Broadcoast's southern cities before dusk, at least.

"It's not a single culture, exactly," he said, finally, as if he'd needed a moment to disentangle his thoughts individually. "It's as many cultures and customs as we have, overlaid across a hideous tapestry of worlds we cannot ever imagine. They have only the most tenuous ties to ours, which is why the diadem is—"

Kharise elbowed him. "Not here."

"Oh, aye," he replied, resting his chin on his wrist. "So, *demons* are acceptable, but not... Well, there's a reason we've stirred all the Scourgelands into action in ours, and it's unsettling, to say the least. Waking him has changed the tenor of war in all the realms."

"Vi hasn't mentioned anything about it to me. She seemed to think the stone wasn't so magical as her mother had led her to believe."

Mehren shook his head.

"It's not what she thinks it is at all."

"Was that what happened, when we..." Kharise paused. "Arrived."

He lifted his head and nodded. "It's the only reason I can imagine. She didn't know, but I can't picture anything else."

Vierrelyne descended the stairs, much of her heaviest gear packed away, but the diadem rested on her brow, scarcely hidden, under her burgundy velvet shawl. The wizard watched her intently, his face unreadable, a grim mask.

She was radiant, in a way Kharise had seldom seen her: freedom, of a sort, looked good on the erstwhile princess. The soft, dark velvet of her dress was tattering at the edges, where she'd cut it, but it still had the fine craft of the royal houses and so it would likely hold a while longer yet. She still wore the boots Kharise had lent her, but that situation was not going to last.

Mehren's gaze finally caught her notice, and the princess was acutely flustered; it wasn't clear from where Kharise sat how the young woman was reading his attention, nor precisely what it was about, but the strange flash she'd observed earlier was no fluke—the wizard's oft-closed right eye looked like the curio twin of the stone in the tiara as he stared at her.

How peculiar.

At the sound of boots in the upper stairwell, Mehren got up and grabbed his pack.

"We should make for the road early."

Kharise followed suit, and Vierrelyne took the cue, though her sadness at leaving without the first consideration of breaking her night's fast was evident.

"We've need of a coster's cart and a cobbler. I reckon there's a village down the road," Kharise said. "There's enough smoke down the hill, we can find both and be on our way."

She could not figure out how to provoke the wizard into starting the conversation she wanted: more of what he knew about the demon in the stone, and how he had come to possess such arcane knowledge.

Mehren went ahead of them and returned with his ruck filled with apples, and a single bunch of grapes which he stashed in his cloak pocket. In the valleys below the Stormwrack mountains, grapes might be plentiful, but to

Mehren, they remained a rare and hard-won delicacy, a golden memory from an era in his own life not worth revisiting otherwise.

Vierrelyne and her dainty feet, piteously blistered, were well-served by a soft pair of new boots, the kind meant for a farm-boy, as well as some field bandaging from Kharise, by the time he'd finished his trading. Mehren chuckled when she showed them to him. Her amusement at having something so ordinary amused him as well.

Thus provisioned, the three made for the trail toward the southern edge of Broadcoast Bay, following a path marked by deep wheel-grooves through rough, muddy soil. The light was hazy, with gathering clouds overhead.

"There's foul weather on the wind," Kharise announced. "My aching elbow seldom lies about such matters. So long as we stay on course, we'll get into the cities on the harbor tomorrow before that thunderstorm, in time to stay dry."

The path was not densely forested, but intermittent clumps of trees on the meadows made for good shade when the early-autumn sun peered out from behind the heavy clouds.

It wasn't until they'd been walking for some time that Mehren felt comfortable enough to ask the princess a question, one he'd held within him since the day before. He turned to look at her, over his shoulder.

"He *is* awakened, isn't he?"

For an instant, her amber eyes showed him nothing but rage, but before he could react, the look flickered away. The shadowed, antlered form of the demon prince was faint in the hazy afternoon light, to Mehren's dimensional gaze, but not totally invisible.

"Yes," she said quietly. "I first heard him in the depths at Stonebrake. I didn't know what it was at first."

"That's what pulled us off-course, isn't it?"

She started to speak but Kharise cut in.

"Don't you blame her for this. We may have gotten out of there just in time, but it wasn't her fault that any of this happened."

"I don't blame her at all, I w—" Mehren froze in his tracks. A flash of bright silver through the trees caught and held his attention. "Something's moving, up ahead, at the tree line. Someone's there."

He pulled his arrow sling from his pocket, and notched a quick spell-shot into it, then cast it into the brush ahead of them. The impact left a cloud of violet haze in the air around the trees, but the wind was strong enough that it dissipated before it changed much of anything.

Once it had, though, Mehren realized with dread that what he'd seen was a glint of armor: the troops from Cascada who were at the tavern the previous evening. Just a few of them, an encampment of some kind.

Deeper in, he saw tall, posted tents.

Where was their—

"It's that nosy wizard!" called a voice from the trees not far behind. The drunken lout from the taproom. "And it looks like he's found the pr—"

Vi hooked his ankle with her boot, and he crashed to the ground with a gasp.

The wizard's hands shook as he searched himself for his dagger. Kharise held her poleaxe, and Vi drew the majestic sword she'd stolen from her father's right hand lieutenant.

Mehren stared in mute horror as Vierrelyne lunged at the grinning lout, her cry of rage alarming for its intensity. The sickening sound as her sword's pommel cracked against his skull, the clatter of armor as his comrades rushed forward... Mehren did his level best to hold it together. He'd been through worse; he'd *done* worse, when asked, when he'd no other choice, but it gave him no warmth.

Why had she gone after him so quickly? Couldn't they sort this all out without further bloodshed? Perhaps, but the Cascadian soldiers leapt upon them in turn and now this was set to be a grislier afternoon than he had anticipated.

Kharise drove back the two who had been standing with the fallen man, whirling on her heels in a display of her nimble strength. The heavy heel of her weapon made as good a bludgeon as its blade. Soon, all three of the rear guards were on the ground.

Vierrelyne roared again. The wild look in her eyes terrified Mehren to his core. Into the forest she charged after the fleeing troop. It seemed to him that her fury went beyond reason. Her physical power was explosive, her sword-arm bestowed with some supernatural range and force. Her every strike shook the ground.

It wasn't right, but he had no words to explain his rising discomfort and nowhere to raise his objections, as the three fought off the Cascadian soldiers. Breaking through the group distracted by Kharise and her astounding, fluid movements, he got into the Cascadian encampment and searched for anything worth pocketing.

Behind the open tents, a tall brunette woman with broad shoulders in the Cascadian uniform red dashed into the clearing and clambered onto the only horse in sight. She surveyed the scene and signaled her horse to bolt through the narrow clearing toward the trailhead.

Where was she going? Mehren tried to figure out the direction. Gauging by the sun... north, northeast. Away from the tavern and the town... no one followed her, and all the other soldiers had thrown themselves into the conflict with Vierrelyne immediately. As if they'd anticipated her, thought they might subdue her. Well, she was certainly not about to let them.

There was enough gear hidden away between the shrubs and trees to make camp for all three of them, including sacks of provisions meant for a dozen soldiers, by Mehren's reckoning. Someone must have come in with a wagon, for there was far too much to have simply marched in without more horses than just the one, and they had likely come several days prior, by how thoroughly it was distributed over the clearing in the thin trees. He noticed, though, that much of it was piecemeal and haphazard. Stolen, probably.

A roar of victory from the other end of the clearing disrupted Mehren's ruminations. Vierrelyne's intense blood rage seemed to have abated, at the cost of half a dozen enemies. He wondered if it was likely there was still another half of a squadron away in the village. Perhaps at that knothole of an inn pissing away their coppers? Mehren hoped not.

It wasn't clear what the Cascadians had been up to in the wake of Talorr's downfall. It seemed strange to him that so many had chosen to stay in the woods, when the village would've been a short ride on the sort of wagon that could haul these provisions and gear.

He didn't like the smell of it—something was off about this place, and the soldiers who had decamped to this position, and until he had a better idea what it was and why, he'd have to keep his deeper suspicions to himself.

Why were they so far out, away from all available resources, yet so well-stocked? Every possibility was uglier than the last. Why had that last one ridden away, in the opposite direction? He didn't like it at all and found little comfort in the survival of this strange ambush.

Vierrelyne's mind hummed with the stress of battle long after they had dispatched the last of the rogue Cascadian soldiers. The camp they made from the stolen goods that evening in the clearing was comfortable enough, but she was animated with the violence and the excitement of Margandrys in her ear, as he relived her great triumph vicariously.

Mehren and Kharise had gone over the items left behind, looking for any sign of marching orders, origin points, coordinated efforts. How many soldiers were there in this detachment? How had they traveled so far?

Nothing much was left in the effects of anyone slain. Their bodies were arranged neatly at the far edge of the clearing, per Kharise's insistence. A trench burial was not feasible, but sky-burial was not uncommon to her people. It was the only honorable option, she'd said, as they had fought and lost with some modicum of dignity, if not of any true honor.

Vierrelyne contemplated the day's events by the light of the evening fire, as Mehren dragged more dry wood into their section of the clearing.

*You were **beautiful** this afternoon.* Margandrys caught her reflection in the steel of her sword, as she cleaned it. She couldn't help but take his whispering to heart, as much as she suspected her feelings as easily played as a lyre. She'd festered in loneliness for a long time, and she'd yearned to be exactly that—*beautiful*—in the time since Alaina no longer said so. She grinned and examined her reflection in the blade, where she once again caught a glimpse of the handsome ethereal figure, barely perceptible, just outside the corners of her perception. The dark and spiteful grin of her mystical benefactor reflected in cold steel.

Mehren looked up from his efforts to line up his rough-hewn dry wedges of oak for a proper cooking fire.

"You shouldn't listen to him."

"I didn't know *you* could," she replied, flaring her nostrils, and feeling somewhat put out to be eavesdropped upon so bluntly.

"I wasn't trying," the wizard snipped at her, and inadvertently toppled his ziggurat of split wood. He sighed. "I can't help hearing him."

Jealousy is an ugly emotion.

"I'm not jealous, I'm concerned." Mehren set himself back to the task of fixing his firewood, and Vierrelyne noticed, just out of her line of sight, how Margandrys fixed his gaze on the wizard, smoldering with enmity.

Once he had created a proper bed for a long-lasting and steady cooking fire, Mehren glanced back up at her, and she could tell he was staring with both eyes, a glimmer of acid green behind his dark fringe.

"Your eye. It gleams," she said, marveling at it.

She'd hoped that she would catch another glimpse and have the courage to inquire when she did. It was too eerie a symbol for her to ignore, even as she felt childish mentioning it. She didn't want to tell him yet of the terrible dreams, nor even the most benign of her night spells, about a young man trapped in a dark place, whose right eye was a locus of great power, a brilliant green gem not unlike the Starprism.

"A polished glass shell." He gentled his fingers over it through the eyelid before opening it again. "It holds the shape of my old eye."

"It's lovely," Vierrelyne blurted out, before realizing she'd said something out of turn. "Oh, I'm sorry. I didn't mean—"

"It's fine," Mehren replied, smoothing his hair back over the right side of his face once more. "I don't like letting most people see; they don't understand."

The seismic shift within her made her heart a trifle lighter. Perhaps he *was* the counterweight to that damned life-defining prophecy. She had been looking for omens even as she'd dismissed the words that had built a cage around her; she hadn't wanted to believe that there might truly be someone who was that fabled Shepherd in Shadow.

"Is that what lets you... See them?"

"It is a spirit lens, but that's not exactly how it works." He cast his gaze low. "I have been given a horrible form of second sight, and the spirit lens helps to clarify what I see, what most cannot."

He sees all the Scourgelands entwined, Margandrys offered with cold, mirthless laughter. *All the realms at once. The realm of bodies, the realm of beasts, the realm of spirits, the realm of dreams; all the worlds in twain. A most powerful and terrible curse. Someone truly **hates** him.*

"For once, the crown of lies speaks truth," Mehren said, his voice rendered small. "I was given a curse by the same horrible zealots who gave me these scars."

Vierrelyne's skin crawled in awkward humiliation. She hadn't meant to pry, but it was as if she'd briefly seen a bridge by which to connect with the eccentric fellow whose uncanny spellcraft had gotten them out of danger at a most critical nadir. She didn't want to pry, to drive him away, but her curiosity was only heightened.

Kharise held out a battered folio stuffed with fragments of handcrafted paper; some loose, some folded, a few curled into cylinders.

"We haven't much daylight left, Highness," she said, as she handed it over to Vierrelyne, "but we can make a start on sorting the contents, at any rate. Maybe we can figure out what this strange encampment was up to."

"Yes," Vierrelyne replied. She opened it and began to skim over the documents inside.

Written in the dialect preferred by the High Prince, she could only decipher the parts written in bold glyph, as the interstitial bits used a formal italic, one she could not sight-read. She felt the blush rising in her high cheeks at this. It wasn't as if she hadn't learned her letters. She sighed and gave a deferral.

"I think these might be too dense to read by firelight, and the sun is setting already."

Kharise gave her a bemused expression and gently took back the folder. "Well, with the Merchant Principalities armies marching your father's corpse back to the palace at Cascada, what do you think is the best course?"

What Vi wanted to say was, "revenge."

What she wanted to declare was her desire to be the one marching that corpse to the ice floe where it belonged, as far from her own mother's sepulcher as she could take it, north to the Frostward Reaches whence his own people had long ago descended. At least there was no chance of his burial at Talorr, for he was too valuable now as an effigy and nothing more, in the grand palace of Cascada, and good riddance.

At the same time, she found herself animated by the fire—something deep within her responded to the flames. She had no love for the Merchant Principalities, and now they were doubtless hunting her as well. To what end, she could only guess, but she suspected that Prince Erenth had seized an opportunity because of some zodiac superstition, some paranoid reading of omens that favored him. Kharise herself had told her: the legend of the princess in the tower was one spread far and wide, and the only thing surprising about it was the truth buried deep within, the stone within the fruit.

"Well, Cascada has marched upon every place my family once ruled, and now it seems Prince Erenth Remaryn has taken everything I ever longed for. I say if the High Prince wants a war, we owe him one," Vierrelyne answered at last, her words slow and calculated.

She listened for Margandrys to chime in, but he had fallen oddly silent. Perhaps he did not wish for Mehren to overhear what he had to contribute.

"We have not an army, Highness," Kharise said with a wry look.

"In time, we may. In the meantime, I daresay I shall not let him think he can best me without effort." Vierrelyne stood up and stretched; her every muscle ached, and she heard the protest of joints whose limits had seldom been tested in recent memory. She could push herself. In time.

Picking over the rations left behind by the erstwhile enemy, she pondered the selection. Some of the bags of produce had turned. She tossed one satchel of apricots to the side, for every one of them was soft and sludgy. A sack of overripe plums met the same fate, its withered fruit unpalatable and covered in some sort of slime. When at last she found a pear that seemed firm and fresh, she bit into it, only to find it grainy and bland on the inside.

"Most of this food isn't worth saving," she said, not masking her disappointment.

She had hoped for some variety. Mehren had outfitted this journey with the most monotonous sack of apples she'd ever eaten. It wasn't as if she'd had no experience with bland and unappetizing food; nearly everything she'd eaten in over a decade had been prepared with an undertone of punishment. Even so, this was wretched. She tossed the pear aside, into the bramble.

It did not escape her notice that something snatched and scuttled away with it, just out of the corner of her eye; something shimmering, with a surreal glow like the demon she'd seen in Stonebrake.

M. Daniel McDowell

CHAPTER 8
STERLING MORAY

MEHREN SCARCELY SLEPT; ALL NIGHT, HE COULD NOT STOP himself from listening, searching for the whispering of that damned demon in the stone. Even the whistle of wind in the dry leaves overhead caught his full attention in the cold darkness. He stewed in his own bitterness at having failed to act, for the demon's very presence was a reminder that he had failed Tobinarde and all the others who had worked so hard at Zalandan in those waning days, before the horns of war had sounded the opening salvos of the apocalypse foretold in the old man's poetry.

In the morning, all three of the travelers took turns examining the various bits of paper: useless marching orders ciphered into a key, with dates long since passed; disorganized inventory lists that bore no resemblance to the tally of strange items found in the campsite; nothing much worth keeping. At last, Kharise turned over a piece of aged, leathery paper, older and more worn and faded than the others. She gave it to Mehren, as the handler of all objects arcane and mystic.

His skin crawled as he folded it open and examined the oxblood lettering and intricate glyphs within.

The calligraphy was crude, and ill-affected by sweat, water, and time, but it was undeniable—a sigil drawn for someone else to use, who could not draw it themselves, drawn by someone as knowledgeable as Tobinarde himself. There couldn't be many people alive with the familiarity of drafting something so intricate, something of such specific and dark utility. The leader of the Astral Circle would recognize this for sure.

To Mehren's less-perfect eye, though, the implications were sinister. Someone had drawn a portal—one which worked in only one direction, designed to lure things from the Scourgelands, the thin places, into this one. Not merely an aperture: this was designed as a temptation. A *beacon*. Someone was instructing them, inviting them in; someone from this branch of this militia used this spell.

No wonder half of the Cascadian soldiers had seemed mad at the tavern. At least one of them veritably must have been quite unwell, courtesy of this deadly spell that was siphoning off some significant force of life every time it was used. Perhaps without even their knowledge, certainly without realizing what it cost.

He flinched when he realized that none of the men in that camp were adept with spellcraft—the drunken one had said so himself: they hadn't brought a wizard.

Naturally they hadn't. No self-respecting delver into the unknowable would handle such a thing without significant safeguards in place: counterspells, at least, or a conduit, a passage through which the demons it brought to this place from the Scourgelands could *return*...

No self-respecting wizard would allow themself to serve as bait. Not even someone so craven as himself, he thought

M. Daniel McDowell

darkly. He might be a clumsy failure who couldn't usher one lousy princess through a mystical portal without a colossal error, but at least he wasn't painting a warpath of endless ruin throughout the waking world by his cowardice.

He turned it over and found that it was inscribed with a note in high formal italics, one that would take some slow reading to understand—and his blood went cold when he realized that the italic hand of this note was clearly the work of his rival colleague.

Carina Betrel was the single best calligrapher in all of Tobinarde's coterie, but she wouldn't draw something so unspeakably vile as this wicked summoner, would she? He shuddered as he tried to read her intricate lettering across the back of the note, smudged with sweat or rainwater:

Do whatever you must do to capture the girl with the gem. Slay anyone who stands between you. Slay her only if she gives you no choice. Recover the gem at any cost. Call upon this sigil for aid from...

He could not read the rest, and he dared not study the frontispiece in too close a reading.

"This is terrible," he said, firmly folding the summoner across its extant creases and placing it in the top inner pocket of his cloak. "Someone in their camp was using a spell they had no business using, a portal designed to tempt the worst sorts of creatures from the darkest realms into our own."

Vierrelyne's soft face went bloodless at this.

"Is that why... is that where those creatures came from. At Stonebrake? Is that what happened to... everyone?"

"Yes, I reckon so, but it's not the only thing." Mehren swallowed hard and flinched. "We also need to talk about your stone, princess. It's impossible not to mention. The demon prince trapped within the Peridot Starprism is..."

"Margandrys," she said confidently. "Crown Prince of all Sundering in Exile."

The wizard pressed his lips together, suppressing the first thought that sprang forward. If the demon introduced himself as *Margandrys*, that was the only prince in exile that Mehren could be certain was not hidden inside that prismatic gemstone prison. The way the power of such a name worked within that particular grim architecture, masking it gave amplification, reflection. An extension.

That still left two of the brothers unanswered for, but Mehren was not equipped to dig into that question yet. Whether Egrendelys or Avadamrys mattered little for now.

"All of Cascada is hunting for you, Vierrelyne. We need to be cautious."

Vi gave him an exhausted sigh.

"It looks as if the next destination for these armies is Estuary City," Kharise said, shuffling the documents in her hands. "Do we follow, or do we forge a different path?"

That must have been the destination for the soldier on horseback, Mehren realized. Back through Estuary City and onward north to the prince himself, perhaps. His blood went cold at the dual realization; if *Carina* had given these instructions, and the rider went north...

He could not be sure that Tobinarde had given her this spell, but he could be sure that she had written it out and given it to these soldiers, with very explicit instructions that nimbly elided their own doom.

Carina had led these soldiers to their death for this.

Vierrelyne stared with an intensity Mehren innately distrusted; over her shoulder, where Kharise could not see, the demon prince who called himself Margandrys stood.

Even in broad daylight, with the early autumn sun reflecting on surfaces that shimmered with unnatural vibrance, a bitter and unaccountable darkness emanated from within him, his eyes a shiny and bright and impossibly vast black. An ethereal handsomeness marked his figure, an impossible perfection to each of his delicate features.

Mehren understood it immediately; the prince was devastatingly handsome, his whispering voice wondrous, deep, persuasive.

He did not like to admit how jealous he was, in a certain light, of the possessive attention that radiated from the demon's shade. He did not like to admit he wished someone looked at him that way in light of his disfigurement; that he longed for yearning admiration.

He was possessed of a fresh bitterness at his scars, at his strange glass eye, at the words he might be called when Tobinarde was fed up with his broad incompetence or Carina was jealous of any of his minor successes; words he would never say himself but were inflicted upon him, even in silence, through a mere glance.

It was clear that Margandrys knew how to cast exactly those words at him.

"I think we should follow, for now," Vierrelyne said at last, her conviction stark. "Endeavor to discover more of their plan."

Kharise nodded. Mehren pulled out the pilfered map, marked up in his nimble calligraphy with his estimations of their travels.

"Estuary City will put us squarely in the terrain of the Principalities, but we can hide in plain sight for a time, Estuary City is an open book," he mused.

If they stayed in Estuary City long enough, he might figure out where to go next, where he might be able to hide; the capital port of the Principalities, with tendrils in every neighboring land, had enough winding passages to get nearly anywhere on the eastern end of the continent, the river capillaries spreading in all directions. It would not be the simplest route to Zalandan, but it might still hold some answers, especially where those strange summoner spells were concerned, so he could not dismiss the idea entirely.

Kharise reflected, as they walked a winding trail through the woodlands, on the stark shift from the forested fringes to the soft sprawl of farmlands, and the starker shift from the farmlands to the first vestiges of the outer limits of Estuary City.

It had been twenty years or more since she'd last passed through the southern hub of the Principalities—traveling from the warm tropics at the Staggering Coast, where she'd spent the last few months of her beloved Noruk's final days, as the aggressive illness never stopped *taking* from him and his very bones ached for the sun. In those days, she had taken in the sprawling river city and its blue and grey banners, its brisk people, and its bustling commerce with great and unwarranted resentment. It wasn't because she disliked it especially, but because a part of her, ever after, hated the world that she had to navigate without him.

Approaching Estuary City from the mountain foothills sprawling with vineyards and pastures, she saw for the first time the abstract beauty that animated those people who loved a place she could not, at the time. One thing to be said for the Principalities: the continuity of a specific vision made it easier to build a city-state with a profile that reflected its own chaotic harmony. Someone had once set out to create a uniform structure across a span of land that resisted anything resembling a straight line. Only the high street succeeded in this ambition. Visible even from this distance, it was a span of cobble between structures that stretched on either end outside of the city limits with only slight undulations around the many bridges that shaped Estuary City's relationship with its waterways. Gleaming stone structures, purpose-built; wide lanes between dense structures to allow pedal-carts, horse-drawn wagons, and waves of people walking between them. Costers' carts and basketed peddlers mingled on the fringe between the rivers of foot and wagon traffic, a slow parade of wares from one end of the main byway to the other. At the city center, alongside fragrant stalls of hot food and tea, were the long row of doors that belonged to the various arms of the city-state, the guilds, and the social orders whose work it was to enact the High Prince's vision.

"I should make for the guildhalls," Kharise suggested. "I suspect I can find out what's happened with all of the soldiers that have marched through here from Cascada and Devere, at least, get some field work in from the ground."

"I should probably provision up," Mehren said, and looked to Vierrelyne, who nodded in agreement.

"I haven't seen so many people at one time since the last solstice ball I was made to attend..." she trailed off. "Can I follow you?"

Mehren nodded. "If you don't mind the walk."

"It's settled. Let's reconvene at—" Kharise glanced around her, looking for someplace inconspicuous, where three strange nomads might not be out of place in such a strange city. "There, the Sterling Moray. A knothole where we'd hardly be interesting. See you at dusk."

Vierrelyne felt as if she might crawl out of her own skin in frustration by the time their feet hit the cobbles on the high street in Estuary City. She had kept the diadem in her satchel with the rest of her armor, and the hissing whispers of Margandrys, even muffled as they were by the cloth, had the power to drive her to great distraction.

"Something bothering you, Highness?" Mehren asked, as he led the way across the busy street toward a cart heaped with late-summer vineyard delicacies. He pulled his own hood over his head, so that it shaded his scarred face.

She wondered if it was to keep people from staring, but here in Estuary City, it seemed to her as if no one paid even the slightest attention to how unusual anyone else might look.

"No, nothing's bothering me," she lied, smiling slightly too hard in the midday sun. She shaded her face with her hand so she might be able to feign the reason for her dismal expression. "I'm not accustomed to so much sunlight and so many city folk."

He chuckled, bemused.

"You are cave-pale, aren't you? We should get you a parasol or something to keep the sun from boiling you alive."

"I'll be all right."

"Oh! Nearly forgot about these. Luckily, they didn't get crushed." He held out a bundle of grapes, blue-black in hue, from his cloak pocket, and she took them gladly.

They were delicious, at least. It made strolling around the center line artery of the city much more tolerable to have something in her stomach, and it helped to have someone else to talk to, just to break up the demanding buzz of Margandrys's crooning, the undercurrent of her thoughts whether she liked it or not.

She'd have to think of a solution, some way to make this bearable. She didn't like admitting it to herself, but the deeper quandary was going to be how she could continue to wear such a crown—for she was much happier wearing it than she was carrying it, and she suspected it was the ease with which Margandrys made his thoughts known to her.

Once they'd found some other, hardier provisions, and polished off the plump grapes, Mehren focused his energy on another task.

"I need to find an arcanist's shop if there's any to be had. In a city this size, there's bound to be someone."

She flashed him a curious smile. "Oh?"

"I just want to confirm a hunch I have, about that spell I found. I don't think it was the only one of its kind. I think..." he hesitated, as if he weren't sure how to say it. "I think the militia from Cascada gave these portal spells to ordinary soldiers, not disclosing what they are, but I need to test a few things, and to do that... I need to replace everything that was in my pockets when we landed in Stonebrake."

At this, Vi cringed. "I'm really sorry about that."

He gave her a thin-lipped smile. "You couldn't have known. Besides, my brushes were in bad shape before I fell on them whilst sliding down a rocky hill. The chalk, though. That was a disaster."

"Surely we can get more—"

"No, no," he said abruptly. "There is but one place for that. Back in Zalandan, in Tobinarde's laboratories."

"Then what use are the brushes?"

"One of them was for inking. Lines, calligraphy; spells like that one we found in the encampment of Cascadian soldiers."

"Could you use a spell like that instead of your spell chalk?"

It wouldn't be safe to travel that way, not with your... newfound alliance." Mehren's tone was pricklier than she liked, considering.

Vi scowled. As they passed one of the finer ateliers, she noticed a hand-lettered announcement and had to pause to read it:

His Majesty of the Principalities, Erenth of Cascada, announces his intention to celebrate his newest wife in the city of her youth: at the center of Estuary City—

Her vision blurred with tears of rage. She blinked and suppressed it; how could she explain it to him? Mehren was still talking to himself as much as to her with his list of sundries.

"So, if we find an arcanist, I need some oxblood ink, some brushes, and a quill." He patted the pilfered crowns in his cloak pocket absently, and she nodded, taking another quick glance at the leaflet in the window, realizing there was a similar one in nearly every window on this street. How big was this event? It'd be here in a week's time.

Mehren navigated the crowds with a dexterity Vi could not hope to match. Even before she'd been locked in a high tower, a fairy tale made horribly wrong—even before her sisters had perished, and her mother—she'd seldom been allowed to roam freely at court. Brabinghar's iron-shod control of Derebor started at home, after all. She had to stop, several times, simply to catch her breath or to let someone pass. He hid his exasperation well, but she knew she was a hindrance, when all he wanted to do was find a storefront that catered to his needs. Any time he noticed that she'd dropped back, he waited patiently enough for her, but she couldn't avoid feeling pathetic and helpless that it was required at all.

Worse, Margandrys seemed attuned to her distress and did his level best to capture and hold her attention. He'd demonstrated a fraction of his strength and agility, lent to her in the skirmish just the previous evening, and it was clear that he had a taste for blood and pain—one that made her wary, but also fed the dark desire for revenge that wound around her own heart, the part of her that wanted to cut the soul out of Erenth Remaryn by hand.

The temptation was high, to don the crown here in the street, just for the endurance Margandrys might lend to her weary legs and blistered feet.

It would not be easy to resist his generosity forever, she knew, which made resisting it in those moments where nothing good could come of it ever more critical. She wasn't going to give in to his urges simply for the sake of his power in a frivolous moment of weakness, not even when it might help her most.

She did not even want to resist it *forever;* she wanted to resist it until it mattered most. That was the difference, she told herself.

M. Daniel McDowell

CHAPTER 9
HIGH STREET

KHARISE ROAMED THE NARROWS OF ESTUARY CITY WITH AN
enthusiastic eye. It was a busy market day, and she
managed to locate a farm cart laden with flatbread, hot
from an oven claimed to be made with a true prairie stone
bed. She ate her way to the mercantile row, listening to find
the kind of conversations that only emerged among
tradefolk away from the ears of customers. Failing that, the
guild halls seemed a worthy choice, and a good place to sit
with the remainder of her bread—quite good, for city-
folk—on the stairwell of the central building.

"You left the tavern at Riverbend with the noblewoman
and the cultist," said a somber voice behind her from the
doorway. "I remember that lovely Plains cloak. High Plains,
I should say."

She curled her fingers over the hilt of her dirk but
relaxed when she saw the figure on the steps: tall man, trim
beard, hair close-cropped to mask his balding patterns.

His eyes were dark; steely but inviting, with lively
creases at the sides. His wide-hemmed grey cloak draped

over broad shoulders, and his boots were the hard-soled, stiff kind Kharise forever attributed to city-dwellers who occasionally found purpose climbing in the foothills.

"Whose business, I ask," she said.

He laughed. "I see. I should have introduced myself. Reyser Gorum, guildmaster and itinerant mercenary sell-sword of the Independent's Guild. I thought you might be here to find a solution to your cultist problem."

She squinted at him, unable to mask her perplexed response.

"I came down to the guild halls to see if I could corroborate some of the truly strange things I saw and heard in the Drought's End the other night. See if there were any reputable tradesmen about, who might confirm some irregularities I observed in the woods between the villages." She paused and drew a deep breath that belied her own disbelief about such things.

Reyser braced his fingertips together, leaning toward her, his head slightly angled to the right. "It sounds like you need to speak to the Cascadian contingent."

"We had a skirmish with some Cascadians on the outskirts of the forests, not terribly far from Riverbend. Something tells me an intelligence officer such as yourself might know about that already."

"Why do you think I asked if you had a cultist problem?" He smirked. "That pest of Tobinarde's was nosing around in the tavern while the Three Armies were still convened at Riverbend before the talks broke down again."

"Were?" At this, Kharise perked up. "What do you mean, before the talks broke down?"

"No, no, lady." Reyser chuckled. "You didn't even give me a fake name, let alone a real one. You don't get to pry."

She sucked her teeth before she mustered a reply.

"I am Kharise gen Valuure; I was born on the fringe of the Unconquered Plains under a dark star that fated me to wander until I one day find what will root me to the earth beneath my feet. So far, it's not been love, nor duty, as both of those things are too delicate for convictions as sturdy as mine." She lifted her chin. Though she stood a head shorter than the guildmaster, she stood tall enough on her own, after all.

Reyser Gorum blinked, then slowly nodded in appreciation. He paused as if he were trying to compose the sentence. "Kharise. It's an honor to know you better."

Well, he knew his plainslander greetings well enough, for as rude as he'd started off. She clucked her tongue at him.

"So. What's happening with the Three Armies?"

He folded his arms and shook his head. "Surely you think higher of me than *this*." He looked over his shoulder, down the alleyway behind him. His body language was stiff, favored his right knee. Suspicious but not paranoid. He was watching for something, but not out of fear. Curious— almost. She'd have to work on him, that was all.

"You'd prefer someplace quieter?" She suggested it in a joking tone and managed to pry a grin out of him.

"I need good lighting, mostly." He gave her a wry look.

Kharise held her chin, mock-thoughtful.

"Not here, though. Someone has you rattled out here."

"It's that obvious? The Guild hall's empty while they're on leave for the evening. I'll bar the door behind us." Seeing her expression, he added, "It's not about you, it's about me."

As a rule, she did not abide a locked door behind her; even in Talorr, nothing sturdier than a broom handle while she spent her hours with Vierrelyne.

Kharise noted, though, that the knee Reyser Gorum was gentling around on was obviously bandaged under his pant leg, and she knew where her wager lay if it were to come down to a close quarters tussle. She followed him inside, hoping she might pry out not solely what he knew, but what it was that had put him on such high alert.

Vierrelyne huffed with indignation as Mehren bolted out of sight once again.

As they left the arcanists' atelier, he looked as if he had seen a ghost. He whipped his hood up from his shoulder, shadowing his face again, and ducked into the crowd so quickly she nearly lost him entirely. He darted across the high street, in the opposite direction, and she had to run to keep pace with him after that.

"What was that?" She wheezed when she finally caught up with him, and at first, he jumped when she put her hand on his shoulder.

"S-someone I don't want to see m-might have found me." He sighed once he'd caught his breath. "One of Tobinarde's other acolytes. I was afraid this might happen."

"I don't think anyone *actually* saw you," Vierrelyne said, wary as she elbowed through a knot of eager marketgoers, trying to stay near Mehren. He weaved through the crowd in a panic that was strange even for someone so nervous as he. "How could they, when no one here even glances at us?"

"I can't be sure, but I think she's here in Estuary City, I'd recognize her anywhere," he grumbled, huddled under his cloak, hood up, with a frantic energy that to Vi's perception bordered on a performance at high court. "I shouldn't have risked walking all through the city like this. I'm such a fool. If she knows where I am, she might tell *him*..."

"You couldn't have expected. It's not..." She paused, trying to piece together disparate thoughts. *It wasn't your fault; you didn't do this on purpose;* but also, she realized, she was grateful for this failure of his, the knowledge that they were being watched, even in such a blank, abstract place as the city. She rather disliked the sense she had that *someone* out there viewed her as a means to an end, a doll with a bejeweled crown and no mind of her own. Freed from her father's tower, she knew that there was no cell she would tolerate ever again, not even the cage of perception.

Mehren sighed but did not break his frenetic pace. "You might be right, but she has eyes and ears everywhere. It was bound to happen eventually. I just wish it hadn't been *her*."

"And what happens, hm?" she huffed. "She tells him where you are? The prophet finds you, and then what?"

"I-I don't like d-disappointing him," Mehren stuttered, and she did not need to see his face to know it for the lie of omission it was.

"We found your ink, and some brushes, even a quill. What else did we need? Why don't we go back t— "

"Shhhh. Yes. We should. It was just off the high street..."

He ducked around, looking for the correct intersection, and grabbed her wrist, pulling her through the crowd with his full attention on the path ahead of them, instead of simply leaving her to trot behind him in agony.

She could not help the sudden shyness that crept over her at his touch; it awakened a vulnerability she thought she'd cauterized away. His hand was on hers, all because he did not want to lose her in this ceaseless river of people.

The Sterling Moray was a short distance away, visible from afar on the high street with its curious sign embossed in a silver etched with age. It looked small and forgotten in the fray of other larger public houses down the same row, but that was no doubt why it appealed to Kharise.

At the front end of the tavern was a row of snug cloches, each with a tall, windowed door and high slatted walls in black. Detailing in tarnished silver leaf was reminiscent of the sign, long snaking ribbons with gaudy fanged eels' heads that bordered the tall, latticed stained-glass window.

Mehren ushered her into the cloche furthest from the door, lit by a single potted candle. It had a long, cushioned bench that wrapped around the interior table on three sides She settled onto the upholstered bench, facing the door, and he returned with two clay steins of heady, dark ale after a few minutes. He sat on the far end of the bench, his right side closer to her, and to the corner of the cloche, she noticed, before he let his hood down at last.

"So quiet here, it almost makes me more suspicious," he said, tapping his fingers on the table before them.

He'd never sat so close to her on this side, close enough to see his old injuries in the stark relief of candlelight, through his curtain of hair. She wished he'd let her look at it, however rude it would be to ask. Maybe she should.

"I need to tell you something important, before Kharise gets back," Vi said. "Something I don't quite understand."

He quirked his head.

"I've dreamed of you," she continued, "even back before I ever met you. I know it's very strange to say it— "

Mehren's voice wavered and his hands shook, but his words were steady, for once. "A prophetic dream?"

"I don't know. A *recurring* dream, one I had for years before all this began." Vi blushed and turned her gaze to the silver details around the window, the eels tangled and chasing each other through gilded waves.

He looked faintly sick. "What *happened* in the dream? It could be all the difference."

"It wasn't... I don't know where it came from. It was less like a *story*. More just an image. I walk across an expansive field, into a valley where I see a river and a little copse of trees, and there's a man, waiting. A young man in a dark, strange forest, a young man with dark hair, and a long scar, and a strange, glowing eye..."

She reached out and pushed his forelock back.

He flinched away from her touch—but Vi insisted, with a *"Please,"* that left her feeling guilty for intruding upon his person, but validated when he agreed at last.

He straightened his posture and pulled his hair back to aim his gaze directly at her. The hard scar tracing from his orbital down his cheek to his lip and chin was a fine little crease that offered his asymmetric aesthetic additional mystery. Other marks and lines she thought might be burns and scrapes.

He'd never shown her his eye on purpose, underneath all that dark hair, not even when she'd asked before, but once Vi saw it, the more she certain she was, wishing she felt less strange about it.

"It *was* you."

"Don't say that. I couldn't be sure of such a thing," he said, his expression solemn. "The realm of dreams is neither real nor unreal."

"How could I see something so specific without some reason for it?" Her voice became soft and quiet; she felt cruel forcing him to show her something so painful—but it was the exact mark she'd seen before. She couldn't simply invent such a peculiar scar—such a peculiar *person*.

His piercing stare, when he faced her again, quickened her pulse. The brilliant green glass of his right eye reflected the light in such a way that it made her feel certain he could see her, through all the realms. She could not help staring back, her heart still fast.

"I don't recall what happened, in the dream, exactly," she said. "I just remembered your face. The eye, the scar. In the dream, you didn't have to hide it from me, but I don't remember why."

Mehren laughed, bitter and half-hearted.

"It was just a dream, Princess. You can be sure it wasn't truly me," he muttered, and dragged his fingers through his hair to set his forelock back in place, nestled over his right eye, resetting himself to the ever-secretive wizard.

Vierrelyne turned her attention to the ale in front of her; it tasted like dark bread, the froth at the top slightly bitter. She could not help herself, though, for she was stuck on the question of what he'd seen and done that so haunted him still, that he was troubled by what she'd confessed.

They sat in stillness for several minutes, until at last Mehren drummed his fingers over the side wall of his empty mug, his expression glum.

"I'm sorry, Vi. I don't like to talk about walking the many realms, but it's not fair of me to suggest you haven't seen something when clearly you have, that's not right. Maybe I should explain. I have some minor talents, but walking the Realms... I learned it to survive."

"Yes?"

Vierrelyne turned toward him, folding her knee across the bench, so she could compress her miserable sore ankle.

"The way I learned to walk the Scourgelands, even the Realm of Dream, other places no mortal should dare to tread," he said solemnly. "It was when the witchfinders came to Beryl."

"I didn't realize you came from the Crystalline Cities."

"Ran from them, really. To my great shame."

"You survived the witch hunts." Vierrelyne let out a sad sigh and put her hand to her face in horror. "Oh, I'm sorry I was so cruel, making you show me that scar."

"Survived."

He laughed bitterly. Vierrelyne's stomach sank anew.

"I guess you could call it that. What good is surviving anyway when I couldn't complete one lousy—" He froze, seeing her face. "I'm sorry, I meant—"

Vi waved her hand. "If you hadn't been at Talorr..."

"I shouldn't talk like this." His gaze did not meet hers. "While the witch-finders held me there—that was how I learned to walk the lands of the unreal. A pathway out when I thought I might die of the pain."

"Is that what happened?"

"I guess I should start from the beginning," Mehren replied. "The witchfinders captured my mentor, said he was abetting their enemy, took all of us as hostages. We were tortured, individually or in pairs. They figured out hurting Istven was the only way to hurt me, so they beat him senseless. Eventually, to death. He wasn't a wizard at all."

"Your brother?"

"No, no." Mehren bit his lower lip. "My first true love. Only true love, really. He... he didn't even know any spells, but they still thought he might be in training, and we were inseparable, until..."

"Is that what happened..."

"My eye? Yes. What they didn't know, couldn't have known, really, was my will to live. My cowardice, my drive to escape. That I could slip from myself, ride the arc of their torments, until at last... someone set me free from it. Tobinarde l'Ete himself. He said he'd been looking for me, that I was his sacred Shepherd." He scoffed at himself.

Vi fondled the ring in her dress-pocket, the signet of the three crowns polished glassy by the touch of her thumb, trying to figure out what she could possibly say.

"When my sisters were still alive," she said finally, "I was told I could have whatever courtship I wanted, because I wasn't an heir nor an alternate. After the carriage accident, I became a curse, a liability, a prophecy made true by the virtue of my singularity. I became the rose in the tower in that stupid story, and for what?"

Mehren furrowed his brow.

"When I was locked away," she continued, her lower lip trembling, "the young woman whose heart enmeshed with mine? We stayed together in letters and rare visits, until she was married off, to appease the Cascadian prince Erenth, never to be heard from again. The only letter I ever sent was returned, in pieces, with frightening things drawn all over them. He already had several wives, but he... he wanted *her*, and he was wealthy, and reflecting on the circumstances, Erenth wanted to make a connection to the western reaches of Derebor for his own ends, no doubt. I never got to tell her what she meant to me, even in the days I told her nearly everything, because I couldn't risk my letters being so bold."

"That's dreadful. I'm sorry you lost her, no matter the circumstance."

"You've had it much worse."

"There's no tournament for suffering; it's not a joust to be won." Mehren tilted his head, at an angle where that demon's eye glimmered its eerie green through his dark curtain of hair. "Would it be better if Istven lived, in a place where he'd never see me again? It might be better for him, but the outcome for me is the same, is it not? I don't see any difference except for a falsity of hope."

"That seems unaccountably dour."

"There's no nobility in self-pity either, Highness." He let out a grim laugh. "If I have to grieve regardless, it may as well be on my own terms."

She put her hand over his, just for a moment, and she felt the sharpness in him softening ever so slightly, like sloughing away crystals of frost. Something in him was warming.

"My grief might be selfish, but it's mine," he murmured, his gaze to the horizon. "The thing none of them could take from me."

"I'm sorry they did this to you."

"It's my turn to say, 'you've had it much worse.' I might have been tortured once, but I can't imagine fifteen years in a cage, no matter how nice a cage it is. No amount of gilding can account for such a thing." Mehren said it softly, and he gave her his full attention, leaning close.

"It's not a joust," she replied, trying to make herself smile. At least he was warmer now. She remembered the signs on the high street windows and felt colder than ever as she thought of that miserable prince adding yet another sad girl to his palatial estates.

She couldn't help the sickening feeling, though, that the mere mention of that despicable prince brought forth the embers of loathing in her core.

The meeting hall for the Independent's Guild was an unassuming space—decorated to give the impression of a continuous if fractious history to the abstract organization heading this operation.

The main gathering room held three long tables of polished ebonwood, each with an assortment of chairs and benches arranged around them in a haphazard fashion that Kharise found charming; none of them matched, exactly, but all of them were gathered for purpose and stained or painted the same dark shade.

The walls were draped in banners under which they had marched, all of them in service to every crown she'd ever heard a song about, and several older than even her songs. There were banners for the far-northern island archipelago Crystalline Cities—Garnet, Beryl, Quartz—and banners to the southern fringes, far east and south of even inland waypoints like Devere; even a long, thin banner of aged black in the same dimensions as the towers known as the Bleak Pillars.

"This is incredible," she said, perusing the various artefacts that lined the walls with great interest, as any bard of her caliber would, however long since her last tune. "The Independents have a rich history, it seems."

"Seems. An *embellished* history, perhaps," Reyser said, giving her an uncertain look. "We wouldn't have a guild hall here in Estuary City if I hadn't insisted on it. There was a time our ranks ran thin enough to justify an undignified retirement, but I thought, *perhaps*. Hang out a shingle and see what kind of trouble comes to us instead of what trouble we can find on the march. As you can see, it works. We do what the Estuary City High Council can't, which is 'most of it,' being honest."

"I don't suppose I can keep much of a secret about my inclinations as a wanderer quite suited to the road myself."

"And yet you do travel with an air of mystery about you." He countered. "What is a woman of your obvious talents doing in the company of the two strangest people in Estuary City?"

Kharise chuckled. "My charges are a secret, however poorly kept. I need to know your allegiances before I speak to such a thing."

Reyser sucked his teeth and clicked his tongue. "Well, it won't take much for me to admit that we aligned with the greater Principalities at the beginning of their deathward marching, if only because they promised us a great deal of wealth and more operating independence than we can ordinarily muster."

"You seem dissatisfied with that outcome."

"It's that evident, eh?" Reyser laughed darkly. "Yes, we received a tenth of what we were promised after the march on Derebor, and not one lonesome copper since. There's a lot of affiliates in the Independent's Guild, and the prince didn't feel he needed to pay them. We, on the other hand, absorbed the cost. The Independent's Guild coffers are, accordingly, running thin."

He looked away, his hands clasped behind his back, and he walked in a figure-of-eight so efficiently, despite his obvious stiff knee, that even Kharise could regard it with genuine admiration and respect.

"If you are looking for an opportunity, then," she said slowly, steeling herself to bridge the moment, "I do have some ideas, but I don't know what I can offer you, exactly. I need to know more about everything, and I'm willing to share what I know with the right person."

She handed him a sterling coin, embossed with the graven image of that tower at Talorr.

"I can't imagine this is worth much in the present marketplace, but I suspect a gentleman of your particular qualifications will understand what this object means, at this moment."

He took it, whistled, and examined it closely, turning it over in his hand and holding it up to squint at each facet. "I will freely concede this was not one of my wildest suspicions. Everything I heard about the fall of Talorr... Well, the bonfire of enmity ran hot for the three armies."

"You know my name; you know my broad history. I should like to know some of yours, Reyser Gorum." Kharise gave him a cold grin. "How did you come to be the leader of such an enterprising outfit as you have here? When did you become the Guildmaster?"

He turned on his heel, interrupting another of his pacing patterns. "Well, that's a funny story, and short, thankfully. When the Crystalline and Sunward Free Cities first got wound up about witch-hunting, my mother and her family took to the road. We stayed in many strange places on the eastern edges of the continent and the northern islands. We were at Stardowne for a brief period and ended up in Estuary City. I came to the Independent's Guild because none of the others would have me, and I was attentive enough and eccentric enough to work the balance books. Time was, sometimes that was the only fellow who made it out alive."

"I can respect that," Kharise replied. "What do you know of the other armies commissioned by Prince Erenth?"

"The forces from Devere are already making moves to break away from Cascada, but I don't know how much of that is talk," Reyser mused. "Their own forces seem to have suffered a surreal number of casualties, unlike anything I've ever seen, like a great shadow seems to stalk not far behind them. Don't know what to make of that."

"We found a Cascadian encampment, not long after we left that tavern." Kharise said it as if she were testing its structural integrity. "In that camp, my wizarding associate found a sigil that he thinks might be the key to how swift and deadly this battle became."

"Did he, now?" Reyser's tone was skeptical.

"He seems to think that there were demons called from other realms of existence, lured to this place." She shook her head. "I imagine a gentleman of your knowledge would turn his nose at such a thing."

"On the contrary," he replied. "You have my full and undivided attention. Your cultist is wiser than he's let on to you, I expect. A lot of those Astral Circle types are quite defensive, with good reason."

She narrowed her eyes.

"And how do you know this?"

"Well, for starters," he said, but paused, as if he was searching for the right words. "For starters, I spent some time at Stardowne because I was in that same cult. For a while. Not a long time, just long enough to realize whatever it was, I wanted no part in it. After that grandiose, self-absorbed bastard flung himself out of his tower, I walked away licking my wounds and made for Estuary City without ever looking back. My mother settled in the outskirts with some of the cousins, I figured it was as good a place as any."

"So. You know the Astral Circle?"

"Only too well, though I am sure old Tobinarde has kept it interesting in the wake of the rest of his beliefs springing to life."

It was Kharise's turn to laugh darkly. "I am beginning to wonder if he is connected to these summoning circles my friend has found."

She startled herself with the use of the word "friend," but it worked well enough, didn't it? She trusted Mehren Tevaht with Vierrelyne, and with the gravity of what the princess held.

"That is a serious accusation. There are many who don't believe the old bastard survived such a terrible fall."

"Don't play coy with me," Kharise replied. "I didn't believe until I met Mehren, but he seems so sincere it's hard to imagine it otherwise."

"*Mehren*, huh? A warded name. That's further than I ever got into that wacky death cult. He's *powerful*, then. Why is he with you?" Reyser paused his pacing to examine a flag on his own walls; a banner that Kharise did not recognize, a plain field of burgundy in a long triangle.

"Because we needed out of Castle Talorr and he offered us a portal," she replied. "And *that* was safer than any other way out."

His expression traveled a range from distrust to intrigue. He put his hand on his chin, his fingers tracing the edge of his beard theatrically. "It was *safer* to hop into a portal to go charging through the demon realms than it was to go anywhere else."

"I said it. I meant it." Kharise stiffened. "And so, you know the last of my secrets."

This brought an actual belly laugh out of Reyser Gorum.

"I rather doubt I'll ever know the last of your secrets, lady." He sat down at the head of the center table and gestured her over to sit next to him. "You mean to tell me the rest of your wandering party of three is comprised of a death cultist from Zalandan and *the Rose in the Tower*?"

"I thought it obvious when I gave you a sovereign from the coffers of the late Brabinghar du Talorr," she replied.

"I thought this coin was something you found in that Cascadian campsite," he said, shaking his head. "This? This changes some things. I don't want to side with the Astral Circle, not even slightly, but *this*..."

"You do still believe, after all these years. After all this evidence proving otherwise." Kharise sighed incredulously, hiding a grin behind her hand as best she was able. "Even feeling superior to those cultists. You *believe* that mad old man, or you once did."

"You know all of Cascada is tasked with finding the girl?" He interjected. "They never did find her, at Talorr. I thought for sure it was because she never existed at all, or if she did, she was murdered alongside her mother and forgotten by all but the most rabid believers. A symbol, a figurehead, a cautionary bedtime tale about vile warlords. I thought for sure she was dead."

"They did not find her at Talorr because she escaped," she said. "But it is true that keeping her hidden will only endure for so long, because she has taken on quite a desperate burden, one that can be guessed at if you believe in the most far-fetched tales of the late queen."

Reyser took a deep breath and drummed his fingernails on the table. "Are you *absolutely* sure you can trust that cultist?" He let out a loud sigh for punctuation.

"He could have walked away at any time," Kharise replied. "I trusted him to walk the city with her today while

I sought out more answers. He's had days to make an escape if he was thinking about it. No, I think Mehren is invested in this, in her. In *protecting* her. For what reason, I can't say."

"You don't think he may try to lure her away from you?"

Kharise grinned.

"Vierrelyne du Talorr is already an accomplished, if unorthodox, swordfighter. What she lacks in experience she accounts for with vicious enthusiasm. I daresay fifteen years in a tower has given her a keen taste for vengeance. No, I do not fear that anyone will take advantage of her here, at least."

"Well. Here's to hoping no one figures out the lady wandering the streets of Estuary City is the Rose in the *Tower*." Reyser dragged his fingers over his face, puzzling over the tableau Kharise had set for him, and for his soldiers, if he was so inclined to take up her terms.

She drew herself to her feet and walked to the door, heavier for the knowledge. "Thank you for your time. I do expect you'll hold what I've told you in confidence?" She placed two more of the silver coins on the end of the table, and Reyser picked them up, examining their heft as he did.

"If I needed to verify some information, where might I send it on to your attention?" he asked. "For curiosity's sake, of course."

"For tonight? I'll be at the Sterling Moray. Come the dawn, come what may." Kharise smirked as she unbolted the door. "A pleasure meeting you, Reyser Gorum."

She could not help but notice that he seemed the slightest bit disappointed at her departure, which entertained her a great deal. She seldom met someone as skilled in the fine art of colloquial intelligence, and this fellow seemed to hold her in the same regard as she held for him.

The walk back to the high street was scarcely notable, save for one curious detail. As she was crossing the street toward the public house, she thought she saw Mehren in the crowd, but when the figure turned their head, she realized it was a woman in a nearly identical cloak, with a riot of blond curls that spilled out of the deep, shadowy hood.

M. Daniel McDowell

CHAPTER 10
INDEPENDENTS

MEHREN'S SKEPTICISM HAD FULLY SOURED HIS MOOD BY THE time Kharise arrived that evening, and he wasn't even exactly certain from where the unpleasantness had come.

By all rights, after two mugs of ale and a well-seasoned trencher of beet stew, he was contented enough, but as soon as the plainswoman turned up with her long list of new discoveries, he felt the same impending sense of dread he'd caught earlier when he'd seen Carina on the high street.

He stood in the corner of their cloche, leaning against the painted hardwood, cradling his empty mug like it was a serviceable shield.

"So, you think we should join forces with one of the armies who marched upon the end of the empire?" he asked. "We should trust this bunch who were part of the sacking at Talorr and Stonebrake, and just continue on with... whatever our plan might be?"

"It would be hard to describe our current movements as a *plan*," Kharise said, her hand braced over the rim of her mug as she sat down across from Vierrelyne. "It's not clear to me what your intentions have been, Tevaht. I could question your loyalties in the same breath, let alone the same sentence."

Mehren gnawed his lip and mused. "I once had grand intentions of returning to Zalandan. I-I don't know what to do anymore. Everything I thought I believed, it's over."

He didn't like to admit that his plans had all turned to powdered chalk scattered across the mountainside, but he felt a sense of urgency around Vierrelyne, and even Kharise, if he were honest; an innate pull to continue on with them, to find out where this tangled net would eventually resolve. There was something deeper here.

He didn't want to admit that the princess's confession, that she had seen him in her dreams, had utterly shattered his resolve. He didn't want to admit that she'd have his very heart if she only said the word.

Vierrelyne remained silent, and Mehren's gut twinged to look at her. She'd barely said a word since Kharise arrived. It wasn't only his own mood he was struggling to balance. Hers seemed as poor as his. Too much ale and time spent in an enclosed space in the dark after a relatively joyful afternoon sightseeing, as if she *weren't* a princess locked in a tower, and he'd closed her up in this dark, stuffy bar at his first inconvenience.

They should've taken advantage of the daylight, but he'd sworn he saw Carina Betrel stalking the streets of Estuary City, and he wasn't willing to risk letting his position be known, not when he hadn't figured out what to do about...

Any of it.

The princess. The demon. The promise. The hideous weapon he'd found in the camp. The thought that Carina could swoop in, find out where he was, find out who was with him... he couldn't risk it. Perhaps if he approached

Zalandan on his own terms, with his own angle. Tobinarde was inflexible, at times, but Mehren had known him to be fair at times as well. He couldn't be held up for his own mistakes if he shaped them into something else, right?

But he could no longer be certain of Tobinarde, either. What if he knew Mehren had failed? What if he'd *sent* Carina out to find him, to clean up Mehren's abject failure?

Vierrelyne sighed heavily and put her elbows upon the table, her chin on her hands.

"I saw a notice in the street today that Prince Erenth of Cascada is taking another wife."

"Oh! I am so sorry, Vi." Kharise's features creased with a knowing look. "This could mean a lot of things, but I know it's not a balm on your wounds."

"It means consolidation of power," she said solemnly, "and it means that Alaina no longer animates his heart, perhaps."

"Who can say? He had several wives before Alaina, remember."

Vierrelyne glared, though not at Kharise.

"In the current moment," Kharise continued, "with their presumptive victories and the vacuum created by the unseating of brittle structures of power, it is hard to argue that it isn't meant to build a further coalition." The plainswoman paused. "I heard some things about their armies that suggests this may be another form of power arbitrage, though."

At this, Mehren quirked his head. "So, their ranks are thinner than they'd like to admit. Even with Devere and Estuary City."

"We lot might be among the few outsiders who know why that is, yes," Kharise mused.

"Apparently he intends to hold the formal ceremony here in Estuary City, in a week's time." Vierrelyne laid her head on the table.

"Why wouldn't he hold it in Cascada, at that enormous palace?" Mehren asked. "Why so far down, in Estuary City?"

Kharise bit her lip and concentrated, her brow knit in furrows.

"Well, I know someone here in the city I can ask about that. In the meantime, lay low. We have enough neutral coins from that windfall in the woods to mark a month or more in Estuary City if we must. I've got us room and board for the night, upstairs."

Vierrelyne gave her such a sad look that Kharise passed her a key, and the princess slipped up the stairs without another word.

The plainswoman took the moment to really study him; Mehren felt the heft of her gaze, as if she were examining him for external signals of future treachery. He leaned into the dregs of his pint of ale.

"When we were in the mountains, you suggested the Crystalline Cities as a destination we might pursue." She said it quietly, as if she were laying the strands of a weasel snare. "But last I'd heard of such things Beryl was still the capital of the witchfinders' general. Hostile terrain for someone with your unique capabilities."

"Likely worse than when I left, yes," he replied. "But at the ports, you could skip from arrivals to departures at the docks, and if you don't mean to be observed as a passenger, you can get to Amberine or Garnet while it's still daylight, most of the time, if you know which boats to take."

"And you think *three* passengers could evade detection?" She shook her head. "What survivor of the witchfinders would ever choose to go back north again?"

"Oh, I wouldn't *stay* there, no."

She did not need to know about the cairn in the valley, he decided, the one marked only with a cipher known to two people, one of them gone; a cairn likely unvisited by the village not far from it, unnoticed in the decade since it had been placed.

"You miss it, though?"

"Asks the plainswoman who spent over a decade with a princess in a tower?" Mehren eyed her over the lip of his mug, needing some hand gesture to shield himself from the deepest reach of her inspection.

"Aye, but I wandered the whole of the Known Lands from tip to tail in the time before that. Just curious, that's all," she replied, with a warmer smile than Mehren expected. "Go get some rest. We've got more to do in the morning."

He could scarcely refuse. For once, his exhaustion might overtake his ragged nerves.

Vierrelyne slumped on the narrow bed in her room. Shabby, unkempt, but worlds above the hard-packed dirt, or a pile of moth-eaten tapestries, or even the camping bedroll salvaged from their spoils of battle in the foothills.

The growling in her pack was so unbearable, though, that she had to get back up and address it, lest the inhuman sounds attract unwanted attention. She had done her level best to ignore his wheedling all afternoon, but with the weariness of the day upon her and some amount of time to herself, the temptation to let his strength rejuvenate her was unbearable. Without a second thought, she donned the thorned diadem, and the demon prince's voice was in her ear once more.

You've kept me waiting so long.

She did not want to dignify this with a response.

Are you angry with me about something?

She clenched her jaw and straightened her shoulders. "What do you know of the prophecies of Tobinarde l'Ete?"

That's not what you really want to ask me. He laughed. *You want to know if what he said about you is **true**. That's not the same. Not at all.*

Vierrelyne fumed. "The Rose in the Tower."

The rose in the tower has thorns of gold, she is a weapon in the hands of the gardener, she carries the burden of the words, she waits for the key.

Margandrys sounded bored.

"The Shepherd in Shadow."

He waits unseen. He holds the key. He walks in ruin, lost forevermore; he knows not the cost, the price he will pay.

"The Crown of the World Unbound."

She gentled her fingers over the spindles of her diadem, aware of them in the lamplight shadows on the floor, spilling over the wall as she tipped her head around to examine them. Her crown seemed taller now than ever.

The Crown of the World Unbound! He parroted it back to her with a cackle. *The final hope of a shattered land, the vestige of another time brought forward into the future, a hidden gem, a sacred truth. What are you playing at, dearest?*

"I don't understand what it is I am supposed to do now. I don't know my purpose. I thought I was meant to do something before my whole world collapsed, and now I feel like I've lost my place. I wanted so badly to be free that I didn't know what my cage shielded me from."

Had you not escaped, you would not have me, he reminded her. *Had you not escaped, you would be naught but cinders—perhaps a prize for that prince of Cascada.* **He** *would don the crown, would he not? Would he fear me as you do?*

Vierrelyne's skin crept with gooseflesh.

"I don't fear you."

You won't let me protect you, even when it would give you more power than you have ever held, even when it would help you. I want to **help** *you, Vierrelyne.*

"I always thought..." She paused, trying to find the words she meant to say, and her skin crawled with dread. "I always wondered what it was that my mother loved about you. I never understood it because she kept it from me."

I'm sure she was right to worry that you would not grasp what it means to be united with someone, to share their vision. It is not an easy gift to carry. That must be why you carry me so seldom.

Vierrelyne fell silent for a time, not sure what to think of the strange gift she had taken from her mother's own grave. She'd assigned a legend, a purpose, a meaning to it in her long and woeful interment, a meaning it no longer seemed to have. She'd been lucky she'd worn it out of the tavern, into that curious encampment, hadn't she?

She couldn't talk it out with Mehren or Kharise, not really. Mehren probably wanted it for himself, didn't he? Wasn't that the *real* reason he'd come here? Did he even care about her at all? Her mind went to the moment in the street, where Mehren had taken her hand, so he wouldn't lose sight of her—was it only because he had a purpose for her crown?

Kharise, well, she believed all of this chaos, this drama, the prophecy itself, was all just nonsense. She'd traveled too much of the Known Lands to have an opinion on anything that transcended them, the Scourgelands and the dominion beyond even there. Kharise believed in what she could see, and feel, and hold.

Vierrelyne felt slightly less exhausted now, the effect of Margandrys's gift in action, but it gave her precious little peace. She sat down on the edge of the bed and removed the crown from her brow. Atop the scarf she'd worn to escape the fires in the tower at Talorr, she rested the headpiece and its demonic spires; she draped the rest of the fabric over its points and contemplated.

It might look less formal, less regal, less demanding, if she wore it with more elements of disguise, but those spires were ever taller, ever harder to hide, as Margandrys slowly recovered his powers.

After taking out her combs and cauls, letting her thick pair of braids rest on her shoulders, the weariness crept back into her bones, and she laid her head down, hoping for some amount of rest, that she might be freed of her terrible dreams of the boy in the darkness, now that she'd finally told him what she had seen.

Something had shifted in the wizard's rigid scheming, in the time since they'd arrived in Estuary City, Kharise was sure of it. What it might be was anyone's guess, but she wanted to understand why. His plans had been deferred for so long now that he'd had to revise, and even those revisions seemed outdated on the face of things. What compelled

M. Daniel McDowell

him now, she could not guess and dared not ask, not until she had her feet under her once more.

She left the confines of the snug, not long after she'd sent Mehren upstairs. She'd have better luck canvassing the locals from the main area of the public house.

The relative quiet of the place, with its thin selection of company and even thinner selection of ales worked against her in this regard. She stood out as a clear outsider, and there wasn't anything to be done about that. She settled at an outer table that gave her a vantage over the rest of the room and composed her thoughts on the day's discoveries.

That Prince Erenth was not fulfilling his promises surprised her not in the slightest. It made an unfortunate sense that he had commissioned so many disparate forces on the promises of future spoils, with the intent to outlast anyone who came to collect on them. Valid, if infuriating, strategically.

What she'd found most surprising was that he had successfully groomed so many disparate forces to join him in the first place, but that was always the way of the Principalities even in a time of relative peace. Cascada's reach was historically limited to the western half of Derebor in exchange for control of her eastern flanks and a light touch from Talorr's tax collectors, but she'd always been the jewel of this side of Broadcoast and with reason, for she held all the region's wealthiest farms and cities.

Once the miscreant Brabinghar broke with that old unspoken tradition of minimal taxation and allotted self-governance, it was only a matter of time before those taxes would be the sundering of relations. And that was before anyone had found out about the strange portals concocted to funnel grand terrors from one realm into the next.

Just when she thought she might head to bed, the guildmaster she'd met on the row turned up in the public house. She noticed he was still favoring that leg. He'd walked all over town that evening, or nearly so, she supposed. Dead stubborn of him, but at least she understood that variety of stubbornness well enough to work around it.

"Do you have *any* idea how many taverns have a name like this one?" Reyser Gorum raised his eyebrows as he approached her, but his grin spread. "I talked to every last body on my roster, every last one of my roustabouts and roughnecks. There are some lingering concerns, but not more than before this new wrinkle appeared."

"Concerns?"

"Well, the collective at the heart of the Independents is *accepting* of a deferred schedule of payment, but—" he said as if he anticipated a flat rejection, "—a job this big, without even so much as a deposit?"

"Oh, now, Mr. Gorum—"

"Please. I have never been Mr. Anything for one day in my life. I told you before, it's Reyser; it's a fine name."

"Reyser. As you like." Kharise grinned, catlike with glee. It was nice to meet someone with such a different decorum than the stuffiness of the Crown. "It so happens that I have some coin I'm willing to put toward the coffers of the collective, as a goodwill gesture, on the promise that there will be more to come if we succeed."

"I don't mean to suggest that I would comment on the color of your coin, but..." Here, he paused as if the rest of the statement was self-evident.

"How many do you need to see?" she asked dryly. "You've seen their color before, good sir, I dare say you are asking after a *number*."

Reyser folded his arms and leaned against the wall.

"You need to get that looked at," Kharise said, shaking her head as she pulled out her coin purse, as surreptitiously as she dared, even with the taproom thin of customers.

"Get what looked at?"

"You have an injury to your leg, one which has progressed over the course of the past day, which means that you should consider doing something different. I can't tell from here what sort of wound it is, but I would give it some thought. I don't *expect* you to for at least another few days, by which point whatever it is may well escalate."

He gave her a thin-lipped stare and shook his head.

"Listen," she said, clucking her tongue. "Let me help."

"And what makes you such an expert?"

"I am a wanderer, a nomad of the Unconquered Plains," she deadpanned. "I know a lot about walking, and you don't want that to get worse."

"Twisted it the other day, on the hike through the mountains back from Riverbend. It's nothing." He waved dismissively, his eyes to the ceiling, but she caught the traces of a grin at the corner of his lip.

"Well, it's your leg." She sighed and counted out a pile of silver coins and passed it to him. "Here's your deposit."

He whistled and placed them in the interior pocket of his jacket. "If you are always this prompt, I might have to rethink the rest of my client list."

"Oh, don't worry, that's a finite resource, until we get somewhere," Kharise said. "For all I know, we're on the wrong track entirely, but I rather doubt it. See what your men find out?"

Reyser nodded and made for the door.

"And get that knee looked at," she added, just as he was leaving. He did not reply, but he gave her a grudging nod and a wave as he left.

She chuckled to herself. Well, hopefully it was merely a sprain and not a gangrenous infection from a week of marching on a sour wound. A part of her that longed for an era long past felt truly at ease here.

She could get used to working with the Independents.

M. Daniel McDowell

CHAPTER 11
PROCESSIONAL

KHARISE MADE HERSELF AT HOME WITH THE VARIOUS FELLOWS OF the Independent's Guild, learning their intricate placement in the grander ecosystem of Estuary City. They functioned as a most unusual detachment, neither a true militia nor merely a congregation of tradesmen. The ranks held stations of all sorts. While Reyser took the lead in more than one regard, he trusted his men to handle all sorts of tasks without his oversight.

There were members of this guild in nearly every shop on the high streets, nearly every office of the High Council, and a number of rank-and-file operatives on the roster whose unofficial title seemed to be Roustabout at Large, a helping hand to anyone who might ask for their aid. These, she noticed, often did such things without a discussion of payment, and she rather suspected Reyser liked it that way. Get paid for the *big* jobs, keep the clean public profile, and maintain order in the most disorderly place anywhere on the Broadcoast.

It afforded him a strange, tidy sort of soft power, one Kharise quite liked, as it allowed her to peer into the inner workings of the city with less scrutiny.

The three spent the week in Estuary City, helping the Guild assemble resources as discreetly as could be done at a dingy tavern inn on the high street. Kharise was not the only one who held the prince's grand plans as highly suspect, for he had still not offered a single coin to those men who had come to his aid. There were no noble-minded Roustabouts-at-Large in the trenches of war.

Estuary City was a safe place for all sorts to hide out, in her estimation. No one here wanted any part of anyone else's business. Kharise kept her ears to the streets and listened for any deeper understanding of the machinations of the Cascadian prince and his most unusual parade plan.

Amongst the rank-and-file, there was a suspicion that the prince's parade had something to do with his debts. A celebration, a show of largesse, it was meant to erase some lines on his ledger with the citizens of Estuary City. There was to be the march, and a concert and show of magic by his court mages, a stage performance; perhaps with music? It was unclear from the outside what parts were meant to be the main event.

Mehren preferred to avoid being seen in the city, so he took to drafting various campaigns and requests for aid by hand, to help the Independents in finding other allegiances, from the relative comfort of the Sterling Moray. He was still shaken by the grim spells he'd found in the camp, Kharise thought. She hadn't gotten him to explain how it was that he understood so many different languages, considering he'd been nearly as shut-in as Vi if what he'd told her of the tower at Zalandan was true. Perhaps he'd used the extra time to study, but it seemed a dour place from his own words.

Vierrelyne made good use of her newfound freedom; the Guild had several skilled swordfighters who were happy to show her techniques outside of Kharise's skill set. The princess's sword confidence and strength were both vastly improved; her speed and dexterity with the blade well beyond what Kharise had been able to build with her, over those many years in that tiny room.

She did not feel comfortable asking, but Kharise got the sense that Vierrelyne was settling into a pattern with the formidable magic in her crown as well. More than once, she caught the distinct notion that there was a conversation taking place, only she could not make out one of the voices at all, as if it were underwater, just out of her range.

The autumn weather had begun to descend in earnest by the date of the event; it was a cold and dreary morning that settled over Estuary City with determination.

Blustery wind and loose leaves were in full effect as the processional from the edges of Cascadian terrain was set to begin at nearly dawn.

It chilled Kharise to her delicate bones just to think of it.

It was set to be a long, curious march, one which snaked through the countryside and eventually onto the Estuary City high street. Mehren had drawn out his map the night before to show them where he expected the bridal train processional would pass.

The guild's workers from the Independent were perturbed, to a one.

"That's a long walk from Cascada," said the man she knew only as Graves, a tall, angular fellow who hailed from somewhere on the plains; not as remote as the Vale, but he'd shed his placename, and she respected it. Not all who wandered did so with a like mind.

"You should know from walking, Graves," quipped Teven, a short man from the street-roaming crew of roustabouts and roughnecks, with the most unique array of body odor Kharise had experienced in her half-century traversing the Known Lands.

"Focus, friends," she rejoindered, and sketched the line of the expected processional over the streets where she anticipated it would pass, with Mehren's stump of graphite wrapped in string. "We should connect with the folks at the city center and see if they're expecting anything unusual. Council went through yesterday, I think."

"Teven," Reyser said with a nod. "Your sister-in-law still on the high council?"

He nodded and tipped his head. "Yeah, boss. I'll go run this past her. They were like cats with their tails on fire last night, clearing all the regular costers' carts out of the central square."

Something ate at Kharise's gut; something about this stank worse than the wharf at evening-tide. Prince Erenth Remaryn, High Prince of Cascada, residing in a grand and mysterious palace at the center of the bustling hub of the Broadcoast, wanting to make an elaborate display of companionship with the people of Estuary City, all because it was the one-time home of one of his several wives?

It seemed to her that Reyser was also skeptical, if for different reasons. To him, it was what they were owed: that the prince had pledged to repay the differences owed to three separate smaller militias who had joined his march on Talorr in exchange for a handsome fee.

"A debt left to rot like that can only fester," he muttered to himself, as he had several times that afternoon, as if he were hunting for the right permutation that might unlock some intention still as yet hidden from him. "I just don't know what he has to gain by all this ceremony. I don't know why the high council likes it, either."

"Never underestimate the power of a promise," Kharise replied with a loud sigh.

Teven leaned in with an observation. "What I want to know is, if there's a wedding party, on the prince's dime, why's he sending the costers' carts to the other end of town? Is he bringing the feast with him through that big parade? Or do the northerners all starve their guests out of common courtesy? Good ol' Mollybrass couldn't answer me that one last night."

Kharise squinted. "I do wonder what sort of party he intends."

"I don't reckon you've heard anything from the high council about that?" Reyser asked Teven, leaning on his right foot; the way Kharise knew always meant something with his lousy knee was still bothering him. "Has there been any discussion about what the actual ceremony or party will entail? Anything more intricate than just, 'city square at dusk'?"

"Not really," Teven replied. "Only about half the council are reporting to service at all right now, still a bunch who haven't come back from—" he whispered "*Talorr*," as if it might wound Kharise to hear.

"I see," Reyser said. "Well, my fellow Independents, I dare say we should endeavor to be present at this wedding festival. I'd like to be wrong about it, but I have a sick feeling in the pit of my stomach and I'm too old to ignore it."

"I know what you mean," Kharise agreed.

"It's some fancy ritual," Teven said. "My brother's wife said it was something from the old days. The women sing and dance, together, to show unity and love? I dunno, with all the money they owe us for that gig in... *Talorr*..."

Reyser shifted his weight and Teven yelped. He looked at Kharise with pursed lips, as if to say, *Well, it wasn't my bum knee that time.*

"Well, since half the high council is still out of service, I dare say the Independents have a responsibility to Estuary City tonight. Watch over everyone, make sure they get home from the city square safe."

Kharise nodded.

"We should probably split our efforts. East and west of the high street, maybe a few individuals at the city square. Mages, if we can spare any."

"How about yours?" Reyser asked. "Haven't seen him at a meeting in days."

"I'll assign him a patrol, if you like," Kharise said dryly. "I'm sure he'll love it."

Dwelling on the bigger picture before her, though, she did not want to think about what Vierrelyne might be feeling over the whole thing, even with the initial surprise of it fading.

Maybe it would be Mehren's job to keep an eye on her.

Buy her a fancy pastry, take her aside somewhere quiet if the evening started to pitch downhill with her, give her something to think about or hope for instead of something to grieve.

It hadn't been clear to her at the time: how badly Vi had taken it when Alaina had accepted the proposition between Stonebrake and Cascada, in the interest of what everyone knew now was a fickle sort of peace indeed.

Vierrelyne had to admit that no amount of light distraction could hold her attention as the processional swept down the high street of Estuary City. Not even Mehren's efforts to tempt her into eating dessert for dinner, nor his attempts to dance in time with the marchers and their music for her amusement, pretending to have terrible rhythm when she had to concede he kept good time with the rest of the dance. It wasn't his fault she wasn't entertained; her feelings had simply hit a boil.

The processional from Cascada was not merely a show of power, Vi thought, as the groups of dancers from the palace's court of entertainers swooped past, horns and bells in accompaniment. She caught a glimpse of the chariots at the end of the processional, and Mehren, for once, was the one left to follow in her wake as she wove through the crowd to get a closer look. To confront her own agonies, perhaps, to embrace what she had truly lost on her own terms.

Did Alaina *never* think of her anymore? Was she alone in her longings? Was her dearest beloved not troubled in any way at the sight of those untold squadrons of soldiers on the march with the intent to take Talorr, to capture Vierrelyne?

It did no good to her to think of such things, but the notion of it would not leave her.

This march was a flaunting of an excess Estuary City never seemed to possess, a wealth accumulated of ages, an accreta of spoils as the throne of the northern and eastern shores. Estuary City might be the central conduit to the Inland Reaches, but the wealth of this strategic place had been sponged off for as long as the Principalities had been allowed a modicum of autonomy. All this had come about in the days before Brabinghar had taken the throne in Talorr those long years ago. He had reinstated the easterly tariffs which likely played a role in his own demise.

Cascada had all but taken full credit for the late tyrant's displacement, and this parade was just another reminder, another opportunity for a show of power. Prince Erenth Remaryn thought himself nimble enough to topple the old ways and strong enough to defend the new ways.

At the end of the procession, the series of opulent chariots rolled, decorated in roses and ribbon, five chariots for five of Prince Erenth's wives from the lesser tributaries of the Prinicipalities. Vierrelyne followed as closely as she dared, watching as Alaina and her sister-wives rode past the crowd. Alaina's face was an upturned mask of sorrow, her fine features drawn with a sadness even more profound than at their last parting. She was dressed in a gauzy burgundy gown, the color of the Cascadian court. Her gaze was turned away from the gathered admirers, her figure as statuesque as the princess remembered, her dark hair in a coif, and the very sight of her brought tears unbidden.

Perhaps she would sing. Surely that was the purpose of bringing someone so talented to such an affair; Alaina had a gift for balladry and poems to music that had been the cornerstone of Vierrelyne's abiding crush, and later of her open admiration, and their courtship, before they had been so coarsely torn apart.

If Vierrelyne could hear her sing, just this once. Her heart ached at the notion of it.

Prince Erenth himself rode in on a black horse, gamely working to entertain the crowd with horseback skill tricks that might seem more impressive at closer range than where Vi stood, watching, as her heart boiled with an unfathomable fury. His shaggy hair was silvering to white at the temples; he had gotten no younger, and yet he had an odd aura to him as he rode around, a vitality he should not possess, one which chilled Vierrelyne to the bone. He seemed lively with anticipation—and why wouldn't he? For this was to be his next wedding, after all.

As dusk approached, the parade route wound into the city square, where observers and revelers alike congregated on the stone steps and milled about on the lawns, while the Queens of Cascada circled around the dais on the platforms at the center of the park, attended by mages in brilliant scarlet robes, too far from the crowd for anyone to hear what direction the women were receiving for this elaborate performance.

Vi trembled with nervous energy, still furious and desperately sad that the woman she one day thought she might marry was nothing more than an accessory to the prince who had torn her world to ruin.

Erenth of Cascada had become a blazing point of fire in her imagination, one she felt determined to snuff out, before he could do the same to her.

She watched the curious show of power, her crown veiled under her shawl, her jaw clenched. Margandrys had accompanied her in relative silence, as if he had known his words would be no more welcome than Mehren's in the wake of this strange spectacle.

Vierrelyne fondled the ring in her pocket-bag, in hope, in wishes, in dreams. They'd both lost too much.

"I heard he cuts their tongues out," someone said, and it made her blood boil—to think it could be true, but also because the indignity it conferred was far too much for Vierrelyne to bear, a needless cruelty even to consider that it was possible.

The five women gathered on the dais, all of them looking dazed and anxious. Alaina did not look at her. Perhaps she could not bear it either.

Each of the women took the others' hands in theirs, a dance of awkward shifting and shuffling at first, until they stood in a ring, hand in hand. The prince approached each of them in turn, kissed them on the forehead, and briefly touched each pair of clutched hands.

A second ring began on the dais below, of the scarlet-jacketed mages who had initiated the ritual. There was an elaborate, gestural dance between the mages, as if they had each learned the steps in a different order.

Prince Erenth returned to his ebon steed, hefting himself back onto his over-elaborate saddle, and taking the reins once more, he commanded:

"Sing."

It was not a song that emerged from the circle on the dais, but a portal, a rift so intense and chaotic that it could only be one of the kind Mehren had found before, enacted with a far grislier fuel. Vierrelyne screamed in horror, one among many in the crowd.

The queens' fear and desperation were not enough to break the spell between them; they were *enmeshed*, their fingers entwined in a spell that had fused them bodily, and a steady stream of foul, bat-winged beasts in every shape and size descended upon the gathered crowd of onlookers through a warped, open rift the color of twilight overhead.

Vierrelyne advanced toward the dais, toward Alaina. Margandrys rang in her ears.

It's too late! You cannot save her. You never could.

"I have to stop them," she replied, solemnly, clenching her fists in rage, centering her feet, drawing a deep breath, and concentrating. "I have to stop this!"

Call it to you, then. The sword, the armor. They are mine when they aren't yours. Summon them here and have your revenge.

"It's not revenge," Vi said, staring up at the women, helpless against the creatures they were brought to this terrible place to summon; the blood rite they'd been forced to do unknowing; the garish spectacle Prince Erenth had made of them.

There is only one thing you can do.

As the torrent of dark, winged creatures flowed from the pedestal, emerging from gusts of smoke and bursting from nothingness into being, Vi lost sight of the prince in the fray, and she cursed under her breath at the surging crowds. Didn't they see what he'd done here, couldn't they feel his strange power?

In her anger and disappointment, Vi called forth the weaponry of the Sundered Princes, with the incantation Margandrys had begun to chant in undertones, and soon the gasps and shrieks of fear were met with the cries of the awestruck.

Her arms over her head, she spoke the unknowable words he whispered to her, of a spell that belonged to only one magic, a bond infernal that had consumed more than its fair share of abiding servants over the course of time.

The white-hot rage she had long attributed to her own mother's temper flowed through her, into her physical being, as the carapace of the demon prince burst forth; cuirass and pauldrons, sabatons and greaves. The raw power of the demon prince flowed into and through her, as if she conducted it with the spell he'd coaxed her to speak.

The sword she had placed carefully nearest the door in her tavern room now rested in her hand, its guard spiked with the malevolent claws of the long-suffering imprisoned Margandrys, *Prince of the Sundered Throne*, and its sweep was grander than she had ever beheld of it before—once merely a sword, but a nice one, now a broadsword with the reach and power of a truly unearthly weapon.

She raised the sword and charged, with a bellow of rage, at the dais where the women stood bound by the hideous ritual, unable to see anything but the Scourgelands, unable to hear anything but the din of... *another* demon, his aura a stark red to Margandrys's vivid green.

What unspeakable horrors had Prince Erenth done?

She wasn't sure where it came from; it was distant, indistinct. It reminded her of Margandrys's intimations when she'd kept him in her rucksack. The voice was deep and its very presence in this place chilled her to the bone. The storm of unthinkable demons erupting from the center of the pedestal was gaining in strength, and Vi knew she had only one chance to break it from its course.

She turned, watching Prince Erenth ride past; swiftly, in the opposite direction. He was getting away. No one understood what she'd seen; she could not explain it in time. The gemstone he was holding, the strange red light; it felt like the same sort of demon presence as Margandrys, but not quite—there was something quite *wrong* about it, but Vierrelyne, in that moment, could not say what it was.

She had to choose between capturing him and saving the women whose essences were enchained in that foul spell, and it mattered not that Margandrys told her it was too late for them—there must be something she could do.

As the sound grew louder, the cavalcade of *hunger* and *death* from the Scourgelands raged on above and around her. She looked out over the crowd to see that there were others readying for this strange and terrible fight as the rest fled, screaming, into the mass of bodies trying to escape from the fleet-winged shadowy creatures overhead.

She leapt into the mages' circle, knocking the women over to break the grasp between their hands. No. These people were bewitched into this, and their hold on one another was unbreakable; a hideous entangling flesh-bond, a grotesque spell she could never hope to undo, not even with Margandrys's hand to guide her own.

I told you, there is but one thing you can do for them now.

Vierrelyne growled. "They didn't do this. *He* did."

Someone wishes to empty the overworlds and underworlds into this world. A demon will not make this distinction. If you think they can be spared, if you leave this spell as it has been completed, you are inviting them to bring the Scourgelands to this one evermore.

She straightened her back and slashed at a winged beast just over her head.

"That's what I need to kill, is that it?"

You will never run out of monsters, Vierrelyne.

The women beneath her writhed, their arms enjoined by this hideous work, and she briefly considered that she should cut them apart, but that was a greater infliction of agony. A stabbing, a neck snapping, that was less suffering than this spell was meant to affect.

These were not soldiers sworn to an unwinnable feat. These were noblewomen in duress, bound by a spell she scarcely understood, but if this foul magic was anything like that dreadful summoner spell Mehren had found... all she could offer them was her mercy and her grief.

The tears streamed from her face as she stabbed each woman through the heart, their eyes already unseeing, their dreams fading from reality into that other realm before her blade ever came near.

The Realm of Dream.

The way Mehren said it, so full of pain and wonder.

Vierrelyne accepted the mantle, as an engine of Death, her role to play in battles she had fought and battles still to come, but she had never felt her monstrosity, the shape of her particular cruelty, sharp as the blade in her hand.

Margandrys cackled with a fury she could no longer comprehend until his voice gave way to a strange and unsettling silence, an absence in her mind, as she cut away the last threads of a life parted from hers too soon.

She could not stop herself, could not end the ritual by any other means. Once she started, once she'd plunged her sword through the last of the suffering wives, through the chest of the first woman who ever understood her—once she'd watched the life fade from the eyes of the first woman who'd ever sung to her, a true ballad, a ballad *about* her—

—her sword grew too heavy to bear.

She sobbed in dismay as the last light faded from Alaina's gaze. Had lovely, melodic Alaina been enspelled this whole time? It was not until Vierrelyne's sword had crossed the plane of her onetime beloved's chest that she'd even seen a glimpse of that light in the young woman's eyes, naught but a moment. Perhaps, if Alaina was lucky, she had known none of it at all.

Somewhere, just behind her ear, the Prince of the Sundered Throne whispered to her, his pretty words thinner than the cascade of her first love's blood over her blade, her hands, her world.

M. Daniel McDowell

CHAPTER 12
AFTERMATH

RELIEF RANG THROUGH MEHREN'S CHEST as he spotted her in the crowd at the dais.

"Oh, praise be!"

When the women had stood and filed into place as one, when the hungriest creatures from the Scourgelands had begun to emerge—Vierrelyne had whirled into action so swiftly, aided by her own dark crown in some battle by proxy. He'd lost sight of her when the crowd erupted into panic and chaos, but now she sat on the high dais at the center of the courtyard. Alone, in the strictest sense.

There could be only one person whose body Vi cradled as she sat, expressionless, haunted by the ghost whose essence spattered across her broadsword. His relief wilted to desperate sadness immediately, as he saw what she'd done, what she'd suffered.

She did not acknowledge him when he approached; he hadn't expected her to, but it confirmed the darkness of her present mind.

"I had to," she said to no one, repeatedly, her lips trembling, when he put his hand over her gauntlet, her other hand clutching the tender place at the side of the fallen woman's neck. Cold dull eyes gazed out over the Realm of Dream evermore.

"I know," he whispered, leaning close to her.

The odor of metal and salt and death threatened his weak stomach, but he swallowed it back. Vi sat motionless.

"She's found the path. She knows the way. She walks the Realm of Dream evermore," Mehren said quietly, his breaths short as he tried to swallow his nausea. He sat with her in silence for a time, until he felt himself strong enough to stand again. He nudged her shoulder and tried to get her to her own feet. "I am so sorry, dearest. You need some rest. It has been a terrible night. Come with me, please."

Indeed, the last vestiges of that terror still stalked the streets of Estuary City, though Reyser Gorum's swift hand, under Kharise's keen guidance, had ended some amount of the horror before it began. The sense of dread, however, had not abated; there were still creatures of shadow creeping among the alleys and loosed upon the land and lurking, but the Guild had mustered enough civilian aid to corner and slay what monsters had emerged so far.

"Vierrelyne. You need to rest, Princess." He patted her hand, more insistent now. "You've done everything you can for tonight. Please. I promise."

Her lips quivered, but her expressionless gaze did not change. He gentled her hand away from the young woman's body, uncurled the armored fingers, and slid his hands underneath the lifeless figure. There was no respectful, proper place for this loss, but Mehren thought, if he draped her onto the dais after he coaxed Vierrelyne to stand, it would be enough for this night.

The woman was beautiful, even in death; he understood only a small part of Vierrelyne's long flame for Alaina, but he knew enough what it was to lose someone so unfairly.

He knew innately what it was to lose hope.

They needed to get out of the square as soon as possible; it was only a matter of time before his nausea would override his keen impulse to protect her. He peeled off Vi's gauntlet so that he could place his hand in hers. It seemed to liven some bit of her at his touch, and he took this as a hopeful step toward coaxing her to rest. It seemed every inch of her monstrous armor was coated in blood and ichor. How had she gotten her armor so quickly?

In the crowd, he had heard shouts of something to do with transformation, and he realized it now, as she slowly got to her feet, that there had been more than one transformation that night, as the spells had unfurled. The women had been entrapped in this fatal portal spell, but Vierrelyne had summoned her armor by the sheer force of the demon in her crown. Margandrys's power over her had grown tenfold in the ensuing chaos and tragedy.

Mehren needed to help her, to pry her out of this state carefully. A bath. There was a bathhouse behind the tavern row; surely that would help, for she was saturated in gore, and this had to be why her mind had leapt away from her. He recognized it, for he had the same power in himself, the ability to ride alongside his physical being when the pain and exhaustion threatened to shatter him.

He had always seen it as a weakness, some frail part of him that wished to escape. Now, he saw it as it truly was, a shield against what would otherwise shatter even the worthiest of warriors.

The crowds filling the high street of Estuary City tended to the injured amongst themselves. As Mehren and

Vierrelyne walked the length of the city to return to the Sterling Moray, the crowds parted around them, with reverent whispering and nods as they passed. Occasionally someone called out in recognition of the battle maven whose enchanted armor had erupted into life in the face of a formidable opponent.

Estuary City itself had been gravely wounded, and he wondered what would come of this.

Mehren led the princess down into the alleyway. The bathhouse entry was lit with lanterns, and it bustled as city denizens sought aid. As they approached, several of the folks milling about stepped aside and let them in, with whispers of what they'd seen in the city square.

"If... If I could purchase any privacy for *her*—" Mehren's hand shook as he liberated the last of his filched sovereigns onto the proprietor's desk. The woman nodded, and shoved the coins back, but Mehren left them; he was too flustered to fumble with them now. She ushered them into a small suite to the back of the establishment, a gated room outside the commons, tiled in hand-cut marble. After lighting the glass lanterns and activating the radiant spell that warmed the bath-stones, the bathhouse proprietor fetched out some soft rags, a drying gown, a small slab of hand-cut soap that smelled of milk and delicate flowers.

"Thank you," Mehren said quietly, and tried to ignore the awkward sensation he got from her warm reply.

He didn't belong here; it should've been Kharise, the princess's long-time closest friend, here to help her out of this dark place. He shouldn't see her like this.

He couldn't *leave* her like this, either.

Mehren knew, within himself, that he *could* help, for he had been here before. He had different wounds, but they had roots alike in the same pain and devastation. He'd escaped a similar pain.

"Princess, please," he said, as she stood, swaying with her uneven breath, her eyes unseeing, her face a mask of horror, next to the long bench beside the stone pool. He guided her to sit, and unpieced her infernal armor, segment by segment, setting them aside until only her under-armor remained, and the tattered blue velvet dress from the time of her confinement. The threadbare fabric gave way under his fingers, shredding in places as he tried to liberate her from it. He lifted the heavy crown from her head, and wrapped it in his cloak, so that he might silence that horrible voice for a time longer. It had *grown*, to Mehren's silent horror. The spindles were taller than his hand.

He realized he hadn't heard its nefarious whispering, in the long walk up the high street, but Margandrys was so drunk with his own hideous powers that he had gone still for a time, one could hope.

Mehren carefully unfastened the delicate combs that held her cauls of maille and beads in place. He loosened the thick pair of braids that held back her dark auburn curls, soaked with blood and ichor, and a fresh wave of weakness and nausea passed over him. *It's not mine, it's not mine,* he reminded himself. *Just help her.*

"Vierrelyne." He nudged her, standing behind her for her own modesty; he averted his gaze, but kept his hand on her shoulder, in the event he had to help her to her feet. "Let's wash some of this away, dearest, please."

He hadn't meant to say it—*dearest*, as if he had the right to make such a bold claim—and for a moment he felt a stronger heave of nausea from these nerves than he had endured all evening. Her breathing changed, at last, and the rigidity in her shoulders finally let go, as if something had given way within her at his words. She stood, wobbly on her bare legs, and Mehren guided her to the bath.

Once she descended into the steaming water, Mehren slid off his boots and hooked his legs over the edge of the bath. He helped her rinse the gore from her thick curls, and handed her the cloth and soap when he felt sure she was awakening within herself, that she was present within.

"Take all the time you need, Vierrelyne. I'll be right here. You're safe. You did everything you could. All of Estuary City thinks you a hero, I reckon." He stared at the ceiling tile, not wanting to know what she might think of what he had to say. "I know I'm not the only one."

She was quiet, the soft sounds of her shifting weight in the water the only reply to his words. He glanced back down at her, just to verify that she hadn't gone under the surface.

Her back to him, he noticed her hair was finally rinsing clean, and that at the crown of her head, there were several streaks of silver-green strands mingling with her fiery red curls. The demon's touch; not so benign as Margandrys promised her.

She turned to face him at last, silent tears streaming down her face, her voice nearly inaudible.

"How could I—"

"Oh, Vierrelyne, I'm so sorry," he whispered back. "You did the only thing you could, you... you spared her from worse. You gave her to the Realm of Dream, and I'm so sorry that it had to be you."

Mehren couldn't fight his own tears as his heart broke for hers. How long had he held that blame within him, after all, when he couldn't save Istven, when he'd barely saved himself? For there were two boys in that grave, after all, but only one body. How long had he suffered and wished it were himself in that lonesome cairn?

He had become Mehren Tevaht to escape it all, when the witchfinder's cruel tests and crueler punishments should have driven him to his own death. It was no comfort at all to know that this feeling did pass soon enough when the soul's wounds laid bare in that moment.

At last, Vi let out a wail of rage and sorrow, an unearthly sound. While her cry was haunting, Mehren breathed a sigh of relief: she was still in there, what she had endured would not be the last of her fire. She looked up at him and put out her hand, wordless. He blushed and tilted his head so that his left eye faced away before he put his arm out for her to grasp. She dried herself slowly, wrenching the water from her thick hair with meticulous effort, and wrapped herself in the dressing gown.

He sat with her in silence, waiting for her, unsure of anything but the certainty that nothing he could say to her, in this moment, could ever be enough.

Kharise had gone into action as soon as the skies had opened and burst forth with monsters, as if that had been her expectation all along. It hadn't, of course. What rational person would expect such a hideous thing?

But she'd known, in her gut, that the Prince of Cascada had sought a way to flush out Vierrelyne du Talorr, and in that regard, he'd achieved his greatest success. Vierrelyne lived, and she held the stone which had given her the power to transform herself in the wake of his provocative display of excesses, his vile sacrifice of wives he had only ever regarded as collectible playthings, talented dolls to perform at his whim, even unto death.

This was lower than she had ever expected Prince Erenth to stoop. She hadn't seen him since the processional. Hopefully Vierrelyne had shown him where he could plant his well-wishes for the folk of Estuary City with the pointed end of her sword.

As they continued their patrol for the dreadful demons, Kharise rounded the corner of the high street with two of Reyser's roughnecks, Ghostnail and Bunny, in tow. Both of them were twice her size, useful in close quarters with the fanged and winged creatures summoned into the city square in this hideous demonstration of power. Bunny was a tall, broad man with range. Even with his short sword, he nearly matched Kharise and her poleaxe at pinning down the snarling beasts. Ghostnail had a sling like Mehren's, but where Mehren lacked the visual acuity for high accuracy, the guildsman had an uncanny sense for where to aim next, anticipating the next movement with a high fluidity to his cast-off arrows.

She hadn't fought in a formation with anyone for years, until she'd been forced into the fray at Talorr, and over the time since that initial tumult, she felt the gentle tug of that practice as it reawakened within her. The movements, the cadence of teamwork was more rewarding than she remembered, each little success building on itself.

"Hail!" Reyser Gorum called out, from the far end of the high street, flanked by four of his officers. "I think we've cleared this end of town. We should circle back to the center of—"

He paused, as the people in the street shifted around and scattered, the various ebbs and swells of folk creating a path for a grand figure, larger than life, her head bowed, an aura of great shadow over her as she walked alongside another draped in a grey cloak.

Vierrelyne du Talorr, in the grand and glowing armor of her demon servant.

Kharise swallowed a deep pang of regret and rage. She should be there for her... but she breathed in relief when she saw that the hooded figure at her side was Mehren Tevaht. Everyone in the crowd seemed awestruck. How could they not in the face of what Vierrelyne had done?

The two walked up the high street, seemingly unaware of the crowds parting in their path, the swarm of supporters in their wake.

"Behind!" Bunny called out gruffly, and Kharise swept into action once more as another bat-winged, clawed monstrosity scuttled off the roof of a nearby dwelling and landed in the street. They would be after these things all night, at this rate. Bunny lunged after it, and made swift work of the creature, no larger than a chicken.

When she looked over her shoulder again, Vierrelyne and Mehren had walked on, the crowd still in awe of her, a hush over those who had borne witness to the avenging angel, the unbelievable transformation that had occurred in the midst of the crisis, the battle-maven whose hand had stilled the engine of this disaster and spared Estuary City the fate of an endless rift portal bursting forth with beasts of every shadowed realm, to hear it told in whispers.

Reyser and his officers rejoined them at the next intersection, near the tavern row, all of them heavy-headed with exhaustion. Two of them leaned hard on one another—she noticed a trace of blood smeared from one cloak to the other and she could not be certain in the dim lantern light which soldier was the wounded one.

"We've done what we can for tonight, I think," Reyser said. "The guild can help with more of the recovery in the early morning. More of my roustabouts will be out of bed at dawn, and we can see to the departed, human and demon alike."

Kharise nodded in exhaustion.

"You took control out here," he said, in a tone of tacit approval, camaraderie. "You knew where to corner things, to prevent it from getting worse. Damage control. Deployment of available forces."

She looked away from him, pointedly, but she could not stop herself from curling her lip in satisfaction.

"You are far more than you let on to be, Kharise gen Valuure, aren't you?" He laughed. "I'm just glad you're on my side."

"I'm on *your* side?" she replied with lightly comic skepticism. "I daresay we do make good collaborators."

"There's a long road ahead, I don't mind saying," Reyser agreed. "We're going to have to do something about Cascada, and I think it's possible that your princess might be the only one who can."

"She didn't stop him?"

Reyser shook his head. "Last pass at the city center didn't show him, anyway. He's a damned coward. I bet he got one look at your princess in her armor, turned tail and fled."

"I don't doubt this was a calculation. A sacrifice he was willing to make in order to draw her out. A significant loss," Kharise grimaced. "We'll talk in the morning. We need to do something serious, something that will punch Erenth of Cascada so hard he swallows what teeth he has left."

"You believe he has a prism, too, then?" Reyser intoned quietly, only for her to hear.

"He must have something, to have called forth such a number of those beasts, even if his abilities would be no match for hers in a fair fight." Kharise shook her head, not wanting to agree with him but knowing that he was not wrong about it. She tilted her head and exhaled deeply. "I must admit, no matter how invigorated I might be, I have also hit the hard limits of my own exhaustion. I cannot summon more of myself tonight."

"Tomorrow." He nodded. "Take care, Kharise."

"Good night."

The crowds were finally thinning off the high street nearest the tavern when she trudged up to the Sterling Moray, and the public house within went quiet as she stalked through with her poleaxe still in hand.

She took a quick basin rinse to relieve her skin of the worst of the night's grime, swallowed a pint of ale that she barely tasted, on a brief pass through the taproom, and made a quiet adjournment to her room up the stairs.

Sleep came for her swiftly, but she did mark it, some hours later, when two pairs of feet staggered up those same stairs and into the adjacent room.

CHAPTER 13
STARDOWNE

THE WORLD WAS DEAD.

How could she still be alive when the world was dead?

The very weight of existence sat on her ribcage while she rested in the bed, the pressure pounding on her skull as she stared at the rafters, wishing the world to collapse around her. She prayed, silently, for an end that would not come, an end she truly deserved, for her most unspeakable deeds. Her hands trembled, her fingers ice-cold, as she tried to pull the coarse wool blanket over her shoulders.

The world was *dead*.

She felt herself scream, she heard herself thrash against the bed, but it was at a remove, at a distance she likened to being underwater, in the deeps of Broadcoast Bay, where no sunlight could ever warm her again.

Whatever horrors she'd endured, in fifteen unthinkable years, she'd endured them with a gauze of hope, and it was this last shred, torn from her eyes, that so distempered her.

The world was dead, and she was condemned to continue on after its light had faded forevermore. She had slain the world herself, had plunged in the blade and leaned upon it until Alaina's screaming ceased, and now she was doomed to her own unending shriek, until at last she was hoarse and exhausted from herself.

She did not know when it was that she fell into dream, but when she woke, there was daylight; and, at her bedside, singing a soft tune in a language she did not know, the man who had helped her find her way home.

Mehren had clearly not slept meaningfully yet, by the bags under his eyelids, but both of those weary eyes were closed as he sang, something that made her think of waves at the shore, that gently lapped fore and back. A folk song, she thought, though she knew nothing else of it. She shifted her weight toward him, and he stopped abruptly.

"Oh. S-sorry, I didn't mean to wake you." Mehren gathered his knees to his chest, looking at her, expectant, nervous.

"Not at all. It was lovely." Vierrelyne swallowed hard, trying to hold down her bitter dread. "I suppose it's a sad song. I don't know the words."

"Aye, one for impossible darkness, for nights at sea when you can see no horizon. A song for nights waiting by the fire for news of a vessel that may never come in again."

She put her hand out to him, and he cradled it between his fingers. "What were those words?"

"Oh." Mehren hesitated. "It's a dialect from the coast of Beryl. Tolven. It's what... What my mother spoke, what she taught us at home, before we learned any Dereborean."

Vi fretted her lower lip with her teeth and tongue. He was from the Crystalline Cities, but she hadn't really taken in what that meant. She felt ignorant for not hearing the intonations and accent she thought of in the context of Beryl. His was quite mild, oblique, as he had clearly traveled widely before he had joined the Astral Circle.

"Tea?" Mehren offered. "The kettle should be ready."

She nodded, and he unfolded himself to fetch her a cup.

Her fingers shook so violently that he put his hand under the mug, just enough to steady it for her to drink. She noticed, as he crouched next to her, he'd pushed his hair back, behind his ears.

For the first time, she saw the pair of gleaming gold hoops in his ears, framed by his soft black curls. In the daylight, the scar tissue on his right cheek was pale, pink, and shiny, with an undulating puckered and silky texture. His wizard-glass eye glowed brilliantly when it caught the sunlight, shimmering like the stone in her crown.

His gaze was fixed on her, his attention full of concern.

He wasn't trying to hide his face from her. In the comfort of the cramped little room above the tavern, Mehren did not need to worry about who might see him, judge him...

Her heart fluttered for a moment.

She'd earned his *trust*. Without that tangle of messy dark hair covering half his face, without his hand hovering nearby, ready to hide himself from view, she got the first real chance to see the whole composition of him, this time in the brightness of day and not the dim candlelight of the tavern cloche.

She gave a bashful grin to the man who'd pulled her back from the demon's brink. Even as Margandrys had tried to steer her into a new kind of pain and suffering, Mehren appeared at her side, not to chide her or belittle her but to support her through an unimaginable agony, one for which he had his own sad kind of foreknowledge. His grin was different when he wasn't hiding half of it from view; the deep scarred crease in his upper right lip prevented a symmetrical form, but it was charming in its own way.

Her face flushed hot with perplexed embarrassment at his forthright aid. She hadn't steadied any of her feelings from the night before. A wave of shame at how she'd treated him before the promenade, a wave of shame that she'd been so dismissive and tried to shed his attention so quickly when all she thought she wanted in the world was a glimpse of the young woman with whom she'd once carried on a brief, intense, imbalanced affair.

She was goaded into hasty violence by Margandrys, and she resented it, even as she knew he was the only weapon she could trust with such a formidable foe as she now knew Prince Remaryn to be. It gave her no peace to know she would have to throw herself into the same maelstrom again, even as she knew she freely would if it'd protect the others, the people who had done so much to protect her.

People like Mehren Tevaht.

"Can I fetch you something from the kitchen?" His own stomach rumbled audibly, undermining any semblance of altruistic intent. He laughed, self-effacing.

She nodded, meekly, not sure she was willing to eat, but willing to try.

When at last he returned, laden with a wooden tray filled with a veritable feast, she felt nervous. He wanted her to eat more than she could possibly stomach. She started to protest, but she was won over quickly by the warmth of a freshly baked loaf of bread, with dishes of honey and creamed-soft butter. There were pots of stewed fruits and a plate of carved cheeses. A bowl of stew anchored one end of the tray, a bowl of poached eggs in a spicy sauce of peppers and tomatoes on the other.

"As much as you want," Mehren said.

She could not stomach the richness of poached eggs, but Mehren made quick work of that dish. She dipped bites of the bread in the stew, a hearty thing made of root vegetables slow-roasted over a long time in a large kettle and seasoned well with fresh-cut leafy herbs on top. Mehren paused every so often to watch her, as if he thought she might collapse.

In her secret heart, in a place she would never admit, this made her feel a sudden, competitive intensity. She was not about to collapse on Mehren's watch. She ate slowly, contemplating, forcing her mind to every corner of the room the second she caught herself drawing inward again.

She had done so with her confinement for fifteen years, after all. She knew how to drown out those relentless insects of futility, whose hideous droning had governed the worst of those times.

Once they'd polished off the last of the slivered cheese and the stewed fruit and the rest of Mehren's selection, her mood began to crumble despite his best efforts to distract and entertain her.

When Kharise appeared at the door, he scrambled to his feet and stood next to the bed.

"Can I get you anything, darling?"

Kharise's concern was writ upon her face.

"Mehren fetched up something to eat a bit ago," Vi said quietly, and Mehren took this as his cue to step away, much to her chagrin.

"I should return the dishes—" he turned away from Kharise, fretting his hair back over his right side, and Vi grabbed him by the waist: trying not to sob, but feeling very lost. She could not stop the tears that did escape.

"Please don't go," she whispered, locking her wrists around his middle. He twitched as if she'd startled him. He leaned into her arms, and she felt his lips on her forehead, the smallest, most accidental of kisses.

"I promise." He gentled her chin with his thumb and forefinger. "I need to run this downstairs and bring up a fresh kettle, but I'll be back before you can truly miss me."

Kharise watched him step away with an appraising glance. Vierrelyne felt the weight of that appraisal and a fresh sense of anguish washed over her.

"I'm so sorry," Kharise said, her gaze forthright even in the face of an agonizing conversation. "I should have been here for you."

"You have more than me to look after," Vi replied, not wanting to accept or reject the apology. She wanted the apology not to hang in the air between them, but to evaporate. She wanted *anything* but for Kharise to see her cry like this, ever again. It was numbing enough that Mehren had seen her, but Kharise? Her mentor had seen her through so much more—so much less—and yet at this moment the mortification was the worst part.

Kharise sat down next to her, wordless, and put her hand over Vi's. She felt her mentor's weariness, even in her hand, and beheld it as its own gift. Survival, in a word: a weight to be carried in the heart forever after.

Mehren returned with a tea tray, and Kharise leaned in and hugged Vierrelyne before she excused herself.

Once he had the large, heavy kettle on the fire again, Mehren returned to the bedside, tray laden again. Just a trifle this time; the tea tray held little dishes of sponge cake soaked in cream, with a crumble of rich, spiced candied nuts on top.

"It's not much, but my mother used to make a trifle like this when we needed something sweet. A little pudding to lift the spirit from the kitchen downstairs."

It was surprisingly spicy: warming and delicious. There was a note of smoke and pepper in the candied nuts. It rounded out the sweetness of the cake and cream quite well, even if she suspected it wasn't how he'd intended it to taste. She ate every morsel despite the fact that she felt like she had just eaten—the sun had gone down already.

Mehren returned to his post beside her bed, this time curled under a blanket. He sang for her again but dropped off around the second rondo of the chorus into much-needed rest, snoring with his chin on his chest.

Vierrelyne laid back on the pillows and stared at the ceiling.

Despite everything she had done, despite the horrors she had wrought with her own hands, the rest of the world was still alive. Now she had to figure out how to keep it that way, even if she had to do it herself.

In the aftermath of Prince Erenth's path of destruction, Estuary City did as it always had: its people made the best of things, and a select number, many of them affiliated with the Guild, stepped in to offer a hand. Kharise leaned into this with both shoulders, as she knew where to apply her best disciplines, and how. It was easier for her to do the physical work of mending than the emotional work of it, perhaps. The Roustabouts at Large made do with that hard work.

Vierrelyne slept for the better part of two whole days. Mehren seldom left her side, not smothering, but attentive, watchful for her strength of will, waiting to see it return. Kharise left him to it, as it spared her some of the harder labor, work that her aching joints nagged her not to take on in those cold mornings at the beginning of autumn: tending the fire, carrying the water, preparing the tea.

The Sterling Moray had become a de facto base of operations, but this condition was not likely to endure well. After several days of brisk foot traffic in the wake of the disaster in the city square, the bustling communications directed to Kharise from every limb of the Independent's Guild threatened to overwhelm the cozy public house.

They needed a headquarters outside of Estuary City, she thought, somewhere that they could strike at Erenth without risking his wrath upon the innocents of the city this time, and she suspected Reyser Gorum might have an opinion on the one she thought would work best.

She sought him out at the guild hall proper, where he had taken to drafting a chart on the far wall that showed where he'd begun his own watch details and other bits of planning. These she couldn't disambiguate without a primer on his handwriting, for he had only two modes of text: block lettering in calligraphic Dereborean, and an illegible, rapid scrawl, sometimes intertwined with the block lettering.

"Looks pretty intricate," she said, reading over his shoulder.

"Not so elaborate as you'd think. Just logistics." He looked pleased, though, that she'd noticed; there was a satisfied grin and an added verve to his step.

"It strikes me that if we are to mount a siege on this scale, we need to find an appropriate repository for soldiers and supplies. Large enough for a garrison, far enough from the lens of the city proper, the sort of place from which we gain an upper hand."

"It seems to me that the guild hall has become cramped in recent days," he agreed.

She pulled out Mehren's map and began to press it flat, screening for her desired target.

"If we are meant to tackle both spindles of this problem, we need a point that settles between the two. Is there any reason not to consider the fortress at Stardowne?"

He looked at her as if she'd just offered him a delicious spider.

"I know," she said. "No one wants to go out there. It's abandoned. It's creepy. It's outside the city. It's still got some cattle roads, though, and it's near enough to Cascada that we won't be repeating the death march of the prince's parade to get there."

"It's *haunted*," Reyser said sternly. "No one goes there because it's a cold and drafty fortress on the high plains. At *best* it's full of mice and the unfriendly spirits of dead cultists. At worst? Bandits, demons, more cultists..."

"That's what's perfect about it," Kharise replied. "No one will expect it from us. City folk out in the countryside. Imagine."

He wagged his finger at her.

"Hey now. Some of us came from far and wide to be here, lady. Yourself included."

She smirked. "I'll write up a timeline?"

He sighed, good-natured. "I half expected you already had, by the way you had this all buttoned up."

"You're just jealous they like my plans more than yours." She tutted at him.

"Oh, I'm not worried, Khar, because I know they aren't going to like this one," he replied with a sharp whistle.

She shook her head. "We need to hit him hard. Decisive. He won't stop now that he knows she's here. We have to find someplace we can protect her long enough to put on a show of our own. The fellows of your little company won't mind."

"They won't," Reyser agreed. Don't you think it's a little risky, letting her keep it? Especially after what happened?"

"Who would you trust?" Kharise narrowed her eyes. "It's got to be someone, and it's not going to be me."

Her heart twinged at the mention of Vierrelyne in the context of that damned crown, after everything she'd been through.

Mehren had started to think of the Sterling Moray as a second home, even with as hard as some of their days here had been. He hadn't stayed anywhere else for so long, in the years since he'd been embraced by Tobinarde and the rest of the Astral Circle. When he still had his spell-chalk, it was safer to return home than to stay away. Without the rigid structure of life in Zalandan, he had felt a little lost at first—following Vierrelyne and Kharise at least made sense on a scale of opportunity. Now, though, he had friendships; with the plainswoman and the guild of oddfellows she'd roped into her employ, but most especially with Vierrelyne.

He'd just gotten into something like a rhythm, some steady pattern to his routine, while he sat with her as she slept through the afternoon, after suffering another wave of exhausting night terrors the evening before. Vierrelyne had lent him her tatting shuttle to fidget with while he sat by her side. He wasn't adept at the motions yet, but there was something therapeutic in handwork, something that kept him alert and attuned, something similar in gesture to the stitches he'd done on fishing nets in his childhood, but different enough to keep his attention. The ever-growing length of lacy knotted black silk cording he'd made with it showed steady improvement in his half-hitch stitches over time. He'd only learned how to do a few of the stitches she'd shown him, but he thought it was pretty.

Kharise came in to see him that afternoon while Vierrelyne dozed, a few days after her hideous trauma at the prince's terrible spectacle. The plainswoman had taken on a lot of organizing for the Guild, in light of the failures of the Estuary City High Council.

"We're moving on a new base, just to ease the strain on the central city resources to organize a rebuttal to Prince Erenth."

Mehren nodded, his lip twitching at the mention of the Cascadian prince. He worked the shuttle quietly for a pair of half-hitches—*over, under, through; under, over, through*—in the hopes that the rhythm of it would help him not to panic at the thought of putting Vierrelyne through something so horrible again.

"We're rebuilding in Stardowne. It's not great timing, but nothing ever is. If we move on it now, we'd be settled before midwinter, and we ought to have the upper hand to march on Cascada then."

The invocation of the place where Tobinarde l'Ete had been reborn gave him a surprising shiver. It was an advantageous location, true, but it was vulnerable; after all, he'd always been told that it was an ambush from one of the nearest city-states, violently angry over those so-called heresies, which had driven his followers into the shadows.

And yet, at his core, with more time than he had ever spent away from the Astral Circle at Zalandan before, Mehren felt as if the storm clouds had parted to let through some light. Something else had taken the place of the cavalcade of bombastic phrases at the core of Tobinarde's teachings. He had let go of the ties that bound him there, for good or ill.

"I'll go," he agreed as he wound the tatting shuttle over his fingertips, passing it through the looped silk thread; *over-under-through, under-over-through.* "I'm still worried about Vierrelyne, but a change of scenery might help her."

"It's quiet and isolated, but we will have the Guild."

Mehren nodded quietly. "Think we'll all fit?"

He measured out the length of lacy cording he'd made; enough for a long pendant, he thought, a token for Vi. He threaded the bead he'd found wedged inside the shuttle onto it—an amber teardrop, the exact color of her eyes. Maybe it had gotten lost or forgotten about, to have ended up where it had, but it deserved to be seen again, remembered, centered. He fed the long end of his chain of stitches through it, and at the midpoint, he doubled the thread through the center hole of the amber teardrop and tied a firm square knot to hold it. He resumed his stitching, endeavoring to make a loop that would work to fasten it.

"Oh, Stardowne has more space than we even need just yet. Plenty of room. Reyser said there should still be fittings for a taproom, though I imagine the place will be mouse-eaten and dirty throughout for a time."

"And then you will want us all to face Prince Erenth again? I hope Vierrelyne will be ready."

"I think so, Mehren. We're moving slowly on purpose." Kharise nodded, flattening her lips, and put her hand to her chin. "Hey, did you ever figure out what happened at the square? It was so sudden I missed whatever touched it off. Vierrelyne couldn't tell me much about what she saw. I didn't want to prod her about it."

"Whatever took place at the city square, there was something more powerful than just those blood sigils our enemy has grown fond of. She said there was something, another stone, maybe, something that upset Margandrys." Mehren shook his head. "Cascada is escalating their tactics. He must have something more powerful than the sigils I found, to do such harm."

"He was trying to get Vierrelyne's attention and succeeded. He was willing to sacrifice all of this to get her to show herself, and she did." Kharise sighed.

"How could she not?" Mehren said, defensive.

"You're not the only one who says they saw signs of something. Reyser thought it might be another summoning stone, another demon prince," Kharise said.

Vi sat up, rubbing her face, and sighed in misery. She yawned before she was able to complete her thoughts. "It was Prince Erenth himself. He has something..."

Kharise leaned closer. "I was afraid of that."

"He was holding a stone, something like mine, but I couldn't get to him in time to see what it was. Margandrys didn't like it." Vi let out another miserable yawn and stretched her arms.

"But I thought there was only one stone of the Sundered Princes, only one Bringer of the Scourge," Mehren mused, tightening the final stitch in his length of tatted cord, binding the ends of the thread together. A nice pendant, he thought, if a bit long.

She sighed and gave another miserable yawn. "I'm sorry, but I can't bear any more of this until I've had some tea, please. I can still hardly roust myself out of bed."

She leaned on the narrow bed frame with one arm, still exhausted and miserable, her eyes bleary. Mehren tucked the pendant into her curled fingers and went about preparing some tea for her at the hearth. The kettle was still hot, and he fumbled around to find the tin of mint leaves he knew to be her favorite.

Kharise walked toward the door with an appreciative nod. "I have to make the rest of the rounds to get the word out about the change in locale. Let me know if you need anything else, both of you," she said, and walked out of the room.

When he returned to her side, Vi had put the pendant on, the stone gleaming in the morning light, with the opposite of Margandrys's malevolence: a warmth, a glow. All the same, he could not help noticing that she'd been crying again, but she'd also taken great pains to hide it; steadying her breath, her face wiped dry, only the misery in her eyes to belie the truth.

Mehren sat beside her as she flipped through her pocket-sized book full of papers—letters, letters that only made her sadder and angrier, and yet, he knew, it was a necessary anger, a flint of her grief. He combed his fingers through her sleep-tangled curls, gently, and plaited her hair for her. Not nearly so skillfully as she could do it herself, perhaps, but he thought it might help her feel less alone, to have some help when everything still felt hopeless.

She did not say anything, and he did not ask, as she gentled the stone between her fingers on its soft knotted lace cord and silently drank her tea.

M. Daniel McDowell

CHAPTER 14
ETUDES

THE PROJECT OF OCCUPATION AT STARDOWNE took over a month in all; the work of building a base that would sustain them all was not a small one, and it was a combined effort of roughly half the guild to establish a safe and livable base out of the stone carcass.

Even with all available hands on duty, Mehren seldom drew assignments to assist the other roustabouts from the Guild; some thought he was too dainty to aid them, while others thought he was simply too strange. Even when he volunteered his help, he was often rebuffed, not tall enough or broad-shouldered enough to prove his mettle in the reconstruction project, even if he was slight enough to navigate the smaller spaces in the fortress.

Mehren, not wanting to be found underfoot while the others worked—and feeling not a little slighted that even mawkish Teven was considered handier than he was—went outside. Clearing brush for bonfires kept him busy the first night, and he quickly realized that the surrounding trees were not so ordinary; they were quite orderly, matriced into rows.

The following afternoon, he spent a fair amount of his daylight with a bushel basket, walking the length of one of the overgrown cobbled paths that led to the orchard he'd found, in the hopes he might win over some hearts and minds by their gullets instead.

The grounds outside Stardowne had at one time sustained a robust harvest of stone fruit for the abbey, but the main orchard had evidently gone feral in its neglected years. The trees had grown tall and wild with no one to prune them back and govern their shapes. There were still some trees with clutches of soft peaches in them, though, the last of the autumn pickings, and Mehren was slight and wiry enough to get them without much in the way of assistance.

As he tested a long and shallow arm branch on the first harvestable tree in the grove, to see that it would bear his weight, he was startled when he heard Vierrelyne call him.

"Mehren? What in all the realms are you doing?"

He flailed as he turned to face her, clinging to the limb above him like a drowning rat might hang on an oar. He was only a few feet from the ground, but he'd rattled himself out of equilibrium.

"Well, Highness, I *was* trying to clear my head and pick some fruit." He laughed; nervous, self-effacing. "I wasn't expecting an audience."

"I didn't know you could climb like that," she said, her cheeks pink from the brisk autumn wind and the last rays of autumn sun alike. She clutched one of the long guard-cloaks over her shoulders with one hand.

"I suppose you wouldn't," he said with a wry grin. He pulled himself onto the next branch, kicked his right leg over it, and released his awkward hold, looking down at her from just a little bit above her head. "I grew up in the harbor at Beryl, after all, my whole family helmed a vessel out of the main port."

"You've never told me anything about it," Vi replied, and as she tilted her head up at him, he caught the pendant glowing in the autumn light, the amber teardrop as golden bright as her eyes. "What's that got to do with climbing?"

"Sails and rigging," Mehren said, cleaving to the sliver of his own history he could safely recall. "I was raised to be fearless of heights for a time, long before I had the good sense to be frightened of anything."

"That sounds more like you, yes," she teased, before she pursed her lips in concentration. "But… How did you get so far from your family?"

"Oh. My mother sent me off from the harbor in Beryl to the nor' easterly mainland in my teens because she got worried when the witchfinders started boarding cargo vessels. They weren't looking for some kid with a knack for… Whatever it is I'm good at… but she wouldn't take the risk. She thought it might help me learn how to work whatever… Ability I had."

He picked a peach and tossed it down to her. She gentled it in her free hand, with some surprise evident on her heart-shaped face as she gently petted the downy coat of fuzz on the surface.

"She sent me to Garnet with my aunt, who took me to the wizards' enclaves. Hadn't learnt to be frightened yet, I guess. Not 'til the witchfinder general got around to scouring the mainland villages."

He silently prayed that would be enough of the story for her, as she delicately sniffed at the soft peach in her hands.

"Eat it, if you like," he said. "There should be enough here for me to carry back the makings of a half-dozen galettes, if I don't waste them."

She blushed and drew her thumbnail over the thick outer layer to break it, then peeled away the skin and nibbled on the soft fruit within. Her excitement at such a simple treat gave Mehren a fresh pang of anguish on her behalf. He remembered when he had thought he might take her to Zalandan and wash his hands of this whole disaster.

From the vantage of past history, though, he knew that seeing her in person had changed his whole trajectory. A shadow of guilt hung over him, with distance from the Astral Circle, but that guilt was tempered with Vierrelyne's own friendship, and what he hoped was a kindling affection—one he harbored deep within himself, too fragile to share; not even with her, not yet.

Besides, none of the stories of the Rose in the Tower had told of her skill with a sword. He'd been unaccountably lucky to earn her approval without meeting her by the pointy end on those narrow spiraling stairs in that hideous tower, in retrospect.

"I haven't ever eaten something so lovely as this," she murmured with her mouth full, cradling the half-eaten fruit in her long fingers and looking up at him with a reverent gaze. "Thank you."

"Well, here's hoping some of Reyser's regiment have a similar sentiment," Mehren replied, lading down a handful more of the soft stone fruit into his basket gently. "I'm rather tired of them treating me like I'm either invisible or a pest."

"A pest! Not even close. I could just about kiss you for finding these," she said. This time Mehren nearly fell out of the tree entirely, in blushing alarm. "I reckon if you merely turned up to the nightly tavern round with that basket full, you'd become the most popular and eligible man among the rousts in Stardowne overnight."

Mehren prayed his own face was less pink than his stone-fruit quarry, and he felt his lower lip twitching madly, in the way in which he knew, from years of fighting it, that it would betray him with a stammer or a stutter if he spoke, so he tucked it between his teeth and reached for another fine clutch of the late-season fruit.

She made a throaty sound of enjoyment as she finished the last few bites that frankly made him lightheaded. He suspected, though he had no proof of this grave accusation, that she'd made that scandalous sound in order to capture his full and complete attention.

However, he'd felt a certain amount of shy sadness that she'd assumed he was only on the market with the men of the Independent's ranks. He knew *why* she had such a notion, but it stung all the same.

He hadn't the courage to clarify that he had eyes for only one person in all of the Guild encampment at Stardowne, and that it was her.

"W-we should get b-b-back soon," he started, silently cursing the wobble in his lip. He fretted it between his teeth and picked a few last peaches in silence before he climbed down and shouldered the basket.

Vierrelyne tried to persuade him to let her carry it, but Mehren insisted he needed to do it.

"As it is, they'll think you helped me," he said, with a dark laugh. "I'll be fine. Here."

He passed her a second peach, fragrant and beautiful, and she held it reverently, close to her chest, as they walked back to the fortress in the dwindling daylight together.

In the ensuing weeks and months, as the Independent's Guild occupied the once-abandoned fortress at Stardowne, Kharise took pride in ensuring that everyone from the Guild felt her personal appreciation, whether in coin or praise.

One of her nightly rituals, once they were settled in Stardowne and the autumn nights grew ever colder and darker, was to keep spirits high as possible through the nightly social in the taproom downstairs.

Her solution for this question of lifting spirits in their compound in the woods was to spend some time herself in the commons with the rest of the guild in the evenings, sometimes with songs of her own, but more often to gather the songs of the individuals who had come to this strange place with her.

There were many such nights leading into the winter solstice. Kharise and Reyser chose that date as the hard line of their march on Cascada.

In the wake of Prince Remaryn's despicable actions, he'd lost more than Estuary City. Now none of the region's trade hubs would offer him so much as a crumb in advance of payment, and Kharise wagered that the dead of winter would be the lowest point in his calendar. Reyser, not inclined to disagree, liked the notion of launching their offensive on the darkest day of the year.

On the night before the Guild was set to raid Cascada and, with luck, drive out that infernal prince and his peculiar demon stone, the songs were louder and rowdier than ever with the undertones of the serious day to follow. The dances were as rowdy as the songs.

Kharise noticed with bemusement, as he dragged her onto the floor for a round, that Reyser's knee was in better shape, at least, but his rhythm had not improved, even with nightly practice.

Vierrelyne traipsed past them on the floor, heavy clay steins in hand as she shuffled toward the table in the middle of Stardowne's taproom, where she settled in next to Mehren, surrounded by Bunny and Ghostnail.

Kharise watched them from the other end of the table, the two of them giddy with mead and, she suspected, their close companionship. Vierrelyne had been engaged to that unfortunate young lady for years, only to have it stolen from her. Kharise remembered likewise that the wizard had lost his heart, and his eye, over a young man's love for him.

They both had wellsprings of pain as terrible as her own, each as painful, both of their tragedies borne of wellsprings of cruelty.

Perhaps it *was* mere friendship between them, but she felt sure the two had much more in common, especially in the wake of recent events. The signs of affection were clear as the first leaves of grass in spring; impossible to ignore but fragile as the ice they grew underneath.

She hid her thoughts from both parties, as she knew nothing good ever came from an old woman trying to nudge anyone together, nor apart, for that matter.

Let them figure it out.

Kharise flashed Vi a grin when the other age-mates from the guild in her midst began to holler and thump their mugs in time, which in turn brought out someone's bowstrings, and someone else a clay jar of beads to shake, and soon the small but loyal coterie had a dance going, which suited Kharise just fine. If someone had a reed pipe for her to borrow, she might have provided another wave of accompaniment for a few of the ranging tunes, but she was not keen to admit how out of practice she had gotten.

All the same, who could ever forget the notes?

The princess went pink as various compatriots from the guild sought her attention between songs, but she only had eyes for Mehren Tevaht, who seemed awestruck at her very gaze. The two sat on the bench at the bend between the two main tables. Bunny and Ghostnail, the elder statesmen of the rousts, held court next to Vi and Mehren with a handful of their partisans clustered around the table, the chatter idling.

After the hours began to wane and the songs grew to a boisterous sort, no longer the ballads Kharise could hum in tune, she made for the stairwell, stopping at the center.

"We march at daybreak, Highness," Kharise called out to her, as she went to settle in the upstairs quarters.

Vierrelyne offered warbling assurances with an affectionate smile on her face as she leaned against the wizard's shoulder.

Mehren, for his part, remained bemused by the proceedings, cradling his stein of mead behind which to hide his ever-widening grin. Kharise gave them a wink and let them be.

Once Kharise had fled upstairs, and the song had sorted into dancing, and most of the guild had either taken to the floor or gone to bed, the dread of the coming day finally descended upon Vierrelyne. As the evening drew thin, she felt a keen urgency not to weather the remainder of it alone.

Mehren leaned against her, his chin on her shoulder.

"It's getting late. We should get some rest."

"Rest, hm?" she replied. "I doubt I can sleep an hour, with what's ahead of us, only..."

"Yes?"

She stood up and nodded toward the door.

He took the cue. They chased each other up the narrow stairs during one of the rowdier numbers. With the dregs of the evening's ale and mead downed, the last few lingering guild members noticed nothing awry as they ran into Mehren's room.

Away from her blessed—cursed—weapons, Vierrelyne felt a quiet within herself, one of which she was seldom aware lately. Training had put her in a constant state of awareness, and tension, for the mission ahead of them.

Mehren stood behind her, his arms around her waist. For the first time since she'd donned the armor and the crown—the first time she had embodied the Scourge-bringer, the first time she had contemplated the Crown of the World Unbound—she felt the *smallness* of herself, in his embrace. She was taller and wider than Mehren, but his hold on her fit perfectly. She leaned her head against his, and placed her hands over his, where his fingers locked together at the narrow of her waist.

He planted a kiss on the small of her neck, just under her hairline, and her breath caught in her throat.

"Yes," she whispered. "Please."

Without the omnipresent whispering of Margandrys, she understood the soft feelings she had about Mehren when the demon's lens was not fixed on her world.

He gently nudged her. "We shouldn't," he said softly.

"I'm sorry, I thought you might want..."

"Oh, I do, more than anything, but I don't want him to lash out at you over it, especially not tonight, when we have so much ahead of us tomorrow."

Vierrelyne pulled his hand up to kiss it. "He won't."

"He knows something," Mehren murmured.

"That I fancy you, that's all." She pouted. "I doubt I can hide it from *anyone*, let alone him."

"Explains why he's so..." He stopped.

"Don't be jealous, please, I can't bear that."

"I'll do my best." He nuzzled against her, leaning his head on hers. "I could almost get used to this."

"So could I." She drew a deep breath and let it out slowly. "I didn't know, when I was locked up in my father's lousy castle, that this was the kind of thing I was missing. Not the fancy ballgowns and pageantry; the friendships, the conversations. The affections..."

"I know what you mean."

He released her from his arms, and she unfastened her hair combs. Her pair of auburn braids spilled out, around her shoulders, the silver strands glinting in the firelight, a flame red cast over them by the dark shadows, a reminder of what she was becoming, what it was she'd already

M. Daniel McDowell

become. She untucked them from their ribbons, letting her hair loose, her braids released of their tension.

He cradled her close once more, brushed back her soft curls and continued kissing down her shoulder, at which she squeezed his arm and leaned into him.

"I don't want to go to bed so alone, not on the night before what might become the loneliest day of my life."

She tried not to think of what it was she had already asked of Margandrys, what he had given her with the false sense of certainty. She tried not to think about the ways she had already lost herself to his accursed whims—and how much she was still willing to lose. She'd lost a drafty castle; a collapsing kingdom; a beautiful woman, a worthless father; a despotic sovereign.

And yet, in the dim light of his room, she beheld the one person she was most reluctant to involve in her mad quest to strike back at the prince, the one other person whose own mad quest seemed to revolve around unraveling this damned prophecy. This curious man, whose gaze had haunted her dreams for as long as she could remember, whose gaze upon her in that moment was unbearably soft, affectionate, longing. She dared not break him of that softness, not when it had saved her life twice over already.

Vierrelyne nudged him onto his bed and loosed him of his waist sash as she did so. Her nimble fingers made swift work of the buttons on his shirtwaist, and she climbed into his lap, leaning over him for a deep, tender kiss.

"More?" Her breath was short as she nuzzled his neck.

"Only if it would please you, dearest," he murmured, "but it'd please me too."

Sleep remained elusive, even in the warmth of a shared blanket on a shared bed.

"What does your name mean, anyway?" Vierrelyne asked drowsily, huddled up behind Mehren, her arm over his chest. "Kharise said it was *warded*, when we met you, but I don't know what it actually means."

"Ah." He paused to think. "Well, I mean, it's what you call me. That little elision in the middle of my name."

"Yes, but how did she know it was warded?"

"I reckon she's heard one before."

Vi sighed. "What makes it a warded name?"

"It just means it's like looking into a warped mirror, it's… a reflection. It's distorted, to protect me from the sorts of things that walk the Scourgelands, the kinds of things that prey on deep names. Maybe you just don't notice the distortion because you've never heard a warded name before?" He clutched her hand tight in his.

"Maybe," she said, not really believing it.

She understood what he meant by distortion—for there was another name, a word she didn't know, but a word that she felt *about* him when she saw him, something she dared not speak though she knew its outline clearly, outside the essence of him she could not rightly describe.

He cradled her fingers in his for some time before he answered. "It's the thing that shields me when I walk through those dark places. The thing that guides me back to

M. Daniel McDowell

the World that Is. Or it used to, anyway. Without my chalk, I haven't traveled in so long."

"Do you miss it, walking the Scourgelands?"

"Not like that, no. It's not a place healthy living things are meant to go, it's..." He hesitated, drawing his thumb across her palm. "It's a place of ancient things, many of them neither truly alive nor truly dead. It's not a place I *want* to go, just a place I've occasion to cross."

"Not where..."

She heaved a sigh and could not summon the rest of the words, but because it was the only question she could ask, and he could answer, even having never heard the rest.

"The Realm of Dream is only one of the Scourgelands, but no, it's not a place I should ever have gone. I know that desperate want." He pulled her hand to his lips, gently kissed her knuckles. "I've tried, and I never should've. It was only hurting myself."

"Can you promise me something?" she whispered, her chin on his shoulder, her fingers curled over his. "Whatever happens tomorrow. If... *if* something happens."

"Yes?" He rested his cheek on hers.

"If you can't fight, if... if things get out of control... I just want you to run. Please, Mehren. Stay safe."

"Vierrelyne," he whispered back with a grin. "Why do you think I *wouldn't*?"

She boxed his upper arm. "I mean it. I... I need you."

"Oh?" he teased. "What in all the realms do you need from *me*?"

"I might need someone to wash the blood out of my hair again," she teased back, and her short sharp fingernails bit his shoulder. "I definitely need someone who understands me like you do. Just. Promise."

"Ow, all right, I promise." Mehren laughed.

He moved his shoulder, to lean on his back, and she shifted around, drowsily, to put her head on his chest. She traced her fingers softly over his scars in the dark, and he held her close, as they waited for what dawn might come.

M. Daniel McDowell

CHAPTER 15
CASCADA

VIERRELYNE DRESSED FOR WAR THAT MORNING, AFTER MUSTER.

Over her armor, over the intricate layers of metal and maille, she wore her usual combs and cauls to hold her heavy curls. Around her neck, her mother's high lace collar. The profile was uncannily perfect, she thought, catching a glimpse of the reflection in the surface of her blade, Margandrys and his approving shade over her shoulder in the dim light.

"Is that..." Mehren attempted to sort out his question aloud, as he laced himself into the only rigid sturdy armor that fit his slender frame: a hard leather shell he wore under his cloak and maille, over his heavy loose black gambeson and bruise-purple shirtsleeves.

"A reminder," she said. "That I was once the delicate creature they would have caged indefinitely. That I can be delicate and sharp all the same, that I am no less dangerous to them now than I was for all those years when they feared a *girl* would ruin the world."

He looked unbearably sad at this, but that was hardly new for Mehren, as he scarcely ever hid his feelings from her anymore. She knew how to read his moods, after his long vigil of care.

They prepared to march with the rest of Kharise's collective contingent, the group that had begun as the guild of odd-jobbers and miscreants who didn't fit a singular billing, Reyser Gorum and his Independents, those of his Roustabouts at Large who could be parted from the day-to-day operations of Estuary City.

It was not the full Guild roster, for there were many who had greater obligations in the city, but those who could throw their shoulders behind this march—Vierrelyne counted fifty before she lost track of who had sworn their hands and shields to this most somber forward movement.

Together they began at a steady pace as the sun rose overhead, providing a single counterbalance to the gathering icy winds. The march through the forest was quieted by snowfall, for which Vierrelyne could only be grateful, the soft tufts of crystalline snow stilling the air about them as they filed from Stardowne that morning. The tension in her chest felt less heavy in the crisp air, but the whisperings from Margandrys in her ear only served to heighten her hypervigilance as they crossed into the forests directly southeast of the palace.

You are as radiant as your mother, dearest, at the height of her powers, at the height of her union with me, as we forged our path through the mountains...

His words, in this place of uncertainty and inevitable conflict, soothed her as the first traces of the arcane began to cross their path—more of the shadowy monsters that only seemed to emerge in this world when they were welcomed in, called forth by someone with dark design.

M. Daniel McDowell

"Ahead!" Someone behind her called out, and the wave descended upon them from the sky.

In the daylight the strange beasts stretched their shadows over the World that Was, as Mehren had called it once. Kharise rallied the front row, poleaxes in hand, to drive them back and strike out as many of the nasty creatures as possible.

It was so unnerving to see these monsters in the daylight with such... vividity. At night, they seemed like little more than perversions of the beasts of the earth, but in the daylight, it was clear that these were creatures of too many teeth: maws of a hunger unending, beyond any satiety, creatures with jaws that could swallow any human whole into fathomless nothingness, creatures that should not exist anywhere in this world.

This first skirmish caught her off her footing. Her urgency to destroy Cascada so colored her vision, it was not until there was a bat-winged horror, the air beneath it sheened with some unknowable foul acid-breath, nearly bearing down upon her. Ghostnail drove it back with a well-planted arrow to the eye, but its shriek of anguish left a wave of strange corrosion in its wake, a green fluid that Vierrelyne knew she must not touch with her demon-bound weaponry if she could help it. Mehren slashed its long, segmented tail with a short sword that sizzled on contact with the thing's hideous flesh. It crumpled in the walking path, its muzzle steaming the snow around it into acid ice.

Once they chased down the lingering horrors, the band regrouped and marched forward in an uncomfortable disquiet, ever onward. The palatial estate at Cascada was already blanketed in a layer of snow, and as the coalition of strange forces moved in, as the first waves of creatures fell to the Independents' front lines, the ambient sensation of frigid dread descended upon Vierrelyne, and all she could do with it was firm her jaw and steady her resolve. She had but one worthy foe in her sights now.

The bitter wind gave an added edge to the foreboding feeling Vierrelyne struggled to suppress. Even Margandrys, ever at her side, whispering his assurances, was silent in this moment, and the softening of the world that ever accompanied such a snowfall left her isolated in her own mind as she contemplated what was still to come.

Mehren marched at her side. For once, because she had mustered the limitless endurance of the dreadful demon within her crown, it was the wizard who struggled to keep pace with her. The thought of his arms around her came to her, in the smallest moment.

A single sliver of jealousy sparked in Margandrys whenever she thought of Mehren now that her affections for him were no longer a burdensome secret. Vi smothered the smug wordless observation immediately. She still could not detangle her deeper feelings about Mehren Tevaht, but she owed him her life, and she suspected, if it came to it, that he would lay down his own in her name.

If it came to that.

What a heavy thing to carry.

Perhaps she'd made a mistake.

Margandrys liked that concession; he did not say as much, but the *bright* feeling, the surge of some dark power that accompanied it, was bitter and hard to ignore.

Did the demon prince truly yearn for her, as he so often confessed? But it happened only at junctures where it was advantageous for him. She did not know what she believed in her own heart, much less his, but she knew she did not have the same susceptibility as her own mother.

You know my heart, dearest. You know what I most desire.

It was cold comfort to know that Abenelle had ridden to the grave with that dark promise, all because the hideous warlord to whom she was chained in life was such a foul prospect compared to salacious, desperate, malignant hope.

Whatever else Mehren was to her, Vierrelyne thought, he was the only person who understood how lonely her existence was, and for that, she was grateful.

He only wants you for what the stone can offer him, he is condemned by all the stars to walk this land in your shadow, Margandrys intoned.

She concentrated her energy on the forward march.

"You said it yourself," she muttered. "Jealousy is an ugly emotion. I need to concentrate."

He is hollow; he would swallow you whole; his yearning for you is only to soothe the great disquiet in his own mind. He is the Shepherd in Shadow and only his oblation will bring an end to this dark age.

Vierrelyne clenched her jaw, remembering such a recent time in her life she was truly alone in every realm, save for the anxious wizard at her side, while he did nothing more than will her back to life in silence. It transcended any of her softer feelings; she would love him to the end of her days for this alone, even if they were both condemned by the stars to suffer alone there ever after.

A fresh wave of something truly dark overtook her, at the thought of that horrific night.

Whatever else came of this day, Vierrelyne would call the same violence down upon Prince Erenth Remaryn if it was the last act of her dismal existence. He had not been the darkest shadow over her life, but to say that he had not been the engine of her greatest despair, even as his actions had freed her—

Well, she would have to return the gesture.

The gates of the palatial estate lay before them, as another surge of strange beasts followed at their heels. Vierrelyne felt trapped by them, but she did not give voice to this sensation. She watched as Kharise and Reyser nodded knowingly at each other and divided their ranks accordingly, each moving in synchrony over the battlefield before them.

"I'm going inside," Vierrelyne said, as the groupings evened out over the snowy field.

Mehren gave her a long, mournful stare. "I wanted to go with you. I have to help them contain these creatures and find the source if I can dismantle the spellwork. I don't know how he's summoned so many, so powerful, in such a short time. It's so much darker than the ones from before. He must have someone aiding him, but—" he shook his head and shivered, pulling his cloak closer against himself.

"It's unthinkable, I know," she agreed.

"I know what you have to do, beloved, but *please*—"

A scream down the hill—Teven? Graves? She could never keep Reyser's men straight once they were out of her line of sight—drew Mehren's attention momentarily, and she took the opportunity to bolt forward, toward the palace gates, before he could appeal to her for a subtler approach.

As she charged inward, Margandrys *pulled, stretched, embodied* the enchanted armor with which she was able to deflect every oncoming blow.

At her brow, the crown formed a horned great helm, shielded with the eldritch energy from the Peridot Starprism itself. She bellowed with rage and delight—his *gifts!* She had only begun to unfurl them before, and now?

Now she could trample every last one of them, drive them into nothingness. Margandrys willing, she would. The gates had lain open when she approached, and with the speed of her benefactor's grand gift, Vierrelyne launched herself through and inside before his guard house was able to seal her out of the palatial estate.

At the marble steps before the palace doors, a wave of panic-stricken spear bearers and bannermen crashed against her sword, as if she had *willed* them there only to be blown backward by the force of her strike, her span extended so far beyond her own ordinary reach by Margandrys's fearsome form. She swept them all back and roared with fury, striking outward, determined only to clear herself a path to those grand doors through these hapless guards.

Inside, she remembered the bland grandiloquence of the Cascadian palace, its colorless pillars of carven limestone, its dark drapery to shield against the bitter coastal winter winds, seemingly unchanged in the age since Alaina's dreadful wedding.

It was not merely the site of one of her life's greatest indignities, but indeed, that did not warm her heart either.

There were none of the monsters within the walls—the prince understood the madness they wrought, then, and he sought to avoid it, to keep it out of the palace. She noticed, though, that it was also absent of the kinds of people who brought life to such an estate; these unchanged decorative features were coated in dust and left in declining repair.

Where was he hiding, in the ruins of his own grandeur?

In his throne chambers, Margandrys intuited. *He expects nothing and believes you to be frail even with my worldly form in your stead; he is indeed the weak-willed creature you have forever pictured in this place, luxuriating in his own ignorance.*

Vierrelyne contemplated. His show of power, the demonstration with his wives—it was a formidable display, but it had cost him. It was a violent gesture, meant to offend the sensibilities of the whole principality, to show how disposably he viewed them all, and on that front, he had succeeded. It was curious that he saw so little need to protect himself with ordinary soldiers, as Vierrelyne stalked the halls, never encountering more than a pair at a time, making swift work of them with her formidable sword, the carapace of the demon's armored form overmatched to the shortswords and pikes of Prince Erenth's guard detail.

"Does he truly think that he is my equal?" Vierrelyne mused. "That he can hide in his tower and wait for the truth to come to him? Is that what he's done? Commissioned the stone tomb of one of your brothers as a weapon of his own?"

Yes. Margandrys laughed. *If he truly wielded the stone of either of my brothers. I have no doubt he believes he does. I know a secret that he does not. Both of my brothers perished in the making of my damned confinement. There remains only one rightful claimant to the throne of the Scourgelands.*

Vierrelyne breathed sharply. An impostor stone for an inferior prince. The irony of it was too delicious, something that reached inside the ugly part of herself and dragged up dark laughter from within. In this moment, it felt right, satisfying, to unify with the destruction.

She smashed through dull collections of decorative pottery arraying the walls, feeling ever more fire within herself as she did so.

The crashing of shards against the tile drew two more pairs of his soldiers from other passageways, and she willed more of Margandrys into herself, welcomed his rage as it widened her stride, gave her the truly brutal reach of the eldritch broadsword between her palms. She had no worthy foes among the dead in this palace.

When at last she reached the throne room doors, she found that indeed they had been barred—though that meant little to her armored fists and shoulders. The demon's fire chased along the edge of her sword, the veil of vivid green magic rippling across the splintered dark wood once she had slammed into it with enough force.

She found Prince Erenth seated upon his throne, alone—not even a single guard. He was smaller than she remembered, even having seen him from afar not so long ago; greyer, more miserable, in his solitude. In his hand, he held his inferior pendant, its blood-dark ruby glinting with malefaction in the dim light of his chambers.

"I hoped you would dignify me with such a visit," he crowed, his voice nasal, smug. "Until my little performance at Estuary City, I thought it might be true, that you had perished at the collapse of Talorr. Part of me hoped it would be so simple."

"But you *knew*," she replied stiffly. "You knew it couldn't be, because I had the stone."

"Oh, I knew *someone* had your mother's stone." Erenth nodded slowly, as if he were waiting for something. "But it wasn't until I saw you for certain that I knew what had happened, after that worthless heretic's plan went sideways at the city square."

"What do you mean?" She snarled. "What plan?"

"Tobinarde l'Ete. He sought to help me, in my desire to break the backbone of Derebor, he was to deliver me the stone and I would raise Cascada as the new seat of empire. When that failed, he sent me the woman with the demon stone. She taught me the spells, gave them to my soldiers."

He gestured with the ruby, and Vierrelyne shuddered.

That fool believes he has a demon stone, Margandrys hissed. *This is something darker and less powerful at once. A soulstone fed on the fat of mere mortals, an unsustainable one at that. A battery made of his every last servant—that is why there are so few who still stand at his aid. He sacrificed them **all** to have a fraction of what I have given you.*

What was he waiting for? She approached the throne, and he elevated his chin, sneering at her, still seated. She realized he was calling the power to himself—he would be armed as she was before she ever reached the steps to the throne. He still thought he had the superior power, because it had been crafted for him, bespoke, by that damned old man in his wretched tower. Perhaps Prince Erenth was braver enrobed in armor; brave enough to make a fatal mistake.

She noticed he did not ever wear the pendant; he held it, and as his armor surged around him, in the fog of demon-light, she observed it was his shield-arm. He knew his vulnerabilities, then; she had a framework upon which she could build her battle against him, she knew how best to draw his final blood.

She stood before him, her sword arm raised, and beckoned. "You sought to take this legacy from me, and it will be your undoing! You sought the fall of Derebor, and you would bring Cascada with it. Someone set you the task of unearthing this."

Erenth laughed. "Derebor was its own downfall. I merely spun the top that collided with its collapsing bricks. Brabinghar would have hidden in that dull and dreadful tower for the rest of his days if it meant he could keep the rest of us under his thumb."

She could defend nothing about the way in which Derebor had been governed, true.

He stood and strode toward her, his sword out. His form was terrible; perhaps born of years of watching instead of dueling. She mustered no sympathy for it, especially when he was so convinced of his own powers. He seemed to think that he held a true stone of the Sundered Thrones, the true prison of the princes, and nothing would dissuade him—not her strength, not her fury, for he was a belligerent and broad-shouldered figure. Not even the knowledge that Tobinarde had freely given to him, in exchange for his part to play in this tangle.

No amount of successful parrying or counterstriking would convince the Cascadian prince that in this instance, he was *thoroughly* outmatched. His force was formidable, thanks to the soulstone in his fist, but as she struck his shield and challenged his balance, she hoped he'd rise to her bait and take a foolish tack against her.

She drew him out onto the courtyard, forcing him to parry a hard swipe that left him off his footing. He squared up again, panting. He'd made an interesting choice, relying too hard on his shield arm in the face of her broadsword, but Prince Erenth had always been one to take an easy path; that was how they'd gotten here. He had thought she'd make it simple for him.

She slashed, and he danced away from her. It was going to be his death. She saw the arc and followed it true.

He stumbled backwards and lost control, striking his elbow on the frozen ground. The pendant sailed out of his hand, behind him, buried in the snow, the shield skidding away to his side. He shrieked as he clawed to take hold of it again, but Vierrelyne planted her boot on his chest. At this close distance, his fear drove the deep creases at the sides of his face. She could smell the sweat-slick strands of his grey hair peeking out from the rim of his helmet.

"You can't! I am the Prince of the Undreamed Ages, I am the future, I hold the true power! I am the uniter of the realms, of beasts and dream—"

"You will never see the Realm of Dream!" Vi thrust her sword into the gap between his helm and his chest plate and leaned on it with the whole of her weight until Prince Erenth lay still beneath her. "You will walk no realm of the future or the past. You will be *forgotten!*"

Margandrys cackled in her ear.

I could say it no better than you have, dearest. Careful—he's still got allegiances from the Scourgelands surfacing in his wake. That stone is no match for what I can offer you, but it is beyond tempting to the weak creatures of the restless dark.

A shriek above her, one that rang off the high pillars of the palace, and Vierrelyne snapped back into action. A hideous winged beast, shimmering in the snowy daylight, darted straight at the ground, toward a distant figure near the edge of the courtyard, in a long grey cloak—Mehren! She charged at it, bellowing, and caught its attention. It shrieked again, its mouth unfurling all the way down its long and slender neck, a long maw dripping with teeth.

She gritted her teeth and lunged, both arms forward. It danced back with better skill and grace than the late Prince Erenth had shown in his last stand against her.

Margandrys hissed with glee and excitement at the frantic movements, as she cornered the creature against one of the interior walls, and slashed until its open jaws spilled forth with ichor that melted the snow and burnt the grass underneath it. Catching her breath, she reflected. Where had Mehren gone? She knew his best strategy when he was out of arrows and other projectiles was simply to run—she'd expressly told him to—but he couldn't have gotten far in this weather, could he?

She would not let it break her, but the instant panic she felt in that moment was undeniable. Margandrys did his best persuasion, whispering his encouragements for her to rally and persevere.

You must go on, beloved, you have many foes yet. Focus.

Reyser Gorum and one of his men—she thought it might be Graves—had cornered a long and leathery beast at the other side of the field. She charged forward once more, and threw herself into it, full-bore, her bones ringing with Margandrys's blessing and glory throughout.

The creatures had overtaken a large area of forest beyond the halls of the palace, as if they had been drawn there, coaxed purposefully. Kharise met her out there, poleaxe in hand, driving back a pair of lobster-clawed creatures with shaggy pelts and ursine bodies.

In the clearing, she found another one of the sigils, with a handprint caked in dried blood, but no sign of whose hand had left such a dark pact upon the world; had they been slain? Had they been able to run?

Did it matter, when the result was the ongoing, continuous shattering of the space between the realms? It seemed clear to Vierrelyne that this was the true threat, the true meaning to the cadence of these assaults.

She stood in her radiant armor, gleaming with palpable menace as she surveyed the field strewn with lesser enemies and fallen allies alike, her enemy's banner in one hand and her wicked blade in the other.

Mehren cowered in terror before her great beauty, her demon-eyed gem as resplendent as her armor, her pallid face a mask of justice and conquest, her diadem a thorned crown, a helm atop her silver-gilt locks. He sank to his knees in the snow and ash, knowing for certain in this moment what he had feared from the first time he'd glimpsed her porcelain face: that he adored her utterly, that he would serve her every whim, for his fate was enchained to hers by that star-damned prophecy.

He *was* the Shepherd in Shadow; he was the one whose place in her grand story was one of profound and injurious calamity, and all because he knew that what he felt was as unquestionable as the decades-old words of some mad prophet, a mad prophet with the same affliction as his own.

If he was half as noble as the prophet had thought, in his many hours of grand visions, Mehren should throw himself before her immaculate blade. Offer his own strange magic, the one he had earned—stolen, in his own words—by his own survival, the future he'd created for himself by overpowering his captors and tormenters, the ones who sought to claim him long before he'd ever heard of this wild

M. Daniel McDowell

quest. If he were not a coward, he would have to offer his blood and suffering to her holy crusade evermore.

Mehren had gotten this far on the strength of his resilience to Death, on his ability to conduct it like the shadows. He had bent that power to her purposes before, but never with such clarity on his role in her grand damnation.

He ached, knowing the blank face of what could only be Death, waiting on the periphery of her grand battlefield, for them both, and it terrified him utterly.

If he wasn't utterly spineless, he might have begged her to slay him, to break the last threads before they were woven into the tapestry. Enjoin the truth of the prophecy into the world—Crown of the World Unbound, reborn anew at the sacrifice of the Shepherd in Shadow.

But Mehren Tevaht was nothing if he was not a coward and so—he fled.

Just as she had asked of him, in the pale evening hours, their arms entwined. It was not the first time the person he most loved in the world had asked him to run, when he had no strength nor instinct for what to do next, after all.

The harsh, crystalline snow bit through his cloak as he went; this squall was not long-lived, but it was bitter, with flecks of ice like knives. He trudged away from the carnage with his heart grief laden. What would it mean to walk away now? To leave just as Vierrelyne's mastery of the demon prince Margandrys truly blossomed into great victories, striking at the heart of each of the Merchant Emirates, and now arriving at the precipice of something newer, *darker*...

Something hideous remained on the horizon; that was abundantly clear to him. There was some aspect of this that weighed on his heart: the nature of the treachery that'd placed Vierrelyne at this terrifying precipice.

There was only one person it could be, to Mehren's thinking: the prophet of heresy himself, Tobinarde l'Ete.

The sigils he'd found, on that hideous paper, pointed in a single direction.

With both eyes open, Mehren saw a flash of something he thought strange: the curling smoke of a demon's essence and a familiar bright-grey cloak of the Astral Circle, dashing through the copse of trees that lined the edge of the palatial estate. He tensed, knowing who it was, and why she'd been here, before he leapt after her, running with every last fiber of himself tightly coiled. It was not an easy task, in the snow where his narrow, pointed boots had little to grip.

Just as he thought he was getting closer his toe caught a stray root and sent him tumbling. Carina Betrel turned and laughed in wicked humor as Mehren picked himself up, trying to brush off the indignity as easily as he could shed the fallen snow and leaves.

"What do you think you're doing, Tevaht?" She strode up to him and scruffed him with his maille. She was so much stronger... how? Carina hefted him over her head, and then threw him sharply to the ground. Winded from the run, let alone the fall, Mehren struggled to pull himself back up. She kicked him, but he grabbed her boot and grappled her to the ground.

"I could ask you the same," he replied, trying to take hold of her wrist, to no avail. She closed her fist, and a flash of red light battered him backward.

The stone, the one Vi had mentioned—had Carina stolen it somehow? Gotten it from Prince Erenth? Perhaps in the heat of the fight it had been lost...

Mehren shivered with dread.

"He trusted you, and you blew it! You couldn't even bring yourself to admit it!"

"It's not that simple," Mehren replied, and she laughed bitterly as she narrowed her eyes.

"Your assignment! That WAS simple, and you still managed to botch everything! Tobinarde sent me out to clean up after your lousy mess, and for what? To find out that you gave the stone to the princess instead of bringing it home! You betrayed all of us! For *what?*"

"I didn't—she took it herself! I didn't get the chance to tell her—" he protested as Carina bore down on him with her fists. He flinched away as she jabbed at him, her strength enhanced by the stone in her hand. If he could just pry her fingers open...

"You couldn't even bring yourself to weasel it away from her. Coward! Since when are you so *noble?* Why are you helping her?" Carina snarled. "Useless! Worthless. It should have been me! I would never have given away something so important!"

He flung himself at her, and she lashed out with her wrist, catching him in the jaw. He fell forward on his wrists and groaned. She pivoted and grabbed him by his messy dark hair.

"We're going back to Zalandan, you and me."

He winced as she yanked him by the scalp and led him away through the forest.

Through the waning daylight, she dragged him toward a shack on the trail outside of the palace center, a one-room hunting hovel in the wild sprawl between the cities. On the wooden floor, Carina had engraved the workings of a portal spell, to save time, just like the ones in Zalandan; this must have been how she'd gotten back and forth. He flailed, trying to wrest back control, as she jerked him around with the hair at the nape of his neck.

"Why didn't you come back to us, anyway, if you *aren't* a traitor? Tobinarde would have understood if something happened. I think you *wanted* to see us fail." She slammed the door behind her and threw him to the floor.

"I—I lost my chalk. It spilled halfway d-down the mountainside, I d-didn't dare try to—" He stuttered, and that only made his panic worse. He hadn't stuttered or stammered in so long, and it was as if being in her clutches again eroded every ounce of his confidence. She smirked.

"You're an adept. Why didn't you use your own blood?"

"With the demon... He's very powerful; he ripped my portal open and dumped us halfway across from where I meant for us to go. It wasn't safe to try again. I'd be letting him set the destination..."

"You didn't betray us for *her*, did you? She's demon-sworn thanks to you. Did you fall for her because she was pretty and sad?" Carina laughed with mirthless rage. "She could never love a sniveling worm like you, Half-a-Face. She was a *princess* and you've made her into a monster. It'll take everything we've got to bring her down now, all because of your weak will."

She battered him relentlessly, until he had nothing left in him with which to fight her, and then she dragged him into the circle she'd engraved. Each line of her carving was filled in with the grotesque chalk of Tobinarde's ossuary, the spell to create the wall of the folds between the realms that would shield them.

His stomach had strengthened over the time he had spent in Vierrelyne's company, but the sight of his own blood on his hands once more blacked him out as Carina closed the circle and pressed her palm, limned with her own dried blood, at the portal's key.

CHAPTER 16
DISSOCIATION

ONCE THEY RETURNED TO STARDOWNE THAT NIGHT, VIERRELYNE was inconsolable.

She had been so certain that she'd seen him— that he'd made it through the worst of the day—she was thoroughly unwilling to broach the idea that she could possibly have been mistaken, not even in the heat of battle, not even with as many other demands as there were for her talents and her weapons that arduous day.

Worse still, she had let the impostor stone, the ruby-red gem Erenth had sought to wield against her, slip through her fingers. Of that there was no sign either, though she did not know what to make of it. The loss of the stone at least could be attributed to the icy layer of snow. The absence of the man whose heart so entangled hers overwrote all her other going concerns.

"Princess," Kharise implored, "they have gone over the whole of that field, they scoured the woodlands beyond. There is no sign of Mehren Tevaht. None of the fallen, none of the wounded. I'm sorry. He must have escaped and gone to ground somewhere."

"Again. I have to look *again*." Vierrelyne seethed, and the stone at her brow glowed its sickly green, brilliant even in the dim light. "I will go out tonight by myself if I must."

Dearest. Margandrys brought out his most supplicant tone. *You must rest. We face more enemies than I had once thought possible. Even in your brilliance, I would ask this one thing. There is nothing to be gained out there in the darkness tonight.*

"I can't leave him. I promised..."

What had she said, exactly? She'd said enough.

Kharise shook her head and sighed.

"I don't like it, either. Get some rest. We'll figure it out in the morning. Perhaps he had to hide somewhere we did not have time to look."

Vi stared into the darkness at the doorway for a long time, as if she might change the hour of day by the strength of her mind alone.

"Perhaps it will all look different in the morning light," she conceded at last, before she stalked away into the recesses of that miserable palatial estate, into a room once used by a woman who had since been bent to an unthinkable torture, an unimaginable fate, to leave this world for the realm of dream under Vierrelyne's watchful gaze, and her impossibly sharp blade.

The princess readied herself to sleep as best she could, but no rest came to take her. She stared into the vastness of stars through the narrow window. Their limitless map was neither soothing nor restful as she contemplated the stark path that lay before her when the dawn finally ascended.

When that day arose, Vierrelyne was no better off than she had been that night; the tension in her core did not dissipate. She reported to muster with the rest of the soldiers from the Guild; she was one of them, was she not?

She sought out Kharise, down in the forward operating space she had carved out for herself in the central atrium of the palace at Cascada. She had already created a detailed plan for the entire campus, from prisoner details and audiences for clemency to the minutiae of kitchen patrol, delegated to Bunny, and the morning roster, delegated to Ghostnail—Kharise was building herself a well-oiled unit of service, neatening the ranks and file of Reyser's quirky organization thread by thread in her grand tapestry.

Vi gave Kharise a bleary-eyed wave and strode over to her makeshift center of command. She had Mehren's map, with several additional lines drawn in with his graphite stump, as well as a series of standing markers resting on its surface. Available forces, reinforcements, fresh reports of monsters sighted nearby... Vi's heart sank anew at the quiet confirmation that none of these markers indicated Mehren had been found.

If he *had* been slain on the field, his body would have turned up by now, and yet, the truth of this gave her no peace at all. Where could he have gone, to be so hidden now? She could think of only one place, but she did not think he would go there willingly—not anymore.

Reyser paced around, his usual morning affability made altogether unbearable to Vierrelyne by the number of tasks that lay before him and his exuberance to tackle any number of them seemingly all at once. She stared numbly at him, her eyes following his circuitous steps.

"No sign of the wizard this morning in any of the fields or woods to the west of us." Kharise said, shuffling a pile of Reyser's notes in search of any additional reports. "I think it's fair to say we will have to move eastward and swiftly so."

"There are countless demons flooding across the forest between here and Zalandan. They know *exactly* where to travel. Are you sure the boy didn't tell him—"

"*Mehren.* A grown man. Just shy and strange. Not unlike some others I've known." Kharise corrected, tapping her toes at him. "And no, I'm certain he didn't. He wouldn't have. His place with the Astral Circle has been fractured since he agreed to follow us to Estuary City."

Vi felt the absence of *why* he'd stayed in her advisor's words.

"It's my fault," she blurted out. "I made him promise me... I made him say he would run, if it got too terrible, I wanted him to be safe, and now... now he's gone."

Kharise blinked and stared at her.

"Dear heart. Mehren was not blindly following your orders. I know I saw him on the edge of the field myself, supporting one of the units afield. That being said, I suspect Zalandan is where we have to go to find him, and soon."

"I think all of this feels less onerous with something to eat first," Reyser suggested. "Let's see what Bunny's got on the griddle and scout things out from there."

Vierrelyne couldn't argue with that, even if the thought of waiting another minute longer filled her belly with stone.

Mehren awoke, foggy and miserable, face first on the slate floor in the confines of a small cell with walls of the same dark stone as the rest of Zalandan. A barred metal door let through long rays of torchlight. His lips were wet and painful, but his mouth was dry, and both of his eyes hurt, in different ways. His left cheek was stiff and aching. His arms were bound wrist to elbow behind his back. He shifted his weight, finding purchase on the wall behind him with his boot heel, just enough to lessen the pressure on his sore ribs.

How had he gotten here...?

He remembered biting someone...

Carina. He'd been punched in the face; kicked, beaten, thrown, slapped... violence earned out of her efforts to drag him off and back to Zalandan with her prize, that horrible red stone. All this because he didn't have the forethought to play dead after the first thrashing she'd given him. No, that was wishful thinking—he would have been dragged back to this wretched castle even if he *were* stone dead, because there were always enough ghoulish warlocks on hand in Tobinarde's coterie to reanimate even the most unwilling.

He wrung his fingers around, trying to loosen his binding. If he could just free his left hand...

The rapid patter of boots on slate flooring outside filled him with dread. There was no time now.

"You're back!" Tobinarde exclaimed with delight in his tone, a tone Mehren regarded inherently suspect.

"Did you miss me, sir?" Mehren tried to stuff down his rising apprehensions. He shoved his hip forward on the stone floor, maille clanking as he tried to leverage his shoulder to get a better view. The master of strange heresies was in rare form, dressed in his best cloak—one reserved for the holidays of his personal sacred calendar, an oxblood velvet that skimmed the floor.

"Mehren Tevaht. My best pupil, and my worst. I sketched my expectations for you in crystalline clarity, and you defeated even my lowest expectations for your success. I tasked you to bring me the princess Vierrelyne du Talorr, and her ancestral weapon, before the fall of Derebor, and you could not even give me the kindness of a swift return to explain your abject failure."

He paced the floor, the soft click of his bootheels on the rough stone punctuating his words.

Mehren coughed but offered him nothing further.

"I sincerely hoped you were dead. I could explain your profound abdication of your role by some cruelty of fates, that the Shepherd in Shadow sacrificed himself too soon to fulfill his promise, and more would be the pity. Surely *Mehren*, of all my talented pupils, would have found his way back to me." Tobinarde paused his circular pacing and strode up to the cage bars. "Instead, I find my most talented disciple seeks to usurp me. Break my prophecy. Perhaps he sought to bend the demon to his own will, because he is also my worst pupil. An impulsive liar, a thief."

Mehren sputtered, not sure which foolhardy accusation to start with, but Tobinarde turned away from him and continued his circuit of the narrow ancillary room.

"What my worst pupil did not know, could not have guessed, is that my plan would proceed apace without his feckless meddling."

Mehren snarled. "That's not what happened."

"Would it be *preferable* to do without this treachery? Perhaps. But even I could not have guessed the princess herself would take the stone." He shook the metal frame, his eyes wild. "What did you *tell* her?"

Mehren fought the tremor in his jaw.

"N-nothing she didn't already know," he said solemnly. "I d-didn't even have to tell her to find it—she'd p-plotted to take it before I ever m-m-met her."

At this, Tobinarde drew back with a scoff. "She *wanted* the Starprism? Knowing what it did to her family, her kingdom? After all this time? She *wanted* it?"

"M-more than anything." Mehren struggled to breathe, still desperate to sit upright, his efforts to no avail. "She even knew... where to find it..."

"And you *helped* her? After everything, this is how you repay me? I should cut every curl from your head for your insolence," Tobinarde snarled. It always worked when you were my best and brightest pupil."

He tried one last time to push himself up, lightheaded from the pressure of the floor. "You said it yourself; I'm your worst disciple. I ruined everything."

"I dragged you out of that witchfinder's hut. I gave you shelter and purpose. I clothed you in the robes of my dearest and most faithful. I gave you your gift of sight between the worlds. I put forth to you a task I entrusted to no one else. I *trusted* you, Mehren Tevaht. And now you discover the cost of your betrayal."

Tobinarde wrestled Mehren back onto his feet, with Carina's assistance. They frog-marched him through the barren halls of their strange, cold fortress, into the old magician's laboratory in the lowest reaches of the keep, a place equally forbidding and familiar to the bound wizard at their mercy.

"I have had to improvise, you understand, in the wake of your treachery," Tobinarde said. "Carina can explain in great detail. If I am to bring forth enough creatures of the darkness in volume and scale, such as I had sought with the aid of Cascada and her forces to bring the princess *here*, to *me*, as I once instructed you, I must use the powers at hand to summon more, and they are so *demanding* to call forth."

The frigid room spanned an entire floor of the great fortress at Zalandan: slab stone tables, hewn from the same dark, flecked stone as the towers above them; sturdy shelves built from long beams of hardwood, laden with the materials of all manner of sorcery, academic and eldritch alike. The place smelled of drying sheaves of moss, aging leather, bundles of herbs and plant matter sourced from all over the known continent, from the Sunward Free Cities to the far fringes of the Unconquered Plains.

There was an inclined service chair at the far end of the laboratory; familiar to Mehren, for it was here that Tobinarde had fitted him, every few years, with the lenses of wizard's glass that allowed him to refine his vision of the Scourgelands and what walked between them in every realm. The two hefted him roughly into it, his arms still bound woefully tight behind him.

Carina bound his ankles together and fastened them to the foot plate. Tobinarde freed Mehren's right arm, but twisted it sharply, catching him off guard long enough to wrench his right hand into a binding cuff.

With his feet secured, Carina pulled up the belt intended to lash a subject into place against the seat-back and fastened it across his chest. Mehren knew from experience not to thrash against these restraints; it would only tighten them, make them ever more unbearable. All the same, he had to fight the nausea and panic building within him.

At last, Tobinarde produced a carven stone plate, a round tablet with a curious tall stiletto blade through its center. It was engraved deeply with a pattern of glyphs and a concentric ring; Mehren recognized it as the same sigil he had found in that fateful camp, the same summoner with no return passage.

"Your prior injuries, at the hands of those hideous cretins, left you with such a unique opportunity," Tobinarde said. "One you've never taken the best advantage of, in truth. If you were less of a pathetic coward, you might have been the greatest of my pupils. You survived a profound torture before."

Unique opportunity? Mehren did not have many memories from that dark time in his life, but he'd thought for all this time that the witchfinder general himself had turned this horrible curse of second sight upon him...

He rested the plate on a table the same height as the right-hand armrest and inched it over to Mehren's side.

"Perhaps your cowardice will protect you again. I had always thought it was some strength within you, but I see it now. It was only your weak will that spared you."

Mehren fought the cresting urge to vomit, fought the wave of panic that followed.

"I *gave* you this gift of sight when the witchfinder general stole your eye," Tobinarde snarled. "I gave you everything you would ever need to be my most powerful disciple. I gave you the whole of your world and you couldn't bring me one lousy girl and one infernal gemstone. I asked you for *so little* and you could not even manage that. Now, you will give me the army of creatures I will need to retrieve the stone for myself and bind that demon prince forever."

He poured a small amount of water over the stiletto, and it flowed down its spine into the pattern of the stone—

it would have been a beautiful device, but Mehren snarled, unable to flinch away, though he dared not look at it, for now he knew the lengths of Tobinarde's intent. The elder wizard grasped Mehren's wrist and shoved his hand, palm open, over the sharp, thin spike, and secured the wrist restraint in place.

The pain and shock of it, the surreal grinding of the blade against his bones, overwhelmed him. He clenched his eyes closed, flinched away from it, howling in unthinkable pain, straining against his bindings.

Even if it were not the sharpest of his agonies at the present moment, he would have trouble looking at it, but no amount of screaming would alter the trap Tobinarde had made of him.

A portal, drawn in blood, meant to summon forth the hungriest of creatures, at the cost of Mehren's sanity, given substance in this world by the slow transference of his own. Not mere shadows, nor drifting entities, as they often seemed when he encountered them in this realm, but the same surging form of energy he had experienced the first time he'd witnessed Vierrelyne's transformation at the hands of the demon prince.

The first of these hideous forms began to wriggle and squirm under Mehren's pinioned palm, and he could not stop himself from screaming as the sensation wormed away from him, with a sickening splat onto the stone floor below.

He looked up as it stretched from a hideous dark worm, dreamlike, on the ground, into a jet-black colossus of webbed wings and claws, and sauntered toward the wide, barred window, where it slithered through into the evening light.

M. Daniel McDowell

CHAPTER 17
ZALANDAN

The following afternoon a small but dedicated group patrol made a swift trail on foot through the forest between the two towers. Two dozen men Kharise had pulled together alongside Vi and Reyser, all to search for the wizard the only remaining place they thought possible. It was a long hike, but the concentrated effort gave her time to clear her mind. They'd eliminated all other suggestions. It had to be the Astral Circle's keep.

"What do you think?" she asked, as the two marched behind the rest of their limited force, with Vierrelyne leading the charge through the snow-dusted narrow pass up into the eastern mountains. "We should probably split forces at the fortress. We certainly can't handle all of these rotten beasts without facing some hard losses if we split up, but if we don't stop Tobinarde first, I don't know that we'll have any choice."

"You go with the princess," Reyser said. "I'll go inside. Once you've got the situation under control out here, come find me, if I don't come back for you first."

"I think we should split up," Vierrelyne replied. "I need to deal with the Heresiarch Tobinarde l'Ete. For all he's ruined. For all he continues to ruin. I will be the death of him if it's the last thing I do."

"I shall marshal the field, then," Kharise agreed. "Someone has to keep these fellows in line. What's your plan, Reyser?"

"I have a hunch about where this latest squadron of bat-creatures came from, that's all. If I'm right, I won't be long."

Kharise squinted at him.

"Promise. I wouldn't want to leave you too long with Teven. He still hasn't gotten a solid grip on that poleaxe no matter what you've been able to show him."

Vierrelyne was silent. Her whole focus was forward motion, a certainty of purpose that even Kharise found intimidating. She had trusted her for so long that this at least came naturally to her, but in the face of a conviction as stern as hers...

Well, she was glad not to be the Heresiarch nor any of his allegiants, she could say that.

Kharise rallied the first line of Independents around her, and pushed forward into the courtyard that surrounded the foreboding tower at Zalandan. She understood, in the terrible tower's shadow, how this foul old man mustered such admiration—and fear. He had carved himself a niche through grotesqueries. No wonder

M. Daniel McDowell

even someone so brilliant as Mehren Tevaht thought so highly, assigned him such inestimable power.

Ah, but she knew—towers could always fall, and someday always would. A tower was but a structure of a sustained effort, susceptible to the whims of the world below.

Hunting down the squadrons of hideous, ink-dark beasts was made lighter by the hands of her comrades, the men in Reyser's ranks whose loyalty to him was conveyed to her effortlessly by his trust in her, and she sought to protect that trust through her actions.

Kharise spotted the young woman she'd seen before, in that same dark cloak as Mehren always wore. She stood with the helmet over her vivacious curls, waiting as if she had an appointment at the gates. Her armor resembled Vierrelyne's in form, but the sheen over this set was a vibrant ruby. She scowled as the older woman approached her with poleaxe in hand.

"Come get me, old lady," she snarled, and Kharise smirked with murderous glee. *Old?* Oh, this simpering infant was not going to *get* to be old for that one. Kharise charged at her and broke her stance readily. Not much of a fighter, more of a braggart?

Those were her favorites.

Swinging her broadsword with reckless abandon, no focus, no control with a weapon of that heft. Not good. Kharise laughed, brandishing her poleaxe. She wasn't going to let this foolish creature get close—the younger woman was heavily armored, which made her dangerous if she closed the gap. She'd *really* have to dance if she wanted to close it, and Kharise was well-prepared to prevent that.

Behind her, she heard the others as they began to engage the various swarming devils above and below, the shadows stretching overhead to block the sun, but never for long, snapping like cut ropes as Ghostnail and his archers held their ground.

It struck her, as she parried this foolish girl's various efforts to press in closer, how long she had believed that there were no such things as demons.

Perhaps they were still just the shadows of someone else's terrible mind—but she had fought them, and they were as real as this feral creature who thought she would get leverage over her, simply by virtue of being larger and heavier in her horrible eldritch armor.

It struck her next that the woman she loved like a daughter was not unlike this demon-ridden creature before her, but better-disciplined, honed to her terrible purpose by circumstance. Half a life spent waiting for the World that Was. Half a life spent waiting for some worthless words to come true.

"Pah!" Her opponent spat in fury, throwing herself forward and twisting the poleaxe from Kharise's arms. She narrowly missed breaking her hand if she hadn't let go and leapt backward.

The shock of hitting the ground might have broken her there and then if she hadn't done it so many times before in her life. The younger woman knelt down, gloating, and Kharise embraced the shattering feeling of her own smallness as this hulking figure stood over her.

She was small; she had *always* been small. And yet, in so many cases, small had always been *enough*.

A small, quiet voice in the ear of the crown, on behalf of a voice that was silenced.

A small pair of hands that nonetheless knew where to put the work, whatever work there was to be done.

A small knife that fit through the gap in nearly any helmet, even one forged of unnatural power; a small amount of force to sever the right cords; a small prayer that even the demon-ridden might still walk the Realm of Dream when last they fell.

She threw the woman off of her, with a roar of pain and anger, and, satisfied that the light in her eyes had gone—to what realm she could not say—she pried the crystal from the girl's palm, and stepped on it, with a silent and solemn prayer; one she had used only once before in her life, but trusted all the same.

M. Daniel McDowell

CHAPTER 18
BINDING

MEHREN TEVAHT HAD LOST ALL BUT THE MOST TENUOUS GRIP ON his reality as the hours passed before him.

He was feral with pain, lost in his own mind, wandering every one of the Known Lands overlaid with the Unknown, the Sundered, the Realm of Dream, the Cairn of Shadows; uglier places even than these, places no one should ever be.

Terror seized him as a shadowy figure approached—him, the chair, the place, the wound, the hand—he shrieked and clawed at—

"Seven hells, what did they do to you, Tevaht?"

Like the violent ending of a curse, Mehren felt himself pulled backward, through time, through himself, wrung like a blood-soaked rag, drained of substance, bereft and in unbelievable, rippling pain. Both of his eyes snapped open, and he stared through all the realms to find he was attended by... *Reyser Gorum?*

He drew a sharp breath and flattened himself against the chair. "What... what are you—" He struggled to breathe, to get the words out. "D-d-don't—I'm n-n-not—"

"Relax, you've got to let me do this carefully, before that monster upstairs realizes I've sprung you."

The guildmaster's voice had an unusual note of warmth behind it, his matter-of-fact deadpan met with a sense of humor Mehren had seldom felt from him.

"Quietly as we can, please."

It demanded absolutely everything within his power to keep himself from screaming as Reyser released the wrist clamp holding him in the hideous trap. Releasing one point of agony only activated the others. The juddering, scraping sensation between his bones only enhanced as his wrist tension sprung free.

"Easy, *easy*," the guildmaster chided him, and took hold of the injured wrist to help guide his palm off the spike without mangling anything further. "He must have had plans for you, after all of this, with how narrowly he avoided shattering your whole hand."

"It feels p-pretty shattered to me," Mehren replied, his voice creaking, as he flinched away once again from the sight of something so horrific, but, for the first time, the nausea and lightheadedness didn't come. Granted, he was sick with hunger, miserable with pain; a single, stimulating visual, even paired with his bodily agony, no longer held quite the same power.

Reyser unfastened the rope at Mehren's ankles, and released the belt that held him under compression. He had to cut the rope that bound his other arm, and Mehren felt a fresh wave of pain so jarring it dissociated him all over again, as the flow of blood to his left arm finally returned after such a long time under compression.

While Mehren worked his left arm back into its socket and tried to restore the sensation to his own fingertips, the guildmaster dug around on the cabinet shelves.

"He's got to have some—Ahhh, here we go," Reyser narrated to himself as he fished out a roll of linen, a strip of wood, and a vial of some sort of unguent. These he brought to Mehren's side, dabbing the unguent onto a scrap of the linen, and massaging it into the open wound. He wrapped this with more strips of linen, stabilizing his injured wrist with a splint after he'd wrapped a few layers of fabric. "Don't move it any more than you have to, it's pretty fragile."

Mehren nodded, trying to wish himself numb.

"The princess is upstairs, I reckon," Reyser said, wiping his hands along the bottom edge of his cloak. "You're lucky, you know. She knew something was wrong, and never let us drop it."

Mehren took a deep breath and tried to center himself well enough to stand upright.

"We need to go help them."

Reyser narrowed his eyes. "Son, you are pale and blue as smoke. You need to rest, or you are going to collapse. Far be it from me to say it but we can't afford that now."

"N-no," Mehren insisted, "It's Tobinarde, he's got the stone from Cascada, he's still trying to summon the war he wanted me to... he's going to trap her, he's going to *use* her..."

"Tevaht. Stay with me." Reyser put his hand on Mehren's shoulder. "All right, if we go upstairs, can you promise me you won't make any sudden moves? If you fell over right now you might just stay that way."

Mehren nodded, still dazed.

"I have to help her. You don't understand, he's—"

"Tobinarde? I understand him perfectly well."

Reyser put his arm underneath Mehren's and helped him to get his footing right.

"It wasn't like I was in his sway for a long time, but I remember what it was like, thinking he had some kind of gift. Some skill for seeing things in the big picture that none of us quite saw for ourselves."

"Yeah?" Mehren felt sick once he started walking.

He inched toward the door with Reyser's assistance, and together they made slow but steady progress up to Tobinarde's observatory.

"He's still trying, he's…"

He ran out of breath so quickly it filled him with fresh despair. If Tobinarde tricked her into letting him close, he was going to use the stone. Worse, if Tobinarde failed, the demon himself might be emboldened…

the demon masquerading as Margandrys would have a foothold into this realm. He'd nearly done it at Cascada; what would stop him now, unless Tobinarde got to him first?

Reyser nodded. "I'm sorry I didn't see it sooner. Didn't realize why it was that all the demons were trying to find Vierrelyne for a *reason*."

"I can't blame anyone for not seeing the whole pattern, the whole plan," Mehren replied. The sounds of a violent scuffle above drew Reyser's full attention. "He buried every piece of it separately, he was trying to hide it… He wanted something *grand* —"

"Well, kid, it sounds like she's grandly beating the shit out of him, not that I'm really surprised."

Mehren could not help but laugh, in spite of the gravity he felt. "I have to get up there, just in case… In case something happens. I—I'll be okay, I promise. I'll go slow."

He leaned against the wall and inched up the stairwell himself, as if to prove his point.

"You don't have to stay with me. Kharise needs your help," Mehren insisted.

It was Reyser's turn to laugh.

"*My* help? No, no. I need *Kharise's* help. That's how we got here. That woman is a force to be reckoned with." He sucked his teeth and patted Mehren on the shoulder. "Not unlike the princess up there. If you won't be persuaded otherwise, well, you two are more alike than you know. Good luck, kid. I'm sure we both need it."

The guildmaster left him to handle the rest of the stairs by himself. Mehren straightened his shoulders with an agonized sigh and pulled himself up, clinging to the wall step by agonizing step, gaining his confidence back if not his strength. Hearing her voice at the top of the stairs, in her clash with the old man and his formidable powers, gave him the burst of courage he needed to pull himself the rest of the way up those long and narrow stairs.

He braced his body in the doorway, and watched Vierrelyne; her form truly formidable, her opponent's only strength his uncanny ties to all the Scourgelands, to every last realm: *the realm of bodies, the realm of beasts, the realm of spirits, the realm of dreams.*

Vierrelyne stood before the old man, sword in hand, as her form took on everything the demon had to offer: his grand scale, his broad-shouldered, wicked spikes, his horned helm resplendent, no heavier than the diadem had been on its own, the jagged peaks of her armor that burred every blade that dared to bite.

She lunged at him, her sword aflame with the prince's ire, sparking in that color she had always thought of as *demon* green. "This ends *here*. The world you worked to ruin, all for what?"

Tobinarde snarled at her.

"It's you. The worthless princess from the mountains. If you had just given him the crown, you might have something left! You stole it from me! You stole *my future!*"

"What future? You've emptied the Scourgelands into this place, you've wrought the collapse of an empire, a dynasty, through your whispers and promises."

"None of them was worthy. Not a single one." The old man shook his fist at her, and this summoned a wave of power she had never seen before—not aided by any power source she saw. "Especially not you!"

He is a most powerful sorcerer, yes, but what he lacks is the unstoppable force we could offer him. Margandrys purred at her. *He covets the stone, forever has, but he does not understand the path to my heart as you do, dearest. He could never give me what **you've** given me.*

"You still haven't told me why." Vierrelyne did not clarify which *you*, for either sufficed.

"I don't owe you that! I don't owe you anything." He threw a book at her, and she struck it back. "This world? This world owes me everything! I built those kingdoms. I gave them purpose. They gave me nothing but ruination!"

"I don't believe you," Vierrelyne replied as she lunged forward, and cut down a wall hanging with the sharp edge of her blade.

*You believe in **power**. You believe in everything you have seen. You believe in **strength**. I gave you **all** of these things. I gave them to you freely because I knew you needed me. Needed this. Dearest, **please**.*

"It was my word upon which they built their wealth, my visions, my dreams!" Tobinarde ranted as he lashed out at her again. "They sundered this land, with all the other lands, in exchange for what I thought would bring me what I was owed."

"You told them to lock a *girl* in a tower until the apocalypse came for us all!" she raged. "You told them to murder my mother! You told them to do this. You sundered this world, Heresiarch! You wrought the devastation, all because you were upset you didn't think to make a castle and a crown of your own at the dawn of the empire? You cannot be so naïve!"

"It was I who united the realms in the first place!" he bellowed. "It was I who brought the Scourgelands to ours. And it was they who brought the war to the Sundered Throne. And now I will take back that power for myself!"

Now you want to fix it? None of this can be undone! You fool mortals have already done your worst.

Margandrys bellowed through her, at him, his rage boiling through her voice.

"No," Tobinarde gasped. "It can't be. I know you, Egrendelys! I command you! I bind you to the spindle of your deep name! I bind you, eternal, to my whim!"

You know NOTHING! roared the voice that dwelt within the stone. *You sought to bind my brothers, you sought to bind me, but you know not who lives on in glittering stone and who was consigned to Death to make it so. You have **lost!***

Vierrelyne felt her own body twist under the power of the grand demon.

His powers had gathered within her, unimaginably vast, enhanced by her conviction, and they had only grown over these long weeks.

She had been a fool, as foolish as her mother—and as she had that notion, a peal of cruel laughter rang through the bell of her helm.

*Oh, Tobinarde! You have lived this lie for so long you cannot remember the World that Was, and you have no place in the World that Is. You meddle in this world because you have **broken** all the others. You are the Poisoning of Worlds, Heresiarch.*

She opened her jaws and hissed with rage, her own shame at falling into the trap, however backward, her trusting that soft voice just long enough...

Oh, dearest Vierrelyne, worry not. This fool seeks to part us, but we shall never be parted again, you shall serve me forever, the demon prince sneered at her, with a sharpness to his choice of words. *No, he should burn, shouldn't he, the Heresiarch upon whose word was impaled an empire? Upon whose word fell every city between here and the castle Talorr? Should he not be made to suffer thus?*

Vi shook her head, her eyes widening in horror, as she raised her sword over the vile old man.

Truly, it could not be argued that the old bastard Tobinarde was not deserving of her heart's ire, but her curiosity at his profound mistake—in misnaming the demon at her brow—was such that it might have stayed her hand if her hand were still her own.

She slashed his throat, and the madman who had bound her to this woeful fate collapsed at her feet, gasping through torrents of his own gore.

It was not long before he lay still, his gnarled fingers clawing at his throat as he struggled against his fate.

It was not nearly so satisfying as Vierrelyne had hoped, but Margandrys laughed, voice full of the cruelty she had, one time, enjoyed.

Mehren leaned against the back wall, still dizzy.

Vierrelyne had lost control of the stone. The demon prince had driven her to the very brink of her abilities, and he was lapping at her worldly and spiritual wounds, siphoning her pain, gorged as a tick, tethering himself into reality by her torment, growing stronger by the moment.

If Mehren did not intercede *immediately*, she would be consumed by his power, and he'd be able to shatter his prison and go free, having shattered *her* first. The thought of losing her now, after everything they had been through... he couldn't bear it, not while he still had the chance to prevent the demon from taking her.

Tobinarde had tried to bind him with the wrong name. It could only be one, then.

Mehren cast about for something, anything, he might use to draft a sigil, to no avail. Only Tobinarde's blood, which was tempting—perhaps his device might work to great effect if the body could be assured of Death—but Mehren knew only too well that the occupation of a demon would lend even the dying the sort of vitality that might keep them alive well past the point of nature's grasp. A body as powerful as Tobinarde's in the hands of someone like the demon prince... His whole body trembled at the notion of it.

No; for the binding to work, it would have to be his own, weakened as he was.

He only hoped his resilience was enough that the demon be truly bound. For the binding to work, he knew what he would have to sacrifice to keep her safe. He could only hope that what there was of himself left to give would be enough.

Of that there was no one who could be less certain than Mehren Tevaht, the last warded coward of the Astral Circle, but the time for such qualms had left them all behind.

It had to be this, and it had to be *now*.

He was careful to open his arm just above the bandage, where he could hopefully stop it from bleeding out too swiftly, the fresh flash of crimson on his forearm still unspeakable to look upon. Mehren steeled his jaw and suppressed the overpowering faintness and nausea forever induced by the sight of his own blood, collecting it and tracing a sigil that, if he understood it correctly, would extract the cursed demon prince, the true Scourgebringer, from the broken binding of the Peridot Starprism... but by the use of his own blood, there was only one place the demon could go, and so there was only one chance to make this right. Only one moment by which the Shepherd in

Shadow could set the known lands free of the endless demons' war and take the Bringer of the Scourge with him.

Only by his own oblation.

He set to work with diligent haste, casting the sigil before him with as much precision as he could wring from his shaking hands.

The work complete, Mehren Tevaht pressed his hands together, still repulsed by the slight tack of drying blood between them, and shouted the name he hoped would be the one to bind the crown prince of the Scourgelands, by the only means he had left.

"*Avadamrys*! Prince of Lies upon the Throne of Dream, I bind you to my will!"

WHAT?! YOU SPEAK THE NAME?!

Vierrelyne roared with the same ferocity as the demon prince as the Verdelite Starprism cracked, and a fierce jet of bright yellow-green demon flame pulsed from the fissure in the stone.

"Avadamrys, o holiest Prince of Loathing, Bringer of the Scourge!" Mehren shouted back. "I bind you to the spindle of your deep name. I call, and you will bend to me! I am the Shepherd in Shadow; I bind you to my fate. I call you to your doom and mine."

*You know not the skill! Worthless worm! **YOU** will bend to my calling!*

Mehren held out his bloodied fingers and opened both of his eyes. He saw Avadamrys as he had seldom before—for he had only known the inversion, the false name, the name of ill-fated Margandrys, the corpse whose quintessence had channeled the creation of the Peridot Starprism in that faraway time, in that hideous timeless realm.

The radiant demon prince's form surrounded Mehren's beloved. Avadamrys was the very embodiment of her holy armor, for the wicked antlers of her helm were his own. The impossibly broad shoulders and spiked forms of her armor all just the dark promise he had made to her, on the night when her desperate cries had broken through the first binding of the foul green gemstone and awakened his ever-watchful eye.

He focused his gaze on that single point—the acid-green stone, embedded in the thorned helm which had once been simply a diadem, had once simply been a warrior queen's token of death, shattered now by the force of a spell he steeled himself to complete.

"Vierrelyne," Mehren gasped. "Whatever happens, promise me you won't let them take it from you. If this d-doesn't work; if you let any of them touch it—"

"I understand," Vi started, her eyes flooding with tears, "but, Mehren, please—"

There was no more time.

As Avadamrys pulled untold aggregate terror from the Scourgelands to fuel himself—the Sundered Lands, the Realm of Dream, the Cairn of Shadows—to build enough of his own quintessence to fully shatter the gemstone prison, soon even Mehren's binding of blood would not be enough to hold such a formidable entity.

*FATHOMLESS WRETCH! I WILL **DESTROY** YOU!*

The rest of the demon's incessant ranting flowed over him, around him. Mehren bent forward, laid his left hand over the sigil, and spoke the words once more, the spell calling upon some darker justice to close this circle, to bind this future, to fulfill this ghastly prophecy.

He bent his head, and fought the words Istven had said, so long ago, so important to him then; they no longer mattered, for he could never outrun his calling, not anymore. Then as now, there was nowhere left to run, and Mehren had to harness that spark which he'd long thought he had captured and tamed, that fear within him that forever governed his wary steps, that way by which he had ridden over and through the Scourgelands so many times before, a visitor in a place unseen by most.

Mehren stared Death in the face for a third time in his short and miserable life—and this time, he grinned.

M. Daniel McDowell

CHAPTER 19
SUNDERING

"NO!" Vierrelyne shrieked.

She felt a harrowing tug from her very core, a shattering, a bone-deep violence, as Mehren collapsed to the ground before her, and Margandrys—no, the usurper, the traitor who had stolen that name and made his brother's name the effigy—went with him, retracting from her and the Peridot Starprism, as if repulsed, as if he was drawn into the lifeless figure before her by great force.

The stone at her brow cracked violently, and Vierrelyne felt a strong energy shudder through her, but it did not leave. She was still armed in the war-gear of the demon prince, though he had departed from it with force. Avadamrys, stealer of his brothers' fates.

Wrenching herself free of the echoing thoughts of Avadamrys, who had occupied so much of her, who had taken so much from her, was not the work of a single day, but she had no time. She thought she might collapse under that strain as well, but she heard Kharise calling out in the distance, leading her forces against the tides of warfare, and this in turn animated Vierrelyne to action once more.

Mehren's cloak shrouded his face, and she resisted the urge to take one last glance into his eyes. It was better to remember him drawn by lantern-light, his features softened by her deep affection and the frailty of her own memory, wasn't it? If she did not look, she would not have to see, would she?

That didn't make it any easier to leave him in the tower, alone with only that erstwhile old fool to join him on one last sojourn into the Scourgelands, a last journey from which neither would return. She straightened Tobinarde's body, laid him on his back; his face a rictus of disbelief, his arms at his chest, his fingers bent to claws at his bloodied throat.

Mehren's body, she trundled with his own cloak, and dragged him into position on his back next to the old man. She hated to look, but it could not be helped. His eyes were closed, his fists clenched, and his arms were still pliant, so she bent them gently at the elbow. When she placed his clenched fists over his chest, the blood on the wound inside his arm only starting to congeal, she realized that he was, however slowly, still breathing, but unable to wake up.

But he... he *extracted* Avadamrys, drew him down, through a portal, which meant... but the demon would never have acceded so willingly, unless... unless he thought he could best the wizard in some other way; in his own terrain, *perhaps...*

Perhaps there was something more to this battle.

She drew her sword, tried to remember the words Kharise loved so well; the lyrics to the song of the sundered love lost.

In her mind's eye, she drew. Not a sigil, nothing like Mehren's meticulous marks. Extending her arm, her sword aloft, she traced her sword over the seam between the worlds, no different from the dozens of times she had practiced in her own tiny cell, no different from the way she had slashed down waves of those enemies who would stand before her, the dance of freedom and tyranny alike.

Nothing.

She cursed, screamed, sobbed in rage.

How was she to find him, before they'd lost everything?

Kharise bolted up the tower steps. She'd heard an unholy explosion, a truly stunning jolt that rang across all of the desolate fortress as the independents had fought off the last of Tobinarde's summonings. The only thing she could hope for was Vierrelyne's safety; that whatever happened, she had prevailed.

The devastation in the tower was profound; smoldering tapestries, shelves of jars and bottles overturned onto the floor, books sliced through at the spine. Vierrelyne stood over two bodies, and for a moment Kharise worried she might have experienced another shock, and truly she had.

Vierrelyne tended to her beloved on the floor.

"Princess?" Kharise said, and relief washed over her at the instant recognition.

"Oh," Vi said, unable or unwilling to summon anything else.

"My dove, I'm so sorry. I'm glad you're safe. I wish h—"

"He still breathes," the princess replied, her shoulders sagging. "He is still warm with life. I—we—can't stay here."

"What do you mean, Highness?"

Vierrelyne shook her head.

"I am not the Crown of the World Unbound, I never was. Kharise, I *am* the Scourgebringer. I am the curse itself. All this time, I thought, that old madman made all of this up, I can *change* this, I can *fix* this…"

"But you still can," Kharise said, as Vierrelyne knelt down next to Mehren's body, as if by her closeness she might revive him.

"No. Without the demon's power, I have nothing," Vierrelyne said solemnly. "You? You forged an army, a following. The makings of a proper kingdom. You've made something worth believing in."

Kharise protested. "Vi, I'm just a keeper of songs from the Unconquered Plains."

"Be unconquered here, in the new free cities," she implored. "I needed your leadership and guidance to come this far, I needed everything you had to offer me, but now, what I need is…"

Kharise nodded solemnly.

"It was *you*," Vierrelyne murmured. "It was always you. We never put it together. You *are* the Crown of the World Unbound."

Kharise's expression stiffened as Vi handed her what remained of the crown. The shattered gem in the diadem fell out and crashed to the floor. She held it like it might still contain the poison of enchantment.

"You know as well as I do what I think of that fool's prophecy," Kharise muttered.

"Which is why it truly must be you." Vierrelyne grew wistful.

"You know what my people, and I, think of kings and thrones."

"All the more reason, for you know another road, a better road," Vi insisted. "You know the stories; you know the myths, *and* you know the truth. You know what it means to be a leader. I never have. I never *could*."

Kharise nodded, the far corner of her lip twisting into a knowing, if reluctant, grin.

"Go back to Estuary City with the Independents. You have my crown and my word, and that will be enough for Reyser and his loyalists," Vi insisted. "You have the makings of something better, something new. Take it while it's still ours. Please. For me."

Kharise nodded, her heart solemn.

She'd never been so bereft of words, or at least of history, to address such a heavy gift as this.

"I promise we won't be gone long, if I am meant to return at all," Vi said, "but I can't leave this place without knowing... Without looking for him."

The princess folded out his arm, where an incision just above the bandage on his wrist dripped, steadily, with bright, living blood.

"I know where he is. Or, at least, how to get there," she whispered. "I just hope I can find him in time."

The form Vierrelyne had taken, in the wake of Avadamrys and his transformation, was formidable. Her armor forever bent to the curves of the great demon prince. Her hair, once radiant auburn, was now silvered with an eldritch green tone.

Her eyes, as ever, were bright-gold and fierce.

Kharise's great affection for the princess was laced with a profound heartache. It had not been so long that she would not remember a quiet, plump girl with a raging fire inside; a young woman molded by ancient fears; a warrior triumphant over all enemies.

She, Crown of the World Unbound, watched as the Bringer of the Scourge set about the oblation of the Shepherd in Shadow, and hoped, for all reason, that this would be the end of it.

Or, with unimaginable luck, a new beginning.

Vierrelyne searched the wizard's cloak, and found a paintbrush buried in one of the deep pockets. Its handle had been snapped off and splinted together with string and sap, its bristles stiff and darkened; with what, she had a hunch. She extended Mehren's arm outward again and dabbed the bristles against the open wound.

She followed one of the concentric rings carved into the slate floor, tracing a faint continuous line, following the one he'd drawn not long before with agitated precision.

She held down her panic as she worked, but she did not know the runes he used for his portal spell. She realized, as she followed his lines, that she needed no outlet, no second ring; her destination lay *within* the grand weft of the Scourgelands, not through.

Vierrelyne drew the runes of his warded name, as best she was able, and put the brush between his bandaged fingers once she had completed the delicate marks.

As she hefted his body into her arms, she drew a deep breath and tried to clear her mind.

He had shown her how to find him before, though neither of them realized it at the time.

She gave Kharise one last look, resolved in the knowledge that the world above was no less sundered than the worlds below, and there remained someone whose radiant wisdom might lift it up again.

The Bringer of the Scourge stepped forward, into the circle drawn in blood, her full concentration on the young man she'd first met in dream, the single person who had understood her as she was—Mehren Tevaht, Shepherd in Shadow, unspoken keeper of her heart.

M. Daniel McDowell

CHAPTER 20
THE WORLD UNBOUND

KHARISE TRIED TO CONTAIN HER SHOCK. WITH EVERYTHING she'd seen in the time since she had evacuated from Talorr, it was not solely the uncanny events of that evening which filled her heart with dread.

It was her assignment.

Her old promise and her new promise; to a girl, now a woman, now a strange ghost she only hoped would return to her before too long.

The sound of scuffling boots behind her in the stairwell caught her full attention. Reyser Gorum, holding his cloak over his shoulder where he'd taken a glancing blow. He was smiling and still had his color; a flesh wound, she thought.

"What in all the realms happened up here?"

He marveled at the destruction in the room around her, chips of stone brick, broken pottery, the worldly aftermath like that of an earthquake.

"The most useless coronation in existence," Kharise grumbled, holding out the shattered crown which once contained the great evils of the Sundered Throne, the Prince of Loathing, that Titled Bastard of myth and legend and song. She hated the sight of it, had since first she glimpsed it between the naif little fingers of her dear friend, the princess of Talorr-in-Ruin.

He stared. "Vierrelyne! What happened, Khar?"

"She's gone. With him. They slew the demon prince." Kharise sighed. "She bequeathed me what remains of this rotten thing before she took off."

"What are you meant to do with it?" Reyser laughed, seeing her horrified expression.

"She thinks I'm meant to wear it, now that it's unbound from this," Kharise gestured at the cracked gem, trying to think of the word. It had been so long since she had been able to think in terms of history and song, and it was inescapable now, as if a decade in uncounted days had locked her world away, at a remove.

Without the urgent burden of the troubled girl who'd become the core of her world, who was Kharise gen Valuure?

"Well, now." Reyser gave her a broader smirk as he pulled the cloth taut around his arm. "I could see you as a queen. Oh, don't give me that look. I mean it."

"Not a queen," she insisted.

"Not a queen, hm?" he parroted. "All right, then, who else do you think is going to take charge of the power vacuum in the Principalities? Let alone the rest of Derebor. The whole of Broadcoast Bay is in turmoil. Someone is going to have to stand up. Someone who knows the region, but also someone who can organize a backchannel."

"I had a lot of help," she demurred. "Not a little of it from you."

"Oh, that's as may be, but I don't go in for any of that protocol stuff. I never did. That's why my guild is called the

Independent's. We don't do decorum, but you? You might hate it, but you lived in the Castle Talorr for how long, answering to all of those people?" He whistled. "You know where the lines are."

"I never went in for it either, myself."

"But you actually have some experience in what to do about it." Reyser squinted at her.

She gave him a long skeptical stare, her lips pursed.

"Think of it. The Crown of the World Unbound. Tobinarde was a rotten old monster, but he did have a gift for a turn of phrase, didn't he? Are you sure you wouldn't want it? Queen Kharise, Breaker of Empire, Builder of Bonds..." He strode over to her and leaned on her shoulder. "Sounds like one of your songs."

"King," she replied, solemnly. "If I must be something, I should certainly not settle, but I do not long for a system of regency, and heirs."

"I can see that." He tilted his head toward his injured shoulder. "Hey. King Kharise, can I humbly beg your royal intercession in the matter of my bicep? I'd ask Bunny to do it, but I'd really like to *keep* this arm."

Kharise chuckled and reached for her kit of field tools. "What in all the realms did you do to yourself," she mused as she dug out a clean rag and a reel of suture.

He looked at her, with a mixture of solemnity and dark humor, the exact concoction of his temperament which she found endlessly captivating.

"Well, Khar, you see, there were these charming little demon kittens, and I thought, 'well, maybe I can get closer,' and then one of them opened its gaping maw of a thousand teeth and swatted at me."

"You're admitting you didn't move fast enough, is that all?" She smirked.

"Yes," he sighed. "At least it wasn't my knee, or I'd never hear the end of it, would I."

The grounds were wild and strange, where Vierrelyne landed; cold and hot at once, an ambient shadow over the whole of the world. This was no place she was meant to be, but she had been here before. Countless times, under the veil of her dreams: the narrow track of dirt beneath her feet the only path back to that thing she instinctively understood to be The World that Is.

From the first time she'd heard Mehren mention it, she knew what he meant, for she'd traveled that road in dreams. She knew this path as well as she knew the terrified boy at the end of it.

The sky above was lightless, the earth beneath her formless, and everywhere around her was the sound of rushing water—so loud she could not hear her own thoughts, though she could not make out the source of it, still somewhere distant down that road.

The body in her arms still lived; she felt the steady beat of his heart in her very bones. The terror rose in her throat, a tremor that brought out only empty sounds.

Where was he?

She had to find the river first; that was where she'd find him. It always was.

It nagged at her that this place remained so empty, so bereft of any sounds or creatures, but it was, after all,

Tobinarde's grand vision to empty this place. To foment the wrath of the living world into everlasting chaos. It was this hideous dream that had led to unconscionable suffering across every plane of existence.

The figure she'd seen so many times before, standing across a dark river; at last, she spotted him, though now this dark river was a wave of sound that crashed all around her, and here the path forward to the young man was clear.

The river lay *behind* him, *beyond* him.

It was her beloved, whose wound was so cursed it tore a rift through time, a rift through reality. She saw him with clarity anew. Here in this liminal dreamscape, the glow of his eye was not merely the attunement of a wizard's glass, it was an unnatural fire which emanated from within him.

He stared at her in terror, in awe, as she approached with his own body cradled in her arms.

Here the scar on his face was impossible to ignore; in this strange place, in his *essence*, it was a livid, raw wound, his hair swept back from it. He held between his hands a strange and vivid green light which spilled from between his fingers. The desperation to hold onto this violent light was writ upon his brow.

She stepped closer to him, an agent of death—or perhaps now she was just another creature of the many Scourgelands, in the raiment of their darkest and cruelest prince. In the clearing, next to that cold, cold river, she laid the body of Mehren Tevaht, still breathing, still alive, whose essence stood outside of it, and that essence stood weeping inconsolably, straining to contain some otherworldly force.

"Finally," she whispered, leaning close. "We're free from this nightmare at last. I know what it means."

"No!" He insisted. "I don't know what will happen if I let him go. Not after everything we've been through."

Vierrelyne bent down close to the body she'd carried across the realms and into this dismal clearing. His left hand, unbandaged, still held something dark, glittering, and alive clenched between his curled fingers.

"Don't touch it!" the haunted figure wailed.

The dark and glittering thing was an enormous black centipede, with cruel pointed legs and pincers, impossibly long and coiled and hideous, much larger than the space it had been given, and once it had squirmed loose of Mehren's tight grip, it scuttled with uncanny fluidity into the dark shape of the river just beyond them and vanished.

"Was that—" He started, and Vi shrugged. She turned to face the strange doppelganger, the essence of the wounded boy who had grown from this place, who had clawed out a warded name to survive his hideous curse, who claimed to be a coward and was anything but; the boy who had become Mehren Tevaht.

"—Then what am I holding? What is this?" His essence reluctantly parted his bandaged fingers, as if he might catch a glimpse before it got away from him.

"You have to let it go," Vi whispered. "Whatever it is, whatever you think it is, it's holding you back. It's keeping you here. Come back with me."

She put out her hand, not sure what to expect. This strange stasis was bound to end; how much time did they have? It couldn't be long.

"I don't know what happens if I let go," he replied. "What if... what if this is..."

The figure knelt next to her, still cradling the violent green light; so much more timid, smaller than the man he knelt beside, but still the essence of someone she loved enough to carry across every realm of reality if she must, an energy that called out to every stitch of herself.

She turned her attention to the body before her, brushed the dark curls away from his closed eyes. "Just breathe," she insisted, and pulled his wounded right hand into hers, gentling the bandage around his palm. She held his hand and whispered the sound she knew, the one that was distorted through the mirror of the realms, the one just at the cusp of her understanding of him, the name deeper than the wards meant to shield him in this unconscionably dark place.

At last, when she thought she might be waiting forever in vain for him to awaken, Mehren gasped and gave a horrible spasm.

He clutched his chest, clumsily, clawing at his face and hair, seeking confirmation that he had survived having cleaved himself across the planes.

"Vierrelyne." Mehren gave her a heartbroken smile before he sighed with deep frustration. "You shouldn't be here, you can't—"

"Of course I can," she said. "And I have."

"You weren't supposed to see me like this, dearest," he murmured.

"I have seen you like this long before I ever knew who you *were*," Vierrelyne replied, "but it is only now that I understand why."

"I didn't stop him in time. I—I was supposed to do my part in this, but I've done it all wrong, and now I don't know how to fix it. I let him go. I can't go back, not without eradicating him... or me—" His voice broke.

"No." She squeezed his shoulder. "We all got it wrong, this whole time. Everything in the prophecy, it's all come true, just not as we expected."

"But how? I didn't kill him, I couldn't. All I did was..."

"Capture him?" Vi asked.

Mehren nodded. "But you can't be here. You're..."

"Kharise is the Crown of the World Unbound. We've done our work to clear the path. Tobinarde's words are undone, the pact is unbound. We're free."

"Not me. What if he's still in here somewhere— what if you can never trust another thing I say again? What if he took hold of me and never let go? What if I'm tainted by..."

Mehren crumpled.

"What if I am just a vessel for an unfathomable evil to persist forevermore?"

"I know him, that creature Avadamrys, better than you might think, even if I only ever knew him by his brother's name." Vierrelyne sighed. "Moreover, I know what it's like to have him in my head, to feel tainted by his thoughts. You aren't alone in this, Mehren. I'm here."

"You should get away from here while you can," he whispered, dragging his fingers through his hair, making strange and stuttering movements as he slowly regained the utility of his body. "Leave me. If we *confine* him to the Scourgelands, consign him to the Realm of Dream, maybe you can escape..."

"Oh no. I carried you in here. I'll carry you out if I have to. You won't get out of this so easily." Vierrelyne replied.

"We *can't* leave this place together, you know," he said quietly. "We can't just slip out. Not like the others can, not like them. The spell I did... It's meant to keep me here. I can't just make a portal to escape."

"We'll cross that river when we get to it. Together."

"If you..." He bit his lip. "If you hurry, you can get yourself back out the way you came, whatever you might have done... It won't last forever, and the longer you've been through it, it fades, but—"

Without a word, she hoisted Mehren into her arms, against his many protestations, against his better advice, and turned her full attention to the long road back to The World that Is; the World Unbound.

If she hoisted, after all,
she might not be too late.

M. Daniel McDowell

ACKNOWLEDGMENTS

This book wouldn't exist without multiple individual cohorts of people I cannot name here without breaking Derby kayfabe, who all encouraged me to take on this mad chase even though I couldn't tell them a damn thing about it the whole time I was doing this.

I love every one of you.

This book wouldn't exist without the diligent efforts of the Inkfort Press staff, all of whom have created something that, to be maudlin, changed my life for the better and showed me what I can do when I put my head down and get to work. Thank you.

This book wouldn't exist without a bunch of other people who both do and do not exist, all of whom made the Inkfort Press Self-Publishing Derby a genuine delight. My sincerest appreciation to S.F. Henne and Laura Huie for profound assistance above and beyond, and much love to A.M. Weald, Baxtor West, Tar Atore, Rien KT, A.J. Alexanders, D. Heyman, and everyone else in the Derby cohort who made the acid-green section of the Inkfort Derby Discord a fun, welcoming place to hang out.

This book wouldn't exist without my newsletter, where I spent a truly astonishing amount of time vacuuming thousands and thousands of metaphorical cats when I could have been writing literally anything else. Thank you to everyone who subscribed, commented, liked a post, all of it. I am a terrible gremlin who yearns for scintillas of approval, and my newsletter, in this regard, gave me every scintilla and more.

This book wouldn't exist without the exceedingly tolerant beloveds in my personal life, whose understanding of my bone-deep compulsion to write books has given them all the good grace to understand when to gently steer me away from my desk and when to get out of my hair and let me work.

Thank you for riding this particular rollercoaster with me.

This book was published as part of the 2023 Inkfort Press Publishing Derby! Check out the other books published in this year's Derby for more great reads.

http://www.inkfortpress.com/publishing-derby/2023-derby-books

M. Daniel McDowell

ABOUT THE AUTHOR

Merritt Daniel McDowell is an inkstained wretch originally hailing from deep in the Rust Belt and presently residing on the East Coast, who has never gotten comfortable living so close to shore, for beyond those coastal waters, there indeed be dragons.

Merritt can reliably be found in pursuit of caffeination at nearly any time of day, up to and including roughly thirty minutes before it is time for bed.

For more information, visit mdmcdowell.com or follow @mdanielmcdowell on just about any social media network.

FLAMESPEAKERS
U N I O N

BESPOKE INDEPENDENT BOOKS
& PUBLISHING SERVICES

FLAMESPEAKER.COM

Printed in Great Britain
by Amazon